D1586699

FRANK MUIR was born in Glasgow. He was plagued from a y⟨
with the urge to see more of the world than the rain sodden slo⟨
Campsie Fells. By the time he graduated, he'd already had mor⟨
the River Clyde has bends. Following short stints as a lumbe⟨
Scottish Highlands and a moulder's labourer in the local four⟨
five years of working overseas helped him appreciate the r⟨
his home country. Now a dual US/UK citizen, Frank spends most of his
time in the States.

Eye for an Eye

FRANK MUIR

Luath Press Limited

EDINBURGH

www.luath.co.uk

C 02 0375031

First published 2007
Reprinted 2007

ISBN (10): 1-905222-56-4
ISBN (13): 978-1-9-0522256-8

The paper used in this book is recyclable.
It is made from low-chlorine pulps produced in a low-energy,
low-emission manner from renewable forests.

The publisher acknowledges subsidy from

Scottish Arts Council

towards the publication of this volume.

Printed and bound by Bell & Bain Ltd., Glasgow
Typeset in 10.5 point Sabon

Acknowledgements

Writing can be a lonely affair, but this book could not have been published without the help of the following. PC Mark Laing and Gayle Richardson of Fife Constabulary, and DI Jamie Harper (retired) of Strathclyde Constabulary, for police procedure. Jennie Renton for editorial input beyond the norm. Suzanne Kennedy for believing in my manuscript and Gavin MacDougall for taking a chance on publishing it. Everyone at the Strathkelvin Writers' Group for unflagging support, but in particular Margot Aked and Sheila Livingstone, whose belief in me kept my writing dreams afloat when I was ready to sink. I cannot thank you enough. Louise Welsh for adjudicating the 2004 Pitlochry Award and miraculously selecting *Eye for an Eye* as winner. Other readers and friends, too many to mention (you know who you are), whose encouragement inspired me to continue. Thanks to each and every one of you, especially Anne. And finally, this book is fiction. Those readers familiar with St Andrews may notice that I have taken creative licence with respect to some local geography. The exact locations of certain private residences have been kept vague for obvious reasons. Any resemblance to real persons, living or dead, is purely coincidental.
Any and all mistakes are mine.

This book is dedicated to the memory of
Gary Thomas Wishart

THE BEGINNING

Rain hangs from the sky in silver ropes that dance on the street and spill from choked gutters. Lightning flashes. His face flickers white. Thunder cracks, a close clap that shakes the windowpane by his head. The centre of the storm is near now, no more than a mile or so to the north, somewhere over the Eden Estuary.

I watch him turn towards me, his eyes small and tight as a pig's. With a drunken grimace he hitches up his trousers, their short legs concertinaed and blackened by the downpour. He moves from the doorway, tries to face me, stumbles against the wall. He rights himself. 'Are you looking for something?' His words are tired and heavy.

'I saw you in Lafferty's.'

'Oh yeah?'

I don't move.

His eyes struggle to focus, and I tighten my grip on the wooden stave tucked behind my right arm. A tremor shivers my legs, for although I've thought about this moment often, I've never killed anyone before.

I step towards him.

As if to show he has nothing to fear, he tries a laugh, but coughs instead. Despite the rain streaming down his face, spittle

I

forms at the corners of his mouth.

The skies flash. The air cracks.

We stand still, shocked by the closeness of the hit.

Then his eyes narrow.

'Wait a minute,' he says. 'I've seen you before.'

I step forward, lift my right hand.

'You're—'

I strike.

The whittled point of my stave pierces his left eye with a sound like wet mud popping. His body stiffens, topples away from me, thumps to the ground.

I follow him down. I am barely breathing.

His left eye fills black with rain that spills down his cheek like ink. I tighten my grip on the stave and drive it deep to the back of his brain, then give a hard twist.

His legs kick. Then still.

I stand, turn away, keep my eyes to the ground.

I head towards Louden's Close then onto Lade Braes Lane, a narrow path hemmed by high stone dykes. I keep my head low and walk with a brisk step. Rivulets of rainwater accompany me down the pathway, like lifeblood flowing from his filthy corpse.

I reach Queen's Terrace, no more than ten quick minutes from home. The downpour will obliterate all trace of my passing. And even if by the slimmest of chances someone finds a muddied footprint somewhere, no one will trace the oversized boots to me. I smile.

Tonight I have started my journey to Hell.

CHAPTER 1

ANDY GILCHRIST STIRRED awake. Something was ringing at the edge of his mind.

He squinted at the Hitachi radio clock on his bedside table and in the winter morning darkness read 5:38.

Not his alarm.

His phone.

Something slapped over in his gut as his wakening mind told him why it would ring at that time of the morning. Had he slept through another storm?

He grabbed his mobile. 'Gilchrist.'

'It's Stan, boss. We've got number six.'

'Where is it this time?'

'The harbour.'

'Shit.' CCTV monitoring of the town was still in its infancy and no cameras were installed near the harbour. The chances of anyone being down there at night were slim to non-existent, but with a rush of hope he asked anyway. 'Any witnesses?'

'No one's come forward, boss.'

'Damn it.' That would be a first. 'I suppose no one from the Division was anywhere near there?'

'We're stretched thin as it is, boss.'

Gilchrist cursed again. He had been on at Patterson for the best part of two months, pleading for additional staff.

And now the Stabber's tally had reached six.

He clicked on his bedside lamp, screwed his eyes against the burst of brightness and scanned his dresser for his cigarettes before remembering he had given up.

'Do we have the victim's name?' he growled.

'Tommy Carlisle told us who it is, but we've not had it confirmed yet.'

'Carlisle?'

'You know Tommy. Owns *The Bitter Alice*. Always first at the harbour. Says he was on his way to load his creels when he almost tripped over the body. One eye staring at the moon. The other, well, the usual. Says it's Bill Granton, the manager of the Bank of Scotland in Market Street.'

'What time was this?'

'5:10.'

'Statement?'

'Being taken as we speak, boss.'

'Granton, was he married?'

'With one son. We've sent Nance.'

Gilchrist drew the back of his hand across his stubble. In years past he'd been responsible for informing next of kin, one of those necessary evils of the job, which no one liked. DS Nancy Wilson would handle it well.

'Granton's wife,' he said. 'Did she report him missing?'

'Nothing logged, but we're looking into it. By the way, rumour has it Granton was gay.'

Gilchrist frowned. To date, the Stabber's victims were all men known to be abusive to women.

'You sure about that?' he asked.

'Not one hundred per cent, boss.'

'Get onto that, Stan,' he ordered, then added, 'No chance of this being a copycat, is there?'

'Doesn't look like it.'

'Have you seen the body?'

'At my feet, boss. Bamboo stave in the left eye. But the

4

pathologist would need to confirm that the brain's been stirred.'

'The press don't know about that. Let's keep it that way.'

'Got it, boss.'

'Has the harbour been sealed off?'

'Yes, boss.'

'And the body?'

'As we found it. But the seagulls are making one hell of a racket.'

Gilchrist had seen only one body with its eye sockets pecked clean by birds. Fifteen years on, he was still unable to rid himself of the memory. He squeezed the back of his neck, forced his thoughts to focus.

'Last night's storm,' he said. 'How long did it last?'

'A good two hours.'

'And that's when Granton was attacked?'

'Looks that way, boss.'

Gilchrist had crashed out, a combination of too many beers and exhaustion from thirty hours' sleep a week for the last two months. 'Have you spoken to Sa?' he asked.

'You're the first, boss.'

'Have her meet me at the harbour as soon as.'

'Got it.'

Gilchrist disconnected and stood up. He lolled his head to the left, then back and around to the right. Steady as a rock. Good.

In the bathroom he turned on the shower and stared at the mirror. Bags under his eyes. Grey stubble. Forty-five going on sixty. Where the hell had it gone? Twenty-seven years with Fife Constabulary. Should he not be looking forward to retirement instead of dreading the day DCI Patterson would kick him out? And that day was not far off. Of that, he had no doubt. Ever since Patterson had suspicions of his affair with Alyson Baird, Gilchrist had known his days were numbered.

He picked up his toothbrush and peeled back his lips. At least he still had white teeth, despite having smoked. His only redeeming feature, he often thought. He dropped his silk shorts and stepped into the shower, turned his face into the stream and lathered Badedas soap against his chest. Eyes closed, his fingers searched for the electric razor he purchased last year on a trip to the States. Battery operated and waterproof. Shaving in the shower was now one of life's small pleasures.

Ten minutes later, Gilchrist braced himself against the cold wind of an east coast November morning. Dawn was still a good hour away and the skies hung low with the threat of more rain. He walked up Rose Wynd to Castle Street where his Mercedes SLK Roadster was parked, and pressed the remote. Lights flashed in the darkness. He opened the door and slid inside. With a twist of the key, the Merc's two-point-three litre engine fired up first time.

He slipped into drive and accelerated onto High Street. Out of Crail, he put his foot down. St Andrews sat ten miles north on the A917 and he would reach the harbour in fifteen minutes. Maybe ten. He noted the time on the dash. Just after six. Sa might already be there.

He picked up his mobile and pressed memo 7. His call was answered on the first ring.

'What is it, Andy?'

He almost smiled. 'Becoming psychic in your old age?'

'Stan called.'

'You sound perky.'

'Been awake for hours.'

'Trouble sleeping?'

'How about you? Hungover?'

'Whatever gave you that idea?'

'Six pints in Lafferty's?'

My God. Was that how many he'd had? 'I left just after you,' he said. 'Which reminds me. Why didn't you stay?'

'What's with the twenty questions?'

'Just taking an interest in your well-being.'

'I'll keep that in mind.'

Gilchrist waited for Sa to continue but she was a woman of few words, a loner with a chip on her shoulder. He had not found a way to reach her yet, even though they had been working on the case together since the Stabber's fourth victim was found with his head staked to the ground two months earlier.

'When can you make it to the harbour?' he grumbled.

6

'That's twenty-one questions.'

'Just be there,' he said, and disconnected.

He gritted his teeth. Sa was his assistant. Not the other way about. She was thorough and hard working, but he needed to feel some mutual trust, feel confident that they worked as a team. But Sa sometimes treated him with a coldness that could be mistaken for contempt. He blamed Patterson for teaming them up. Patterson had known Sa was difficult to work with and it was his perverted way of saying, *try screwing the ass off of that one.*

Sebbie opened his eyes.

He clicked on his bedside lamp, but the bulb had blown two weeks earlier and he could not be bothered to replace it. He tried reading his watch, but it was too dark.

He ran his fingers through his thick, greasy hair. He had not showered for over a week. He felt his penis press against his Y-fronts. He was always hard in the mornings, it seemed. Ever since that stupid bitch Alice had ditched him, he was always hard. But it was no longer Alice he thought of when he masturbated. He thought of her.

He slipped his penis out.

Every time he masturbated now, he masturbated to her. She was such a classy bitch with her polite accent and long dresses that hid tiny braless tits and came down to sandalled feet with skin the colour of cream and he bet she never wore panties when she worked in her shop and if he pushed her dress up and up and over her thighs she would...

He lay still for several moments, then cleaned his hand on the pillow and rolled out of bed. In the bathroom he switched on the light and blinked against the brightness. His bald chest was slathered with strips of white that trailed to his pubic hair. He slid his hand down to his stomach then slapped his fingers against the wallpaper. Wet streaks covered old stains.

He turned on the tap and splashed cold water onto his hands. A quick rub down with a smelly towel, and Sebastian Hamilton was ready to face the world. He did not bother to wash his face or brush his teeth. No need. He had done that last night. Besides, now he had made up his mind, he felt good.

His plan was simple. That classy bitch might think she was beyond his reach, might think she would never let him touch her. But it didn't matter what she thought.

He was going to have her anyway.

CHAPTER 2

GILCHRIST PARKED HIS Merc behind the ugly harbour-front building and stared at its bland facade rising like a grey wall in the pre-dawn gloom. The structure looked out of place.

What he loved about St Andrews was its history, its links to the Reformation and executions for heresy by burning at the stake, its hidden lanes and ancient walkways, its stone dykes and ragged ruins, its narrow alleys and foot-worn steps. And often, when he left the pub, aglow from one too many beers, if he half-shut his eyes he could almost believe he was in an earlier century.

He removed a pair of rubber gloves and coveralls from the boot, pulled up his jacket collar and pressed the remote as he walked along the harbour. An icy wind forced tears to his eyes. He stared off to the dark horizon of the open sea. A lifetime ago, it seemed, he had often walked this way with his children, Jack and Maureen clutching their tiny plastic buckets and floppy spades, determined to dig holes in the golden-brown beach of the East Sands or search for jellyfish and crabs in the receding sea pools. Which reminded him, he had not heard from either of them for several days. Or had it been longer? He made a mental note to call them later.

He breathed in the aroma of salt and fish scales, the strangely pleasant stench of decaying kelp and seaweed. To his side, the sea clapped the harbour walls, and it puzzled him that the sounds and smells seemed new to him somehow, as if the harbour's intangible familiarity had eluded him until that moment. He walked past groups of fishermen crouched by lobster creels. One of them grunted and nodded and he nodded back. But he knew from their unhurried actions and tight-lipped silence that trapping lobsters was the last thing on their minds that morning.

Up ahead, from the lambent glow of an adjacent window, he recognised the silhouettes of Sa and a uniformed policeman. As he neared, he saw what looked like a bloated heap of discarded clothing on the quayside. The lighting vehicle had not arrived yet and a lone photographer prowled the body like a tempted lion, camera flickering like the visual remnants of last night's storm. Three Scenes of Crime Officers in white coveralls were preparing to set up the inflatable tent.

Gilchrist reached the corner of the building.

'Where's Stan?' he asked Sa.

'Gone for a pee.'

'Police Surgeon been notified?'

'On his way.'

'And the pathologist?'

Sa tutted, which Gilchrist took to mean Yes.

He eyed the scene. A closed row of plastic traffic cones lined the street. Another row of taped cones surrounded the victim. Examination of the body should not commence until the Police Surgeon had confirmed life was extinct, but Gilchrist pulled on his coveralls and gloves. 'Don't suppose we need anyone to tell us this one's not breathing,' he said.

When he stepped over the tape, the photographer lowered his camera, as if in deference.

Granton was wearing a dark blue pinstriped suit beneath a fawn overcoat. It had not rained for several hours, but his clothes were sodden. His right eye stared skyward, lid half-closed. His left, a congealed pool of blood and blackened matter, housed a wooden stave. It always surprised Gilchrist how calm the

Stabber's victims looked, as if they had been talking to a friend who had changed into a fiend all of a sudden and stabbed them unawares. Or perhaps having a stave driven into the brain rid the body of mortal rictus.

Gilchrist took hold of Granton's left hand. It felt cold and wet. Rigor mortis had not fully set in and the skin felt as soft as a woman's, an indication Granton had never done a day's manual labour in his life. Gilchrist twisted the hand over. In the dim light, the skin shone wet and smooth and hairless. Manicured fingernails glistened as if varnished. No wedding ring. Only a depressed mark on the meat of the ring finger where the ring had been slipped off.

Gilchrist looked up at Sa. 'Did you notice this?'

'No wedding ring?'

'What do you make of it?'

'Took it off to get bum-fucked.'

Gilchrist wondered if he would ever understand Sa. He remembered when they had been teamed up by Patterson, she had looked squeamish over the body of the Stabber's fourth victim, in Burgher Close. But at the post-mortem she had watched with the attentive curiosity of a student as the pathologist slapped a dripping brain onto the scales.

Gilchrist felt in Granton's right-hand coat pocket. Nothing. The other was empty, too. From the inside suit pocket he removed a burgundy leather wallet. He placed it to his nose. The leather smelled new. He ran his finger over the embossed monogram on the top corner. WBG.

William Granton. But what did the middle initial stand for? Perhaps his family name?

Gilchrist opened the wallet and counted ten crisp twenty-pound notes. 'Two hundred pounds,' he said. 'That's a lot to be carrying.'

'Maybe that's what you have to pay these days.'

'For spending the night with another man?'

'Who said anything about spending the night?'

'Granton's wife never called the Office to say he hadn't come home.' He looked at Sa. 'So it might be reasonable to assume she never called because she didn't expect him.'

Gilchrist flipped through the wallet again. Other than the usual credit cards, all bearing the imprint of William B. Granton, the wallet contained nothing else.

He stood. 'No money taken.'

'There never is.'

'And no driver's licence.'

'Maybe he doesn't drive.'

Gilchrist frowned. Most people carried their licence with them. If Granton lived within walking distance of the bank, maybe he had no need of a car. Or maybe he did, but kept his licence at home. Or maybe he had been banned. Which did not seem likely, somehow. But it would not be the first time Gilchrist had been fooled by superficial innocence.

He stared along the harbour wall that jutted into the sea like a giant's stone limb. Spray drifted on the wind. During last night's storm the sea must have thundered onto the pier. He stepped back over the tape.

'What was Granton doing out here?' he asked.

'Meeting his shirt-lifter?'

'Here?'

Sa shrugged. 'Why not?' She looked away. Gilchrist found himself following her line of sight, along the path that ran up the slope to the ruins of Culdee Church and past the Abbey wall. By the light from a street lamp, he watched Stan walk towards them, mobile phone pressed to his ear.

'But why here?' Gilchrist asked Sa. 'There must be a thousand places in St Andrews for two adults to meet in private without the risk of being seen.'

'This is one of them.'

'Hardly.' Gilchrist found his gaze being drawn to the end of the harbour pier. Over the years he had come to trust this sixth sense of his. So, why the pier? It might be a discreet place for Granton to meet a partner, but surely they would never have sex out in the open. In the middle of a downpour.

'Boss.'

Gilchrist turned.

Stan clipped his mobile shut. 'Someone saw him.'

'Saw Granton?'

'Saw the Stabber.' Stan's breath clouded the air. 'Sam MacMillan. Painter and decorator. Lives on South Street. Not far from Deans Court.'

'Did he get a look at the Stabber's face?' Sa asked.

Stan shook his head and ran the back of his hand under his nose. 'Wouldn't say. He called the Office about ten minutes ago and said he wanted to talk to someone about the Stabber. He asked for you, boss.'

Gilchrist frowned. Over the past months his picture had been in the newspapers and he had often been quoted as Detective Inspector Andrew Gilchrist of the St Andrews Division of Fife Constabulary's Crime Management Department, senior investigator in the Stabber case. By his side, the photogenic Detective Sergeant Sa Preston. He never liked to see himself in the newspapers, always thought he looked tense, as if he was not in control of his emotions.

The way Stan looked at that moment.

Beth Anderson wrapped a peach coloured bath-towel around her naked body. In her bedroom she picked up a jar of Dior moisturiser and squeezed out a dollop. She rubbed it in, breathing in its light fragrance and loving the way it left her skin cool and moist.

She let the bath-towel drop to the floor and studied her figure in the mirror. She had never fallen pregnant, although she'd had a few scares as a teenager, and she exercised often, which kept her stomach trim. Not quite washboard abs, but flat enough not to bulge over the top of her knickers.

She stared at her breasts, cupped a hand under the right one, which she thought hung lower than the left, and pushed it up. Much better. She always thought her breasts were small for the rest of her body, as if they belonged to someone more slender. She slid her hands down over her waist, settled them onto her rump. She squeezed. Still firm, she thought, but too wide. Yes? No? Her mother had assured her that one day when she was in the throes of childbirth she would be pleased to have inherited wide hips. But having a family was not top of Beth's list. In fact, now she was fast approaching the big four-oh, it was pretty close to the bottom.

She threw on a pair of white jeans, flat black shoes and matching leather belt. A peach cashmere twin-set, purchased for a steal in the States last year, topped it off. She pulled on her light-tan suede jacket and left the house, umbrella in hand.

She had breakfast in the Victoria Café, near the corner of St Mary's Place and Bell Street. During the summer months the roof-top patio was one of her favourite places to eat. But in November the patio was closed and she took a table by the window. She knew the menu by heart, so when the waiter approached, his black-brown eyes glistening with pleasure, she said, 'Fruit and a croissant, please. And a pot of Earl Grey.'

'Certainly, Miss Anderson. Anything else?'

'No, thank you.'

'May I?' He slipped a small glass vase onto the table, pulled a cut rose from his pocket as if by sleight of hand, and popped it into the vase. 'For you.' He stood back, both hands over his heart. 'With all my love.'

Beth felt her lips pull back in an unrestrained smile. 'Thank you, Brian. That's lovely. Thank you.'

'When I serve the most beautiful woman in the whole of the British Isles, the pleasure is all mine.'

'You're crazy.'

'Crazy with love.'

Beth chuckled. 'But the answer is still no.'

'Ah, but one of these days,' he said, 'you'll surprise yourself and say yes. No?' Then he pirouetted and crossed the wooden floor towards the kitchen.

Beth watched him go. Brian was young enough to be her son, but it felt lovely to be treated with such romance, and so revitalising to live a romantic dream from time to time.

She fingered the rose. Red. Which stood for lust. Not love. Brian was full of youthful hormones, but in the two years he had been employed at the Victoria Café, not once had he been anything other than a gentleman. He had told her his romantic side came from his father, Baldomero, a hot-blooded Spaniard who had divorced Brian's Scottish mother when Brian was ten, and now lived in Gibraltar with a Spanish beauty from a once wealthy family that had lost its land and property when Franco came to power. It made her own seem mundane. The years were racing by while she stood still. And as she felt that familiar heaviness encircle her heart, she knew she had to make a change.

That evening, she thought. She would end it that evening.

CHAPTER 3

GILCHRIST OPENED THE door to the larger of the two interview rooms and followed Sa inside, a polystyrene cup of coffee in his hand. The room was nothing more than four walls painted a light shade of blue, large enough to accommodate six metal chairs with black plastic seating. A low table centred the floor. Two small windows looked onto North Street, high enough to permit privacy from passers-by.

Sam MacMillan sat alone on a seat in the corner, a white-haired man in his sixties. His complexion, ruddied from decades in the east coast wind, took years off him. He glanced at Sa, then fixed his gaze on Gilchrist as if comparing the man in the flesh with the photographs in the newspapers.

Gilchrist sat in the chair to Sa's right. He sipped his coffee. It tasted hard, like an espresso. But it worked for him. He leaned forward. 'I'm Detective Inspector Andrew Gilchrist.'

'Aye, son. I know.'

'And this is Detective Sergeant Sa Preston,' Gilchrist added. 'I'm going to tape this interview. All right?'

MacMillan nodded.

Sa pressed the *Record* button on the micro-cassette recorder. Gilchrist cleared his throat. 'The date is Wednesday, November

27th, 2002. The time,' he stretched his arm, 'is 8:16 am. Those present are DI Gilchrist speaking, DS Preston and interviewee, Sam MacMillan. Although Mr MacMillan offered his statement, he has been advised that he can have a lawyer present, but has waived that right.' Gilchrist looked at him. 'Is that correct, Mr MacMillan?'

MacMillan nodded.

'Please speak for the record,' said Sa.

'Aye,' MacMillan said. 'That's correct.'

'What would you like to tell me, Mr MacMillan?'

MacMillan took a quick breath. 'I seen the Stabber.'

'Where?'

'At the harbour, like. Last night.'

'Please speak into the recorder, Mr MacMillan.'

'I seen the Stabber murder Bill.' He raised his hand in a clenched fist and brought it forward in a hard stab. 'Bill dropped to the ground like a sack of tatties.'

'Did you get a chance to see the Stabber's face?'

'I did. He was just a boy.'

'A boy?'

'Well, a young man. Like he hadnae started shaving yet.'

Gilchrist kept his eyes on MacMillan. His team had remained divided since the first body was found in Thistle Lane. Some argued that the Stabber was male because of the strength required to drive a stave through the brain. Others were convinced the Stabber had to be female because the victims were all men known to have been abusive to women. After the third victim was found staked to the ground behind Blackfriar's Chapel, an FBI profiler was adamant that the Stabber must be two hundred pounds and six foot plus. Without a witness, no one really knew. Gilchrist felt a surge of excitement. MacMillan had just given his investigation the jolt it needed.

'Where were you when this happened?' It was Sa.

'On the pier.'

'Was it raining?'

'Pelting it down.'

'How close were you?'

'Sixty, seventy yards away.'

'And you saw the Stabber from there?'

'Aye, lass. I did.'

Given MacMillan's age, Gilchrist wondered just how good his sight was. Good enough to identify a killer, at night, in a storm? He doubted it. Any defence lawyer would tear him apart in court. He noticed a faint mark on the bridge of MacMillan's nose. 'You wear glasses?' he said.

'Aye, I do. But only for reading.' MacMillan picked up a pair of binoculars from the floor. 'I seen the Stabber through these,' he said. 'I've been a bird-watcher all my life.'

'May I?' Gilchrist reached for the binoculars before MacMillan could respond and read the manufacturer's printed label on the end of the lens swivel pin. Bushnell. 10x50. He put them to his eyes, confirming what he suspected and handed them back.

Silent, MacMillan took them.

Gilchrist tried to keep the disappointment from his voice. 'How long have you had these?' he asked.

'This pair? Eleven years.'

'You like them?'

'Aye.'

'You carry them around with you?'

'Never go outside without them.'

'Even at night?'

'Aye, son. Even at night.'

'Not a lot of birds at night,' said Gilchrist. 'Watch bats, do you?'

MacMillan shook his head. 'It's a game we play.'

Gilchrist frowned, puzzled. 'Go on.'

'I've known Bill since we was toddlers. We grew up together, went to school together, been friends all our lives. Close friends, like.' Sad eyes shifted beneath bushy eyebrows.

Gilchrist studied him.

'Did you know Bill was homosexual?' he tried.

'Homosexual? Sounds better than poofter.'

'So you knew?'

A shadow settled behind MacMillan's eyes. 'Aye, son.'

'Would it be right to assume that you and Bill were...'

MacMillan's nostrils flared for a brief second. 'Aye, son. It would.'

'And that's where you and he met? At the harbour?'

'I go out for a walk every night. Been doing that for the last forty years. Never missed a day, come hail, rain or snow.'

'Even in thunderstorms?'

'Even in thunderstorms.'

Sa leaned forward as if to ask a question and Gilchrist surprised himself by pressing the flat of his hand against her thigh. She sat back.

'No one knows about me and Bill,' MacMillan whispered, then dabbed a thick finger at the corner of his eye. 'I dinnae think I could stand the looks.'

'Tell me about the game you played,' Gilchrist said.

MacMillan took a deep breath.

'Every night, I take my midnight walk. On Tuesdays I go to the harbour and wait for Bill. I never know if he's going to come or not. That's part of our game. Sometimes he does. Sometimes he disnae. He likes it that way.' Teary eyes held Gilchrist's. 'I would walk out to the pier and watch through my binoculars. I would be out of sight. But Bill knew I was there. I was always there. He hadnae come by for nigh on three weeks, the longest time yet. Something told me he would come last night. You know what I mean?'

Gilchrist nodded.

'I seen someone walk down by the Abbey wall. I thought it was Bill. But I wasnae sure. I was too far away and it was bucketing. When I got closer I seen by the walk that it wasnae him. Then I seen him, up by the shorehead.'

MacMillan picked up the binoculars and Gilchrist noticed the yellow taint of nicotine on thick fingertips. He would have given a hundred quid for a cigarette at that moment. He took another sip of coffee. It tasted even more bitter.

'Bill would walk to the harbour wall,' MacMillan went on. 'All innocent like. As if he was staring out to sea. But he would be looking for me. Then when no one was around he would unbutton his coat and he'd...' MacMillan lowered his head.

'But he didn't get a chance to do that last night,' Gilchrist whispered. 'Did he, Sam?'

MacMillan shook his head. 'No, son. He didnae.'

'What happened, Sam. Tell me.'

MacMillan gripped the binoculars. 'Bill heard something. He turned around. I didnae know what was going on at first. Then I seen someone walk towards him.'

'The Stabber?'

'Aye.'

'Was that when you got a good look at him?'

'It was dark. But, aye. I could see fine well. The Stabber was young, like. Just a boy.'

'How could you tell?'

'I'm no altogether stupid.'

'What was the Stabber wearing?'

'An anorak. With the hood up.'

'Colour?'

'Dark green. Or blue, maybe. It was dripping. And jeans. Tight jeans. Even though Bill was looking away from me, I knew he was talking by the way his head moved.'

'You had a clear view?' Sa again.

'Not too clear, like. I kept having to wipe the lenses.'

'Well enough to identify him?'

MacMillan stared at Sa. 'When Bill was stabbed, he fell flat on his back. Down like a sack of tatties he went. And just then, the skies lit up.'

Gilchrist held his breath. He glanced at the recorder. It was still turning. He resisted the urge to look at Sa, could sense her tension. 'Do you know who he is, Sam?'

MacMillan grimaced. 'I seen his face. Pure evil, it was. But I just seen it for a fraction of a second.' Then he shook his head. 'If I seen him again, I wouldnae be sure.'

Gilchrist slumped back in his chair. Something stirred within him, flared to anger. 'Why didn't you call the police? You'd just witnessed a murder, for crying out loud.'

'I couldnae think straight. Bill was dead. I couldnae do nothing for him. I had to walk past his body to get off the pier.' He shook his head. Tears welled in his eyes. 'I couldnae even look at him. I havenae slept all night for thinking about it.' Then he buried his face in his hands and his shoulders heaved with his sobbing.

Gilchrist pushed his chair back and fought off the urge to shout to the skies. If MacMillan had called right away, they might have been able to trap the Stabber.

He glanced at Sa. She was staring at MacMillan, her face pale and drawn, as drained as Gilchrist felt. The case was taking its toll on her. On both of them. They'd been at it seven days a week for the last two months. Eighteen hours a day. Minimum. They couldn't keep that up forever. No one could. And that bastard, Patterson, hadn't called yet. But that would come. As surely as the sun would—

'I followed him.'

Gilchrist stared at MacMillan, his mind demanding to hear the words repeated. But Sa beat him to it.

'You did what?'

'I followed him. The Stabber. I was on my way home when I seen him ahead of me.'

'Are you sure?'

'Aye, lass. I recognised the anorak. And the tight jeans.'

'Did he see you?' asked Gilchrist.

'No, son. He went through The Pends. It's a wee bit bendy. And I kept well back, like. He walked past Deans Court.' He shook his head. 'Just like the Devil himself.'

'Where did he go after that?'

'Into North Street.'

Gilchrist felt his gaze being pulled to the front of the building. The Office was in North Street and so was the University. Was the Stabber a student returning to St Salvator's Halls of Residence? But they had these Halls covered last night. Or had the Stabber slipped down one of the side streets, maybe headed back to the town centre? He would check the CCTV recordings.

'And then what?' he asked MacMillan.

'He was walking fast. By the time he turned into North Street he was a good bit in front of me. I didnae want to get too close, like, in case he saw me. But when I turned into North Street he was gone.'

'Gone?'

'Vanished.'

'You never saw him?'

'No.'

'Did you see anyone?'

'I didnae.'

'After he turned into North Street,' said Gilchrist, 'how long did it take you to reach the corner?'

MacMillan shrugged. 'Fifteen seconds. Maybe more.'

'Maybe a minute?' asked Sa.

'I'm sure it wasnae that long, lass.'

'Where were you standing when you last saw the Stabber?' Gilchrist asked.

'In The Pends. By the entrance arch.'

'We'll work it back,' Gilchrist said to Sa. 'Get some feel for how far the Stabber could have walked in the time it takes to reach the corner of North Street. Carry out door-to-door enquiries. Turn out every house in the street, if we have to.'

Sa leaned closer. 'Maybe the Stabber ran,' she said.

'Why would he run, lass? He was walking. Fast, like. But just walking.'

'Maybe he knew he was being followed.'

'No, lass. I've told you.'

'Did you see any cars?'

'I didnae notice. I was looking for someone walking.'

'So, you're not sure?'

'No.'

'Maybe he just drove away.'

'He would have had to have gone some to jump into a car, start it up and drive out of North Street before I reached the corner.'

'Was he old enough to drive?'

'I'd say so.'

'Why would you say so?'

'He didnae look like a wee boy. More like a young man with

a baby face.'

'But you never saw his face.'

'No clear enough.'

'And you never saw a car.'

'I wasnae looking for a car, but with all these questions you're firing at me, I'm no so sure any more. I just cannae remember.'

'Perhaps he had a car parked down a side street,' Sa pressed on. 'Did you hear a car?'

MacMillan's face clouded. 'I'm sorry, Mr Gilchrist.'

Gilchrist stood up. The interview was over. 'Your eye-witness account will be of great help to the investigation. I appreciate you coming in and talking to us.'

'I'm sorry I never chased after him,' MacMillan said. 'That's what Bill would have done.'

Something in MacMillan's tone struck Gilchrist. The Stabber's five previous victims had all been rough men, drinking men, and up until that moment he had no reason to believe Granton was anything other than a mild-mannered bank manager.

'How was Bill with women?' he asked.

MacMillan shook his head. 'Bill might have looked like butter wouldnae melt in his mouth. But he could be a bad-tempered bugger when he put his mind to it.'

Gilchrist held MacMillan's eyes and knew the old man's words had just put a different light on things.

CHAPTER 4

A BITTER EAST wind sliced Sebbie to the bone as he walked through the West Port, pulling his tattered combat jacket tight around his shoulders. Damp seeped through the soles of his trainers and forced him to curl his toes.

He passed the blackened ruins of Blackfriar's Chapel, its arched supports and vaulted roof a sixteenth century work of construction ingenuity. He felt his stomach spasm and that familiar sickness seep through his guts like acid. He should find out what was wrong. But what could the doctors do? They had not been able to help his father. So how could they help him?

At Queen's Gardens he crossed the street and sat on a wooden bench in the slabbed area that fronted the Town Kirk. From there he had a view along South Street and up Logie's Lane through the covered walkway that led onto Market Street. Sometimes she would come that way, down through the alley and past his bench, then left onto South Street towards her shop. Other times she came from the West Port.

A man in jeans and a grey sweatshirt walked past, holding a tongue-lolling Alsatian by a leather leash. He had a sausage roll pressed to his mouth. Shards of pastry fell to the pavement like flakes of brown snow. Sebbie watched him strut along Logie's Lane towards the covered walkway, the mouth-watering smell of cooked meat and onions enticing him like a Siren's call. The Alsatian lifted a leg at the corner of the pend and Sebbie turned to—

Shit.

He shielded his face with a hand, but she walked past on South Street without so much as a tiny glance his way.

The stuck-up bitch.

He waited until she passed the corner of the Town Kirk before he followed. He hooked a thumb under the waist of his jeans and tugged them up. They seemed looser. Maybe they had stretched. Maybe they needed a wash. But the washing machine that was left in the house after his parents had...

After they had...

Even now, three years later, he still found the correct expression confusing. After his parents had died, or, after his parents had gone. Neither was strictly correct, since only his father's body had been found, shifting along the West Sands on the incoming tide, skin as white as porcelain, a red slash like shocked lips on his neck. Sebbie had refused to believe his mother was dead, too. She had disappeared. She had run away. He had tried to convince the police of that. How could they say she was dead?

But the police named her as prime suspect, convinced she had slit his father's throat then fled the scene, maybe even the country. Without any physical evidence, no one knew. Two years later to the day, the case had been closed. That was a mistake. And now that useless detective, the skinny one with the white teeth and the good looks, was going to pay.

Sebbie ground his teeth. Payback time. He walked along South Street, eyes glued to the wobble of her rump. Something warm and cosy settled in his stomach and pressed its way to his groin. He almost smiled.

Payback was going to be fun.

Beth put a fresh filter in the coffee machine, topped the water reservoir, then chose five CDs for her shop's CD player. Her customers often complimented her on her choice of music, little-known jazz bands, singers, pianists, music every bit as accomplished, if not more so, than commercially successful artistes. She switched the CD onto shuffle.

Loston Harris sang mellow in the background as she turned her attention to the countertop. It always annoyed her that customers pressed their fingers to the glass when pointing at something they wanted to buy. She gave it a short squirt of Windolene and a stiff rub with a paper towel then walked round to the customer side and did the same with the front panel.

Something caught her eye. She turned.

He stood with his face pressed against the door. Both hands capped his eyes, restricting her view of his features. She thought he was checking to see if the shop was open, so she tapped her wristwatch and mouthed, *We don't open until nine.*

He lowered his hands and twisted to the side. For one confusing moment, Beth thought he was going to slam his shoulder against the door. Then a clenched fist thudded against the glass, and the panel rattled as if about to burst from its frame.

She rushed behind the counter and lifted the phone from the wall. She had the police on speed dial and was about to press in the number when the man ran off. She held onto the receiver, her heart fluttering.

What was that all about?

She eased the phone back onto its cradle and almost tiptoed to the door. She scanned South Street but saw only couples window-shopping, a small boy kicking a ball across the road, an old lady searching her opened handbag.

It struck her then that she had not even noticed what the man had been wearing. If she was ever asked, all she could say was something dark. Perhaps an anorak. And that he had looked young.

She glanced at her wristwatch. 8:55. Cindy would be along any moment. She flipped over the CLOSED sign and unlocked the Yale. She opened the door as she always did, to make sure the handle worked from the outside. Last year it jammed and the shop had been open for an hour before she realised customers were turning away.

She gripped the outside handle then let go with a squeal of disgust. She looked down at her hand in disbelief then rushed through to the back of the shop and vomited into the wash-hand basin.

At the conclusion of MacMillan's interview, Sa handed the micro-cassette tape over for typing. Once it was in report format, MacMillan would be asked to review it then sign it as his formal statement.

Meanwhile Gilchrist checked with the CCTV Officer, only to be told that the system had blacked out during last night's electrical storm. Gilchrist wondered, as he made his way to DCI Patterson's office, if that was one reason the Stabber attacked only during wild weather.

'The ACC's been on the blower,' Patterson told him. 'And the shit's piling up, Gilchrist. McVicar doesn't want to hold a full press conference yet. In the meantime you are to make a preliminary statement to the press. They're waiting in the car park. With me so far?'

'Yes, sir.'

'You are to feed them crumbs, Gilchrist. Teeny weeny crumbs. You got that?'

'Will you be present, sir?'

'Only you.' Patterson's lips almost pulled into a smile, and Gilchrist felt as if he was being set up. 'Tell them a full press conference will be held in the lecture theatre at HQ this afternoon. And try not to fuck up this time. Oh, and Gilchrist?'

Gilchrist raised an eyebrow.

'See me when you're finished. There's something we need to discuss.' And with that, Patterson returned his attention to a file on his desk.

With grim resolve, Gilchrist walked along the narrow hallway to a door that opened onto the car park. Patterson wanted to discuss his resignation, he was sure of it. But first, he had to fight off a pack of hyenas with teeny weeny crumbs.

Gilchrist hated press conferences, hated being centre-stage, a problem that first developed at school. At thirteen he had towered above his classmates, a gangly pimpled youth with bony shoulders stooped in a constant battle to avoid standing out. Girls giggled and whispered whenever he walked into class and, convinced he was a freak, he could not look anyone in the eye without blushing. He grew only one more inch, to hit six-one by fourteen. And that was it. No more growth spurts. As his friends caught up, his embarrassment eased off. But even now, thirty-one years later, he still suffered from the occasional flush.

He stepped out into a drizzle as fine as mist and scanned the sea of faces. Portable lights were set up by the entrance archway, where four cameramen balanced mobile cameras over their shoulders. Gilchrist repressed a grimace as the unkempt figure of Bertie McKinnon wriggled to the front of the crowd. A local journalist renowned for his fiery polemics on anything he regarded as abuse of public office or a waste of public monies, murder investigations were not his forte, but that had done nothing to stop him pouring vitriol on the perceived shortcomings of Fife Constabulary.

Gilchrist avoided McKinnon's feral stare, mounted the makeshift podium, braced himself and started to speak. He confirmed that a body had been found by the harbour and that the Stabber was a suspect, then parried a barrage of questions that demanded gory details, reporting only that the M.O. was indeed that of the Stabber. He fought off the persistent clamour for the victim's name, refusing to reveal the identity until the family had been notified.

Then he heard McKinnon's voice, harsh and rough as a smoker's bark.

'If you can confirm nothing else, Inspector, can you at least confirm that you are no closer to catching the Stabber than you were when his first victim was found in Thistle Lane?'

'Every day brings us closer,' Gilchrist replied.

'Four months later and you're no further on.'

'I can assure you he will be caught.'

'But when, Inspector? The public need an answer.'

'We're doing everything in our power to—'

'*Everything*?' Cruel eyes grinned back at him from above a dirty beard that bushed to the neck of a threadbare sweater. Grey hair slicked back in a greasy ponytail. Blackened teeth parted beneath a moustache yellowed from forty years of sixty a day. 'Have you given any thought to turning the case over to someone who could deliver results?'

Before Gilchrist could respond, McKinnon added, 'Have you been asked to step down?'

Gilchrist caught the gleeful tone of victory and in that instant knew that Patterson had confided in McKinnon, had told him he was about to be kicked off the case.

Gilchrist tried a wry smile. 'Not yet,' he said.

Laughter fluttered into the damp air.

'Are you saying you expect to be removed from the case?'

'I haven't heard anything to suggest that. Have you?'

'We understand St James's Palace has expressed concern about the lack of progress.' A woman's voice from the back.

Gilchrist looked up, thankful for the respite from McKinnon. The American accent did not surprise him. Ever since Prince William had commenced undergraduate studies at St Andrews University, the town had become a haven for royal-watchers. With the young royal residing in the same town as a rampant serial killer, this made for international news.

'What are you doing to reassure the Palace of Prince William's safety?' she asked him.

'Prince William has nothing to fear from the Stabber.'

'How can you say that?' Her voice snapped with such emotion that heads turned. 'This town is gripped by fear,' she continued. 'A fear that grows each day the Stabber is allowed to roam the streets. Any one of sixteen thousand residents will tell you they're afraid to go out at night. How can you possibly say Prince William is not in danger?'

Gilchrist tried to keep his tone even. 'Firstly, Miss...'

'Reynolds,' she hissed. 'Jennifer Reynolds of *Newsweek*. And it's Ms.' The word buzzed.

Gilchrist felt the dry warmth of a flush creep into his face.

Focus, he heard his mind order. Focus on a response. He stared at her. 'Prince William in no way fits the profile of the Stabber's victims,' he said. 'Quite apart from that, he is protected by his own security personnel at all times.'

'How does that fact help the other sixteen thousand residents of this town?' she persisted. 'Is it or is it not safe for people to walk the streets at night? Especially during a thunderstorm?'

Gilchrist felt his face grow hotter and decided to be non-committal. 'On the whole,' he said, 'the streets of St Andrews are as safe at night as those of any other town.'

'But this isn't any other town,' sniped Reynolds. 'This is the town in which the future king of England is attending university.'

Gilchrist felt his flush evaporate, as if a wind had risen from the East Sands and chilled the air. 'Britain,' he announced.

Reynolds frowned.

'St Andrews happens to be in Scotland,' he said.

Someone whistled the opening bars of 'Flower of Scotland' and Gilchrist decided to draw the conference to a close.

'One last question.'

He turned his body to shield his face from the cameraman by his side and nodded to a grey-haired man in a dark blue suit, white shirt and bold red tie.

'Can you confirm the rumour that the Stabber is a young man, perhaps even a student?'

'Who told you that?'

'Do you deny it?'

'No comment.'

'From that response, can we assume the rumour is true?'

'No comment.'

McKinnon's gravelly laugh rasped.

'No further questions,' said Gilchrist, and stalked from the podium, ignoring the cries that erupted in his wake.

He slammed the door behind him.

How the hell could he control his murder investigation when one of his own team was talking to the press?

CHAPTER 5

My father hit my mother.

I was five years old when I first saw him hit her, too young to understand why she was lying on the kitchen floor, crying and screaming with her legs curled up into her stomach, arm flailing while my father pounded away at her with his black boots, white spittle drooling from his bristled chin, eyes red and wild and crazed as a raging bull.

I now recognise that single point in time as the moment when the hatred first began, like some cancer seed that floats in on a cold wind and settles deep in the soul to germinate into something foul and evil.

Nothing ever seemed the same after that. My father never lifted me and spun me around anymore. I never saw my mother smile again. And my brother, Timmy, developed a stutter that stayed with him the remainder of his short life. As for me, I started punching and kicking Sandy, my one-eyed teddy that had been passed down from Timmy.

When Sandy stared at me dead-eyed, the way my mother did, I battered him the way my father battered her. When Sandy stared back at me still, I took a kitchen knife and stabbed out his other eye. I cried when Sandy had no eyes. Until I realised that without eyes, Sandy could not watch my hatred grow, or see the pain spread like a fungus over my mother's wrecked face.

Poor old blind old Sandy.

Three weeks later, I stabbed out his brains.

Gilchrist burst into the main office and stomped to his desk.

He faced his team.

'Everybody,' he shouted.

He waited until the group formed a loose scrum in front of him, then stared at each of them in turn. Young eyes gleamed back at him. 'Someone's been talking to the press,' he said, 'and I don't like it.'

Eyes shimmied to the side. Someone coughed.

'Let me make this crystal clear. No one is to discuss this case with anyone outside this room. And that includes all senior officers, no matter who.' He caught DS Nancy Wilson frowning. 'Got a problem with that, Nance?'

'Does that include DCI Patterson?'

'You're not listening.'

Nance looked to her shoes. Someone chuckled, Baxter, perhaps. Stan almost smiled. Sa raised an eyebrow.

'Every single scrap of information that leaves this office will leave this office through me,' Gilchrist said. 'Even if the ACC himself asks you about the case, you will direct him to me. You are following orders. Plain and simple. Is that clear?'

The group gave a collective mumble of confused consent. His orders violated police protocol, but he had made his point. Any more leaks and he would go nuclear.

'All right,' said Gilchrist, 'let's move on.' He turned to Baxter. 'Has traffic done its bit?'

'North Street's blocked off from Deans Court to College Street, sir. And all side streets and lanes in between.'

'Each point manned?'

'Closed to the public.'

'Nance?'

'Sir?'

'Warrants?'

'All in order,' she said. 'Eighty-two in total.'

'Good. Stan?'

'Boss?'

'See to it that our media friends out the back are kept from the area.'

'Got it, boss.'

'You've all been briefed, so you know what we're looking for. Anorak, dark green or blue. Jeans. Probably still wet from last night's storm. But don't bank on it. The staves could be from bamboo furniture, a bookshelf, a decorative screen, so anything that looks like it could be dismantled and whittled to a point, check it out. Look for shavings in the rubbish, the fireplace, marks on floors and walls. Be nosy. Snoop around. Don't hold back. The smallest clue could be all it takes to nail this case. But remember, MacMillan has identified the Stabber as a young man. So anyone younger than thirty is to be considered a possible suspect.'

'Sir?'

Gilchrist eyed Nance. Other than Stan, she was the brightest of the young breed.

'How reliable is MacMillan?' she asked. 'I've read his statement. It was coming down in buckets. He's an old man. He was some distance away. He thought he saw a young man.'

'Meaning?'

'What if he's wrong? From a distance, a woman might be mistaken for a man.'

'Are you suggesting we should disregard his statement?' Sa asked.

'No. I'm saying he saw the Stabber's face only during a flash of lightning. He could be wrong. That's all.'

'Nance is right,' Gilchrist said, scanning the faces. 'We don't know who or what we're dealing with. Best bet is someone young. We've a lot of ground to cover. So let's get on with it. And Baxter?'

'Sir?'

'Watch those manners of yours.'

Baxter coughed.

'Right,' said Gilchrist. 'Debriefing's at six,' and left the room.

Two minutes later, eight plainclothed detectives and ten uniformed police constables spilled from the Police Station and marched like a band of vigilantes up North Street towards the Abbey end, where they split into pre-assigned pairs, ten to the north side, eight to the south.

Gilchrist eyed the stone wall that bounded the Abbey ruins and felt his gaze settle on the archway that defined the start of the road known simply as The Pends. 'When the Stabber turned into North Street,' he said, 'MacMillan was standing at the entrance arch.' He glanced at his watch. 'Time me.'

He strode down the shallow incline at the pace he imagined MacMillan might take. When he reached The Pends, he stepped behind the crumbling entrance support and checked his watch. Thirty-one seconds. He eyed the entrance to North Street and visualised the Stabber turning the corner. Once again, doubt crept through him. The Stabber could have known he was being followed, regardless of how cautious MacMillan had been.

Gilchrist walked back to North Street, faster this time, twenty-five seconds. 'Right,' he said. 'The world record for the two hundred metres is less than twenty seconds. Assuming the Stabber's not the fastest human on the face of the planet, then somewhere between here and two hundred metres is where he must have gone.'

Sa stared off along North Street. 'Presuming he didn't drive off, of course.'

Gilchrist followed her line of sight. The spire of St Salvator's, where Prince William resided, pierced the roofline like a marker that defined the limits of their enquiries. The Stabber could not have run that far in twenty seconds. Maybe Sa was right. He could have turned into North Street and driven off. Or hidden for a while, then driven off.

That was possible.

Gilchrist guided his team into action.

Stan crossed the street to join WPC Liz Gregg, his partner for the door-to-door. Baxter and Clarke approached the first door on the left, armed with a warrant. Young and Mann the next. Stan and Liz stepped up to the first door on their list and Gilchrist caught Stan's hand touch the back of her jacket, an almost unnoticeable contact that spoke volumes. Patterson had pronounced sexual relations forbidden between staff, on threat of termination. But as long as the job didn't suffer, Gilchrist was happy to keep quiet.

Wilson and Gray reached the top of a short flight of steps. From an opened doorway, a young woman with blonde hair and blue denim jeans frowned at them.

Gilchrist turned to Sa. 'Did you talk to Patterson?'

'About what?'

'MacMillan's statement.'

'That's old news, Andy. The ACC'll have a copy by now. What's your point?'

'He talked to McKinnon.'

'Patterson?' she sneered. 'He talks to everybody.' Her gaze locked onto his in an unfamiliar moment of intimacy. 'I wouldn't give Patterson the time of day,' she went on. 'He's violated the integrity of your investigation. You should file a complaint.'

'He'd deny it.'

'I'd support you.'

'I didn't know you cared.'

'You're being set up, Andy. Patterson wants you off the case. You know that, don't you? And I don't like it.'

'What's in it for him?'

Sunlight burst through the grey clouds and Gilchrist noticed one of Sa's eyes had more flecks of green in it than the other.

'Safety,' she said. 'His.'

Gilchrist frowned.

'You threaten him,' she added.

As Sa's words fluttered through his mind, he realised how little he knew of her. She had lived in St Andrews most of her life, never married, and lesbian rumours did the Office rounds from time to time. Gilchrist had never given them any substance

35

and something in the way she now looked at him strengthened his belief.

'Come on,' he said. 'Let's go.'

Sa turned, and Gilchrist found himself staring at Wilson and Gray as they stepped inside. As the young woman in blue jeans turned to close the door, Gilchrist thought he caught a glint of recognition in her eyes.

'You should call the police.'

'Cindy, I don't even know what he looks like. What do I tell them?'

'They'd have your call on record. If it happens again—'

'Don't.' Beth closed her eyes, pressed her hand to her mouth. 'Don't say that.'

Her body gave an involuntary shudder.

In the small utility room at the back of her shop, she had run her hands under the tap for a full minute, scouring her skin and fingernails with a nailbrush, washing her wrists and forearms with hefty squirts of antibacterial soap. She had dried herself off and looked in the mirror, checked that nothing had dripped onto her clothes. And when Cindy arrived she had asked her to give her the once over, too.

But the worst part had been swabbing the door handle, the glass panel, the entrance tiles, with soapy water, then sluicing the area down with disinfectant. Afterwards, she had trashed the gloves and washrag.

She shuddered again at the thought of it.

But how could she file a complaint?

Finding the words to tell the police that someone had ejaculated on her door was beyond her. Without a description, what could they do? And she had unwittingly destroyed all the evidence. She had no option but to work through the rest of the day as if nothing had happened. But despite her outer resolve, she could not rid herself of the unsettling feeling that continued to sweep through her.

What if the man returned?

What then?

CHAPTER 6

GILCHRIST KEPT HIS finger on the doorbell longer than considered courteous. He was concerned by Mrs Granton's failure to answer following Nance's visit to break the news.

'See anything?' he asked Sa.

She shook her head.

Gilchrist stepped back.

The cottage's roughcast facade shone white in the morning light. A brass coach lamp, polished like new copper, hung by the side of a varnished door. A gleaming brass nameplate was engraved with the single word Inverlea. A stone wall ran along the boundary and hid the rear garden from passers-by.

Gilchrist peered over.

A tidy lawn with crisp edges, the flowerbed turned over for the winter. Pruned shrubs stood against the opposite wall like shorn heads. A patio door lay open to reveal several dark inches of interior.

'Back in a tick,' he said, and gripped the cold stone.

He swung his legs up and over and leapt onto the gravel path that edged the lawn. He brushed moss and dirt from his hands and stopped at the sight of an elderly lady at the patio window. Behind him, Sa cleared the wall and landed on the gravel with the grace of an acrobat. Without a word, she walked past him, her feet crunching the pebbles, and faced the patio door. The woman barely reacted, as if she was watching a play, rather than two strangers invade her property.

Sa pressed her mouth to the gap in the patio door and said, 'We were concerned when you didn't answer.'

The woman stared blankly, as if she had heard a sound but was unable to locate it. Sa opened the patio door wider.

'May we come in?' she asked.

'Of course, dear.'

To Gilchrist's surprise, Sa stepped inside, put her arms around Mrs Granton and gave her a hug, patting her like a mother clearing wind from a baby. As they parted, Mrs Granton glanced at him and smiled.

'Come in, Detective Inspector. Please. I've heard so much about you.'

The living room was redolent of flowers and fresh polish, the air thick enough to taste.

'Have a seat, dear, I've got a pot brewing,' said Mrs Granton, then walked into the kitchen.

When he heard a cupboard being opened, he said, 'What the hell's going on?'

'Liz is my aunt,' she explained. 'Not my real aunt. She was best friends with my mother.'

'So you knew Bill Granton?'

'Yes.'

Gilchrist recalled her reluctance to look at Granton's body. Now it made some sense. 'Why didn't you tell me?'

'Would it have made a difference?'

Gilchrist chose not to answer and sat on a beige leather sofa that felt creased and soft. On a polished side table stood four framed photographs of an aged corgi. On a wooden bookshelf, another two. But no family photographs, or any evidence that Mrs Granton had shared the house with a man.

'So you must know Sam MacMillan as well,' he said to Sa.

Sa shook her head. 'His name cropped up but I had no idea he and Bill were so, how do I say it, close.'

Gilchrist glanced towards the kitchen. 'Did Mrs Granton know about her husband's relationship with MacMillan?'

'If she did, she chose to live with it. She's a devout Catholic. Divorce was not an option.'

'Children?'

'Only the one. Alex.'

Alex. Alex Granton. Gilchrist ran the name through his mind, but could not pull up why it sounded familiar. It would come to him.

'Do you know where he lives?'

'Glasgow. Last I heard he was a nurse in the Royal Infirmary. Never married.'

Mrs Granton reappeared carrying a large silver tray laden with a pot and cups and two side plates heaped high.

'Some home-made shortbread,' she announced.

Silent, Gilchrist watched her fuss around them, filling three bone china cups with the weakest of tea and asking whether they liked milk or sugar, and would cubes be all right, and how many. It seemed surreal to think that her husband's corpse now lay in the Police Mortuary in Dundee.

When everyone was served, Mrs Granton sat in a floral-patterned chair by the fireplace, patted down her pleated skirt and took a delicate sip.

'Okay, dear,' she said to him. 'Why are you here?'

Gilchrist hesitated at her odd behaviour, then said, 'Firstly, on behalf of Fife Constabulary, I would like to offer our deepest sympathy over the tragic death of your husband...'

'Another, dear?'

'Pardon?'

Mrs Granton nodded at his side plate. 'Would you like another finger of shortbread?'

'No thank you, Mrs Granton, I'm—'

'Call me Liz,' she said. 'Please. Everybody knows me as Liz. Liz Cockburn.'

'Cockburn?' he repeated.

'That was my name before I met William.'

The name niggled somewhere in the depths of Gilchrist's mind. 'And you were married for how long?'

'Forty years next March. The eighteenth.'

'Forgive me. But why would everybody know you as Liz Cockburn?'

'Because that's my name.'

'Yes, but why not Granton?'

'I've never liked Granton. I much prefer Cockburn. It sounds so much more Scottish, don't you think? Another piece of shortbread, dear? It's my own recipe.'

'No, thank you, Mrs, eh, Liz, I'm all shortbreaded out.'

She smiled. 'I can tell Sa was right about you. She said you were a nice man. There's not a lot of you around.'

'I'm sorry?'

'Nice men,' she said. 'You're few and far between.' Her eyes misted over, then she blinked and said, 'More tea, dear?'

'No, really, Mrs...'

'Liz.'

'Right. Liz. No. Thank you.' He glanced at Sa. He could have been a mouse between two cats. He forced himself to focus and said, 'I was told you declined to identify your husband's body.'

'Alex can do that.'

'Your son?'

'I called him this morning as soon as I heard. He said he'd be very pleased to identify the body, and that it wasn't before time.'

'Are you saying Alex was pleased to hear...'

'Not pleased, dear. Delighted.'

'Oh.' Gilchrist sat back.

'He didn't like him.'

'Did he have good reason?'

Mrs Granton glanced at Sa, and Gilchrist had a sense of Sa having given her permission to speak out. 'He knew William hit me.'

'He *hit* you?'

She tilted her head back in an act of silent defiance. 'Yes,' she said. 'He hit me. Many times.'

Gilchrist leaned forward. 'I'm sorry, but I have to ask. How, exactly, did he hit you?'

'Usually with his fist. Never in the face. William was clever that way. Sometimes he would whip me across my back with his belt.'

Gilchrist struggled to keep his voice level. 'How long had that been going on?' he asked.

'Since before we were married.'

Gilchrist clawed a hand through his hair. He wanted to ask why she had married someone who beat her, but instead said, 'Were you ever injured?'

'Often. William once cracked six of my ribs. I was in bed for over two months.'

'What did you tell the doctor?'

'That I fell down the stairs.'

'And he believed you?'

'Why wouldn't he?'

Something swept through Gilchrist then. A sense of the futility of it all. 'And the belt whippings?' he pressed on.

'I never went to the hospital unless anything was broken. He fractured my arm once.'

'And you reported none of this to the police?'

'No.'

'What about Alex? Did he do anything?'

'He threatened to report William to the authorities.'

'And did he?'

'No.'

'Why not?'

'I asked him not to. William said he would throw me out of my home and leave me penniless if I reported him.'

'But surely you—'

'It was my choice, Inspector. For better or for worse. Those were the vows I took. The worse was the beatings. But the better was full of kindness. William could be the most charming man at times.' She smiled, and the years seemed to fall away from her. 'Most charming. And that's the way I would like to remember him.'

Something in her tone told Gilchrist the meeting was over. He stood. Sa did likewise.

'No need to get up,' he said to Mrs Granton. 'We'll let ourselves out.'

But the old woman struggled to her feet with a dazed smile that had Gilchrist thinking she was not all there and that forty years of beatings had finally taken their toll.

'I may come back later for a statement,' he said to her.

'Oh, that would be nice, dear. Do let me know when, and I'll have some fresh shortbread ready.'

'Right. Okay. Sa?'

'And there's no need to climb over the wall,' Mrs Granton added. 'The front door's always unlocked.'

Outside, the wind felt light and fresh and free of the sense of gloom that cloyed the Granton's cottage. Gilchrist chose not to speak until they turned onto South Street.

'Tell me, Sa. How can we help the public if they're not willing to help themselves?' He shook his head. 'Abused for all these years by some, some...'

He sniffed something in the air. Cigar smoke. A tourist in a Stars and Stripes tracksuit and running shoes stood at the edge of the pavement, newspaper stuffed under his arm, fat cigar tucked into the corner of his mouth.

Gilchrist fought off the urge to nip into a shop and buy a packet of fags. Just twenty. That's all. He would make them last, take one a day for the next three weeks. The tourist stepped off the pavement. Gilchrist inhaled, then opened his eyes, surprised to find he had closed them. Was this what his life had come to? Sniffing passive smoke like some tramp trawling bins for food? He had never believed he suffered from nicotine addiction, but at that moment the strength of its grip shocked him. Was physical abuse an addiction, too? Did wife-beaters have an addictive need to bully their victims? If so, Gilchrist despaired at the depth of their turmoil. He started to walk.

'Didn't you know she was a victim of abuse?' he asked.

'Not until recently.'

'How recently?'

'Only a few months—'

'I find that hard to believe—'

'What are you trying to tell me, Andy?' Anger blazed in Sa's eyes. 'That it's all my fault? That I should have found out sooner? You heard her. Bill was a sneaky bastard. He hit where it wouldn't show. How the hell am I supposed to know, when she wouldn't even let her own son report it? As far as I'm concerned, that bastard got what was coming.'

Gilchrist said nothing.

'Did it ever cross your mind that the Stabber might be the best thing that ever happened to this piss-pot of a town?' she went on. 'Maybe we should just let him run wild and kill all the abusers in the country. That way we'd be rid of the lot of them.'

'You know that's not the way.'

She flinched.

'Look, Sa—'

'Fuck off, Andy.'

CHAPTER 7

HE RETURNED BEFORE midday and spied on her shop from behind a car on the opposite side of the street. Annoyance flitted over him like flies on his skin. He scratched the inside of his left arm and drew blood from an old scab. An elderly couple stepped into the entrance alcove, and he held his breath as they took hold of the handle and pushed inside.

The bitch. She had cleaned it up. The thought of her fingers touching his sperm stirred something deep inside him and he felt an overpowering need to see how upset she was. He had changed his clothes and now wore an old white sweatshirt, curry-stained on the left sleeve, and black jeans that hung loose around his waist, and felt sure she would not recognise him.

Her shop was an upmarket novelty store. Two Laurel and Hardy face masks centred the window. Mobile phones designed as Ferrari sports cars, bars of soap, multi-coloured chameleons, reflected off stainless steel shelves. A CD rack that looked like some skeletal saxophone hugged the corner.

Through the glass he saw her talking to a customer. She smiled an easy smile and tucked loose strands of blonde hair behind her

44

ears. He gripped the handle.

Inside, the shop smelled of potpourri and was crammed from floor to ceiling with photo frames, posters, face masks. Wooden puppets with glossy painted faces lay lifeless on flat surfaces, or hung limp from hooks in the ceiling. Shelves glittered with ornaments, stainless steel pieces shaped into objects that looked like bookends, bottle openers, key rings. All of it priced way up there. Jazz segued over the ambient buzz of voices.

He stood with his back to the counter and studied the shelves. Not much took his fancy, except perhaps the painted motorbike carved from wood, with wheels that spun, handlebar that turned and a minuscule Harley Davidson logo on the—

'Can I help you?'

Sebbie's breath locked in his throat as he stared into grey eyes that levelled with his own. Her height surprised him. For a moment, he thought she recognised him, then teeth as white as sun-dried bone appeared from beneath moist lips.

'It's handmade,' she said. 'I have three others. Would you like to see?'

He nodded.

She reached for one of the upper shelves. Long fingers clasped another model, larger than the one he held.

'Here.' She handed the model to him and stretched up for another one. A sliver of white skin flashed at her waistline. He caught the pale swell of her tummy, the finest of blonde hairs at her navel, and lower, a glimpse of black at her panty line. He felt his mouth dry up. Black panties. He never imagined she would wear black, had thought she would wear knickers as white and clean as the image she portrayed.

But now he knew. Black. The bitch. The dirty bitch.

'Here.' She held out another model. 'This range is one of our bestsellers,' she said. 'They're popular with collectors. One told me he had upwards of fifty. And going up in price every year.' His fingers looked rough and unclean beside hers. He read the hand-printed price tag.

Seventy pounds?

'Do you collect?'

'Uh, no, I, uh, was just looking.'

'Your arm's bleeding.'

He frowned at the bloodstain on his sleeve, then looked into her grey eyes. But it was the top of her black panties he saw. He smiled, almost laughed, then turned to the shelves again. 'How about that one?'

She seemed to hesitate for an instant, stiffened then faced him. Her eyebrows flickered.

'Excuse me.' She drew away. 'I have to...'

She returned behind the counter.

Silent, he watched her, intrigued by the hesitant tug of her lips, as if she was holding back a smile. What would he give for that bitch Alice to see him walk into a restaurant with her on his arm? He thought he saw her whisper from the corner of her mouth. As he turned to replace the model, he brushed against a CD rack, which toppled onto a shelf with a hard crack.

'Fuck.'

The word was out before he knew it. A couple shifted away. From behind he felt the bitch's eyes crawl over him.

'Sir?' A fresh-faced girl with green eyes that stung appeared by his side. 'Would you like to buy something?'

'I, uh. No.'

'In that case, I'll have to ask you to leave.'

At the counter, the bitch stood with her back to him, her hand on the phone.

'Now, sir. Please leave.'

He spun round to face her.

The young woman stepped back, but kept her nerve. 'The door's that way,' she said.

As he strode off, he clipped something, heard the hard clatter of a metal ornament hit the floor. But he just kept walking, anger swelling inside him.

'Fuck you,' he said. 'Fuck you, you bitches.'

PC Norris said, 'DCI Patterson would like to see you, sir.'

Gilchrist had worked with PC Norris on the body on the West Sands. Three years ago as best he could recall. He wondered if his own face had ever looked as smooth. Long before his lungs felt the choking fire of that first cigarette, no doubt. Something contracted in the pit of his stomach. The urge for a smoke, or maybe it was just the mention of Patterson's name.

'When?'

'Now, sir.'

He glanced at his watch. 12:35. He had ignored Patterson's earlier instruction to report to him, and was now back on North Street assisting in the door-to-door enquiries, surprised Patterson hadn't hounded him down before then.

'Tell him I'll be along as soon as I've finished.'

Norris's lips twitched. 'He said you would say that, sir, and I'm to let you know he's ordering you to report to him right away.'

Gilchrist wondered if he should tell Norris to piss off. Or better still, tell him to tell Patterson to piss off. But Norris was only doing his job. 'Take over,' he said to Sa. 'Norris will assist you.'

Patterson's office was located on the upper level at the west end of the building. As Gilchrist mounted the stairs, an image of McKinnon's grubby face whispering into Patterson's ear manifested in his mind and he struggled to shake off the sick feeling in his stomach. He rapped his knuckles against the door. Hard.

'Come in.'

Patterson's office lay in perpetual twilight, the slatted blinds never fully opened. The main source of light came from a Tiffany lamp with a butterfly design, which cast a greenish glow onto an A3 blotter.

Patterson sat behind the desk, his attention focused on a document pressed flat to the blotter with his left hand.

Gilchrist watched him scan it with literary pride, then place his hands to his mouth in a fleshy steeple. In someone intellectual, that pose might suggest thought. Patterson looked as if he had frozen mid-clap.

'You're not popular with the press, Andy.'

'I'm not trying to win any contests.'

47

'I'm told the conference was a fiasco.'

'Depends whose side you're on.'

'Not sure I would have recommended handling it the way you did. Restricting access like that.'

'Who gave permission to break the barricade?' Gilchrist asked, louder than intended.

'I did.'

The arrogance of the man continued to amaze Gilchrist. He had tried to keep the press from infiltrating North Street and encumbering their enquiries. Why close the street to the public if the press could stroll its length?

'You talked to McKinnon,' Gilchrist said.

'About what?'

'Don't play dumb with me, Mark.'

Patterson's eyes flared for a moment then died. 'How many's that now?' he asked.

'How many's what?'

'Stabber murders, Andy.'

'You know it's six,' he said.

Patterson pressed his steepled hands to the tip of his nose. 'Six.' He paused. 'Is that it?'

'Is that what?'

Patterson unsteepled his hands and placed them flat on the desk as if to examine his fingernails. 'Is the tally going to reach seven?' he asked. 'Or a whole lot more? Are we just expected to sit back and watch you fuck up day after day?' His face reddened as if something was squeezing his collar. 'Would it be unreasonable of me to expect an answer?'

'Not at all.'

'Well, dammit, what do you have to say about your incompetence?'

'The answer to your first question is that I hope the tally doesn't—'

'*Hope*? Good God, man, don't tell me all we've got to go on now is *hope*.'

'Would you like me to continue? Or would you prefer I wait until your blood pressure settles?'

48

Patterson let out his breath in an audible sigh then tried a quick smile. But he was asking too much of his nervous system. 'That's what I've always disliked about you, Andy. Your insolence. Your maverick contempt for authority.'

'Depends on whose authority.'

'Defiant to the last.'

Gilchrist did not like the word last, but said nothing.

'Let me explain the gravity of the situation to—'

'I know how serious—'

'Shut up.' A hand slapped the desk. Patterson's face paled. 'I've had Assistant Chief Constable McVicar on the phone. St James's Palace has been in contact. In case it's slipped your mind, Prince William attends university in this small town of ours.'

Gilchrist waited.

'I have been advised that the Queen is concerned over her grandson's safety. I've done my utmost to assure all concerned that the Prince is in no danger, but the Palace remains dubious over the lack of progress in the investigation. They've asked...' He sat back, studied his fingernails. 'They've asked that you be replaced.'

Gilchrist had been anticipating this moment ever since Patterson got wind of his affair with Alyson Baird. And now it was here, he felt nothing.

'I've agreed, of course. Detective Chief Inspector Christian DeFiore of the Scottish Crime Squad is driving up from Edinburgh. He should be here in about an hour. I've told both ACC McVicar and Chief Superintendent Greaves that you'll give DeFiore full and uninhibited access to all files and matters of evidence, and that by tomorrow evening I expect you to be in a position to step aside and let him take full control.' Patterson smirked. 'Is that clear?'

Gilchrist stood up.

'*Sit*. I'm not finished.'

Gilchrist ignored the demand.

Patterson leaned forward, so his face came out of shadow. At that low angle, his pockmarks looked like tiny scars. 'Unfortunately, we need to go through a PR exercise,' he said. 'I've prepared a press statement giving your reasons for stepping down.'

'Which are?'

'Your health.'

'What's wrong with my health?'

'The Stabber case has taken its toll on you, Gilchrist. You've been advised by your doctor to take some rest.'

'Nervous breakdown? That sort of thing?'

'Well done. Any more of this and you'll go up in my estimation.'

'Would that please me?'

Patterson's jaw twisted, sending a ripple of shadow across his cheeks.

Gilchrist pressed both hands flat on the edge of the desk. It gave him an odd sense of pleasure to see Patterson look up at him. 'I don't like it,' he said.

'It doesn't matter what you like, Gilchrist.'

'It does to me.'

'You'll do as you're ordered. For God's sake, man, St Andrews has been the focal point of the national news ever since that royal brat set foot in the place. And while he's here, the last thing we need is a serial killer racking up his score because of your incompetence.' Patterson's nostrils flared, and Gilchrist had an image of fire and smoke billowing over the desk. 'Whether you like it or not, Gilchrist, you will take medical leave.'

'There's nothing wrong with my health.'

'I know that, for Christ's sake.'

Gilchrist shook his head. 'I won't do it.'

'All right,' said Patterson. 'If that's your decision.' His manner was too calm for comfort. Gilchrist waited for the sting. It came in the following breath.

'Let me put it this way, Gilchrist. Medical leave gives you the chance to have your job back when the case is solved.'

Gilchrist felt anger burn his face. The thought of grabbing Patterson by his hair and slamming him nose first onto his desk was almost irresistible. 'And if it isn't?'

Patterson seemed not to notice Gilchrist's emotional struggle, and shrugged. 'Alternatively, we could just fire you.'

'For what?'

'Incompetence. Insubordination. Poor time-keeping. Screwing secretaries. Like me to continue?'

'That's your prerogative.'

'I've never liked you, Gilchrist. You've always known that. But others more senior than I seem to hold you in high esteem. They value your abilities as an investigator, of all things.' He chuckled. 'Mind boggling, if you ask me.'

Gilchrist almost laughed. He saw it now. Patterson wanted to fire him, but his hands were tied by others more senior. 'I'll tell you what I'll do,' he said. 'I'm off the case. Not for medical reasons but because you think I'm incompetent, the worst DI in the history of Fife Constabulary.'

Anger flared in Patterson's eyes, held for a moment, then vanished. It really was amazing to follow the man's thought process. Patterson pushed his seat back and stood, as if to intimidate Gilchrist. But at five-ten, he was a good three inches shorter. 'Okay,' he said, 'but you'll have to suffer the consequences.'

'For what?'

'Your failure to perform.'

'And the consequences are?'

'Demotion.'

Gilchrist walked away.

'Get back here, Gilchrist. I'm not finished with you yet.'

Gilchrist reached the door, opened it, then faced Patterson. 'I'm doing you a favour by stepping out of the way, Mark. So don't push your luck.'

'I'm warning you, Gilchrist—'

'Do you know what your problem is?'

Patterson's head jerked.

'You're so hell-bent on trying to even some imaginary score that you've forgotten what the game's about. But let me tell you this. One word about a nervous breakdown, and I'll sue you personally. I'll hit you so hard you'll wonder why you ever wanted to play the game in the first place.'

Gilchrist eased the door shut and took the stairs two at a

time. Outside, he felt strangely elated. North Street was still closed. Overhead, a flock of seagulls wheeled from sight, leaving the echo of their harsh cries on the breeze. To his right, four women huddled in a concerned cluster, whispering.

He crossed the street and stood with his back against a wall, waiting for Sa to appear. Ten minutes later she stepped from a door into the brightening sunlight, PC Norris behind her.

'Any luck?' he said to her.

She shook her head. 'Everyone we've interviewed saw nothing and heard nothing. Maybe the others are having better luck. We'll find out at debriefing.'

'I won't be there. I'm off the case.'

'Patterson fired you?'

'Suspended.' He walked away, fingers by his ear in a make-believe telephone receiver. 'Call me later on my mobile. Oh, and some guy by the name of DeFiore is coming up from Edinburgh. He's with the Scottish Crime Squad.'

'What?'

'Your new boss.'

CHAPTER 8

The leather whistles through the air and smacks my mother's buttocks. I flinch at the strike and start to cry. My father twists the belt with a deftness that is startling, and hits her with the buckle end. I think he will stop when he sees she is bleeding, but the sight of blood seems to drive him on. He shifts his stance and whips the buckle hard across her face. Her left eyeball bursts, weeps black and red.

I scream. Timmy's hand crushes my mouth, pressing so hard I think he is going to burst my lips.

My father turns his head. Eyes as dark as the Devil's look into mine. He stumbles over my mother's body and lunges towards us.

Timmy whimpers, drops his hand from my mouth. I pull at him but he stands there, his skinny body shaking. Something warms the soles of my stockinged feet, and I realise he has wet himself. I try to make him move, shout at him, but it's as if he is glued to the spot.

I push the window open, wriggle onto the concrete sill. Timmy cries out. I leap.

I never see my father again. Five days later, his body is

recovered from the water's edge. Nor Timmy either. His head was crushed by a blow to the back of his skull.

Gilchrist fought off the urge to walk to Lafferty's and spend the rest of the day drowning his sorrows. Instead, he walked back to The Pends and stood in the shelter of the crumbling archway. He eyed the grey stone wall and iron railings that bounded the grounds and cemetery of the ruined Cathedral and tried to imagine what MacMillan might have seen as he followed the Stabber into North Street.

He visualised flickering skies, rain thrashing the road, a body hunched against the wicked night, anorak hood tugged tight. He followed the ghost in his mind and reached the corner of North Street.

He stopped, checked his watch. Twenty-nine seconds.

He looked along North Street. The huddles of worried neighbours had dispersed. Two uniformed officers were walking towards the Police Station. His gaze danced along the row of terraced houses on the north side of the road and he wondered why he always looked that way. Why not to the other side? He studied the old stone façades, tried to imagine what MacMillan had been too late to see, and came to realise that thirty seconds was just not sufficient time for someone to disappear from view so completely.

Had MacMillan's eyes failed him? Had he been blinded by the rain? If not, where could the Stabber have gone?

Gilchrist felt his gaze pulling back to The Pends. From where he stood, he could see the left of the arched entrance. But from the other side of the road, that support pillar would be hidden. Which would mean the converse was true, that someone taking shelter behind that pillar would not be able to see that side of the street.

Gilchrist's mind crackled with possibilities. What if the Stabber had not turned into North Street, but slipped across the road, as he was doing now, then into the lane that paralleled the Abbey wall and continued towards the hill overlooking the harbour? That would mean he was backtracking, completing the circle around the Abbey ruins and heading back towards the scene of the murder where Granton's body lay.

Gregory Lane, on the other hand, ran almost perpendicular to North Street, down to the cliff front, a six-foot high stone wall on one side, a combination of gable ends, walls and gates on the other.

Had the Stabber escaped down this lane?

MacMillan's natural instinct would have been to seek shelter in the lee of the stone wall. The storm had come in over the Eden Estuary, and with the rain in his face he would have been hard put to see the murderer slipping into the lane.

Enlivened by that possibility, Gilchrist entered Gregory Lane. Along the left wall, he noticed the indentation of two gates, one near North Street, the other close to the exit at the cliff pathway. On the right, the lane formed the short side of a triangular complex of terraced houses and open courtyards. Had the Stabber gone into one of these houses? Or through one of the gates? Or used the lane as a shortcut to the cliffs? Or was Gilchrist's theory just a theory, and seriously flawed?

As he walked along the lane, Gilchrist felt hesitant, like a child creeping through a forbidden room. His sixth sense was telling him something. Beware, it whispered. You are close. When he emerged at the far end of the lane, he crossed the asphalt path and gripped the metal railing that ran the length of the cliff face.

Sixty feet beneath him, sea rocks glistened dark and wet. Gulls drifted by on invisible trails of wind, heads turning as if searching for their nests in the rocky face. The tuneless clamour of bagpipes came at him on the breeze. By the ancient ruins of Culdee Church, a lone piper paced back and forth. The sight of Scottish busking at its most ethnic brought a smile to Gilchrist's lips.

He spent the next thirty minutes investigating the residential complex bounded by Gregory Lane, the Abbey wall and the cliff path. It seemed to him that the courtyards were too open, windows from one house backing onto another, providing no privacy or obscurity, even at night.

He approached the ruins of the castle, focusing on the houses that overlooked the sea. He ambled like a tourist interested in local architecture. He took in the glistening paintwork, the washed steps, even ventured up to the windows and capped his hand to his brow as he peered inside. A thin face with hollowed cheeks reflected back at him, making him think that perhaps the pressure of work had indeed overtaken him. Maybe Patterson was right. Maybe someone with fresh input would solve the case in a matter of minutes. Maybe pigs would fly.

Most of the houses looked empty, but the shiver of a curtain in a downstairs window caught his eye. A ceramic nameplate announced the resident as McLaren. He gave a quick rap.

A woman in her fifties wearing an apron powdered flour-white opened the door.

'Mrs McLaren?'

'Yes?' she asked, with more than a hint of impatience.

'I'm Detective Inspector Andy Gilchrist of—'

'I'm in the middle of baking.'

'I won't keep you long.'

She yielded with a sigh. 'I suppose it's that young one you'll be wanting to talk to then.'

Inside, the warm smell of baking reminded Gilchrist of Saturday mornings at home as a boy. Mrs McLaren tilted her head to the ceiling and shouted, 'Ian. Come down here.' She glanced back at Gilchrist. 'God knows what'll become of that lad. Does nothing but sleep all day. Then when it's time to go to bed, he goes out.'

'Was he out last night?'

'In all that thunder and lightning? Not a chance. He's more scared of getting wet than that cat of hers next door.' She stomped into the kitchen. 'Ian,' she shouted again. 'Get yourself down here. Right this minute. It's the police here to see you.'

Gilchrist heard a stampede of thuds down the stairs.

'What is it, Mum?'

A teenager stood in the kitchen doorway, barefoot and stripped to the waist. Ribs corrugated his sides. A tattoo of sorts stained his left bicep. Denim jeans that seemed to defy gravity, covered stick legs.

'This is the police, Ian. Tell him.'

Mrs McLaren, her back to Gilchrist, sprinkled flour over a wooden board and banged her rolling pin onto the work surface. 'And don't go telling lies, now. Do you hear me?'

Gilchrist tried to soften his manner. 'What do you have to tell me, Ian?'

The boy rubbed his upper arms. 'Nothing,' he said.

The rolling pin thumped onto the wooden board.

'It might be warmer in the living room,' Gilchrist said, sure that the boy would not talk freely with his mother close by.

Gilchrist took a chair by a tiled square on the wall, all that remained of the original fireplace. An electric fire with a wood-stained top centred the hearth.

The boy stood by the chair opposite.

'Would you like me to put the fire on, Ian?' Gilchrist asked.

Ian shook his head.

'You're shivering.'

'I didnae start it.'

Gilchrist almost frowned. 'I didn't say you did.'

'He hit me first.'

'Self-defence, was it?'

'Aye.'

'And where and when did this fight take place?'

The boy grimaced. 'Outside the Whey Pat. Last Friday, like. I've already been up at the Police Station.'

Gilchrist saw no bruises. Probably a minor tussle. 'Did you win?' he asked.

The boy's fists clenched, then relaxed. 'Aye.'

'I'm not here to talk about the fight, Ian. I want you to tell me where you were last night.'

'Upstairs.'

'All night?'

'Aye.'

'Not go out at all?'

Ian shook his head. 'It was raining. I cannae stand the rain. I cannae stand this place.' Gilchrist was not sure if he was talking about his home, the town, or Scotland, or all of the above.

57

'What did you do all night, Ian?'

'Played my guitar until it got light. Then I went to sleep.'

Gilchrist nodded. As a boy he had taught himself a few chords, but felt embarrassed singing. He found more pleasure in writing songs, though he hadn't tried to sell any, never even knew he could.

'Have you asked her next door?' the boy was saying.

'Who's *her*?'

'Lex Garvie.'

'Lex? She a friend of yours?'

'No.'

He leaned forward. 'Why should I ask her?'

'She keeps odd hours.'

'Does she?'

'Aye. And I know for a fact she was up late last night.'

'How do you know that?'

'I seen her.'

'Where?'

'Out the back.'

'In the storm?'

'Aye. After midnight.'

'Doing what?'

'It looked like she was feeding that stupid cat of hers.'

Gilchrist frowned. 'What's stupid about the cat?'

Ian shrugged. 'They say she's a witch.'

'The cat?'

'No, Lex Garvie.'

'Who says she's a witch?'

'Just some of my friends.'

'Not the ones you fight with?'

'No.'

'They play the guitar, too?'

'Not all of them. Tam plays the drums. He's dead good, so he is.'

'What makes them think she's a witch?'

'Just stuff.'

'What sort of stuff?'

Another shrug.

'I see,' said Gilchrist.

'You dinnae believe me. I can tell.'

'I'm too old to believe everything I hear first time now, Ian. Growing older makes you cynical.' Gilchrist waited, but the boy offered nothing more. 'I'll look into what you've told me, Ian. You've been extremely helpful.'

'Can I go now?'

'Back to bed?'

'I was listening to music.'

'Sure.'

Gilchrist returned to the kitchen.

Mrs McLaren told him she had watched television, to drown out *thon racket* from upstairs, then taken a sleeping pill and gone to bed. There was no Mr McLaren. He had died in a fishing accident seven years earlier. Gilchrist thanked her for her time and declined her invitation to try her Madeira cake.

'Are you sure you cannae be tempted? It's straight from the oven.'

'Positive, Mrs McLaren.'

'If that's the way you feel, then.'

Outside, the wind had risen. Gilchrist switched on his mobile. He had missed a call. Jack's number flashed up.

At last. His son had finally deigned to call.

But Gilchrist had too much on his mind to call straight back. Something was niggling him about Nance's comment.

From a distance, a woman might be mistaken for a man.

Is it possible MacMillan saw a woman?

Gilchrist was intrigued to meet the witch next door.

Sebbie stepped onto the West Sands, an expansive stretch of beach that rippled to the sea. He crossed puddles that glinted as dull as pewter, his worn trainers casting shallow prints that welled like his mother's eyes. He reached the shoreline and breathed in the smell of salt, the faint stench of seaweed. A breeze bristled his hair and sent a shiver through him.

The tide had turned. The sea was creeping shoreward.

He scuffed the damp sand. It was here on the West Sands that his father's body had been found. The memory of that day seemed unreal now. But the sand was real. The sea was real. The air that chilled his lungs was real. His loneliness was real, too.

With his toe he sketched a human shape and remembered how his father had lain there, his flaccid skin as white as milk, his body emptied of blood through the red gash in his neck. Water lapped at Sebbie's feet and the advancing tide obliterated his imprint of his father's left leg, then dribbled along the ruts in the sand, taking the left hand next, then the arm. Two minutes later there was nothing left.

Even when the sea splashed his toes, Sebbie did not move. Not until a wave lapped over his ankles.

Further up the beach, he kneeled, scooped a handful of damp sand, ignored the wind, the cold and the advancing waters. Within a couple of minutes he had dug a hole some twelve inches deep, its shallow sides collapsing from seeping water. He pulled off his trainers and crammed them into it, his fingers like metal tines, scraping deep into the liquid bottom. He pushed sand back in and flattened and patted the surface until all that remained was an area smoothed of ripples, darker than the surrounding sand.

As the waters edged over his covered spot, it struck him that his symbolic tribute had filled the sense of loss he had harboured since the day his father's body had floated in on the surf three years earlier.

By that simple action, some burden had been lifted. And he saw then that he needed to pay tribute to his mother, but a different type of tribute, a get even type of tribute.

Someone had screwed up the investigation.

Now that someone was going to suffer.

CHAPTER 9

'LOOK AFTER IT for fifteen minutes, Cindy.'

Beth pulled on her suede jacket. As she opened the door, the pungent stench of Dettol caught the back of her throat. With an overpowering need to breathe in fresh air, she rushed across the tiled entranceway.

Away from the shop, she tried to recall what the man had looked like. She was no good with faces. Never had been. Names, yes. Which helped her in the shop. Customers liked that she remembered their names. It made them feel as if they were visiting a friend. But faces, no.

He had sent a CD rack crashing to the floor. Nothing had been broken, otherwise she would have had no hesitation in reporting the incident to the police. But something in his manner had upset her.

She had noticed his expression in a wall-mounted mirror as she reached for one of the wooden motorcycles. Since her summer vacation she had lost over six pounds, so her jeans were slacker than usual, and she had caught him leering down the gap at her front. She was certain of that.

But would any man have done the same?

Then she saw the answer in the memory of his eyes. They had scared her. Dark and fierce, as if they had no need to blink. And his hair. Matted, as if it had not seen a brush in months. His fingernails, too. Black with grime.

She crossed onto Abbey Street and walked downhill. It felt good to get away. The shop had been her mother's dream. Not Beth's. At the age of twenty-three Beth's future lay in interior design and she had applied to Heriot-Watt University in Edinburgh. Before her letter of acceptance came through, her father had died of a massive heart attack at the breakfast table. Unwilling to leave her mother alone, Beth delayed the start of her career for a year.

A small insurance payout provided the cash for her mother to buy the shop. But six months after opening, her mother had complained of blinding headaches and a puzzling inability to control the movement of her fingers. Within four weeks she was diagnosed with a malignant brain tumour. The speed with which the cancer overpowered her was frightening, and three months later Beth buried her mother beside her father in a small cemetery on the outskirts of town.

By then, she had found to her surprise that she liked the shop. A change in products from miscellaneous domestic knick-knacks to exclusive accessories aimed at the wealthy American tourist market resulted in a feature in the local newspaper. It helped, too, that she was dating the editor, an ambitious, self-centred individual. And it now seemed incredible how close she had come to marrying him.

She turned left onto The Shore, the road that led towards the harbour, and five minutes later felt the sea breeze on her face. The Kinness Burn ran by her side. With the tide out, it looked nothing more than sodden mud and a trickle black as oil. A family of swans nestled in the grassy bank on the far side, beaks tucked under their wings, as if sheltering from the wind.

Beth removed her mobile from her pocket, unsure for a moment if she should make the call, then on impulse punched it in. A man's voice invited her to leave a message and number.

That was it. No confirmation that by doing so he would call back.

'Hi,' she said, and tried to keep her voice lively. 'I'm calling to remind you about tonight. The West Port Café. Eight o'clock. See you then.'

She slapped the silver casing shut and walked on, her thoughts filled with the imminent meeting. But in The Pends a memory came back to her of grimy nails and clotted hair and eyes as black as pools of ink. And it struck her then that she had seen the young man before.

After walking the length of Gregory Lane several times, Gilchrist's sixth sense was compelling him towards the end of the lane, close to where the 'witch' lived.

He had often wondered if the Stabber might be a woman, but had been ridiculed by Patterson when he raised that possibility after the third victim, Henry McIntyre, *a vile excuse for a man*, according to a neighbour, had been found behind Blackfriar's Chapel with his head staked to the ground, clutching his wallet as if he had been about to pass over money. *Why else would he have opened his wallet?* Gilchrist had argued.

He checked the brass nameplate. A. Garvie. Alexis Garvie? Lex? He eyed the upper level. No movement. He rapped the brass knocker. It echoed like a hammer-blow.

The door swung open to reveal a blonde-haired woman in a grey sweatshirt and black spandex. Bare-footed, tanned as if she had spent a few weeks on the Costa del Sol. Beads of perspiration dotted her forehead. Sweat stained her chest.

He had seen her before, he was sure. 'Ms Garvie?'

'If you're selling anything, I'm not interested.'

He noted the English accent. Yorkshire, as best he could tell. He tried a smile as he held out his warrant card. 'Detective Inspector Gilchrist. I'd like to ask you a few questions.'

Her eyes widened as if in expectation of being charged and handcuffed and marched to the nearest cell.

'Is it to do with this Stabber thing?'

He nodded. 'May I come in?'

'Do I have a choice?'

'It won't take long.'

She turned away, leaving the door wide open, and it took him a moment to realise he was expected to follow.

The house smelled of soot and furniture polish. Bright rugs covered the backs of the sofa and chairs like oversized antimacassars. More hung on the walls, unframed canvases of reds, greens, yellows, blues.

In the kitchen a television sat on the counter top, its volume muted. A reporter mouthed to him from St Andrews harbour then slipped from view as the camera panned the length of the pier.

'Tea?'

'No thanks.'

'Do you mind if I have a cup?'

'Of course not.'

She filled a kettle. The water drilled into it, as if to emphasise her displeasure at his presence. The kitchen window was ajar and looked onto a tiny garden area that ended at a stone wall. A black and white cat sat on the window sill, as if deciding whether to enter or stay outside.

'What's his name?' Gilchrist asked. 'The cat.'

'Pitter.'

'Peter?'

'No. *Pitter.*'

Sun burst onto the back garden, and Pitter's eyes closed.

'That's an unusual name.'

'That's what I thought.'

'You didn't name him, then?'

'He's a she, and I inherited her from a friend.'

'You live alone?'

'Is this it?'

'Is this what?'

'The interrogation.'

He gave her a small smile. 'You could say.'

'Well, in that case, yes, I live alone. I'm not married. Never have. Never will. Don't have any children. And don't want any,

God forbid. Just a cat. That's enough trouble, thank you very much. You've already been introduced to her. I've lived here for two years. Moved up from London. And before that, Tadcaster, Yorkshire. Don't have a mortgage and design websites for a living. Don't charge much, so it's not much of a living. But I'm happy.' She pulled open the fridge door and a waft of cool air brushed his legs. He moved to the side. 'Except, this bloody kitchen's too small.' She pressed a can of apricots under an electric can opener. 'Anything else you'd like to know?'

He watched her shove a teaspoonful of bright orange fruit into her mouth. 'Were you at home last night?' he asked.

She nodded. Another spoon-load.

'Alone?'

'Uh-huh.' Juice dribbled from her lips and she turned to the sink, grabbed a paper towel and dabbed her chin. She loaded up the spoon again, held it out to him. 'Want to try some? They're delicious.'

'No thanks.'

Something tinkled and he turned as Pitter padded onto a folded tea-towel by the edge of the steel sink and sat down.

'She sees the tin. Thinks she's going to be fed.'

Gilchrist smiled. 'Friendly?'

'Very.'

He reached out and stroked the top of Pitter's head, worked his fingers down and under her chin. He felt her throat vibrate with delight.

'Keep that up and you'll have a friend for life.'

He scratched some more. 'Why Pitter?'

'Pitter patter. She was one of two.'

'What happened?'

'Nothing,' she said. 'A friend has the other one.'

'The friend who gave you Pitter?'

'Uh-huh.' She opened the cupboard door under the sink and dropped the emptied can of apricots into a plastic bag. Then she dabbed her lips with the paper towel and dropped that into the plastic bag, too.

'Boyfriend?'

'You're joking.'

Garvie's blonde hair, short at the back and sides, was spiky on the top. Perspiration darkened it at the neck and ears.

'You keep yourself fit.'

She nodded. 'I was exercising when you knocked.'

'Exercise a lot, do you?'

'Try to. No more than a couple of hours a day, though.'

'That's a couple of hours more than most people.'

'Still not enough.'

'And at night?' he said. 'Do any exercises then?'

'Rarely.'

'How about last night?'

She shook her head and reached for a teapot. 'Sure I can't talk you into a cuppa?'

'Positive.' He eyed the coloured rugs in the lounge. 'Travel a lot?'

'Used to. In my last job.'

'Which was?'

'Chartered Accountant.' She smiled. 'God, I hated it.'

'Doesn't it pay well?'

'Money's not everything. But it paid for this place.'

'Why give it up?'

She shrugged. One hand held a mug, World's Greatest Lover printed on the side. The other, a ceramic teapot. 'I couldn't stand the sexual innuendo,' she said, and tipped the teapot. A stream of golden brown tea steamed into the mug. 'It's different for a man. Men get laid. Women get fucked. But what do I care?' she added, 'I'm gay.'

He was not altogether surprised by her blunt admission. 'So,' he said, 'Patter must stay with your partner?'

'I'd heard you were good.'

'That's an odd thing to say.'

'St Andrews is a small town, Inspector. And you're the small-town hero.'

'We all have our crosses to bear.'

'And your reputation precedes you.'

'In what way?'

'You always get your man.'

Or woman, he thought.

'Besides, I've seen you about.'

'In the pub, no doubt.'

'And on the telly.' The sinews of her neck stood out like rods of flesh as she turned to the window.

The strength of her physical attraction unsettled him.

'No one likes us,' she said. 'Gays, that is. No one likes to have us living next door.'

MacMillan's words came back to him. *I dinnae think I could stand the looks.*

'Ever been called a witch?' he asked.

She laughed without humour. 'You must have been talking to young Ian next door.'

'Why would he call you a witch?'

'It's not Ian. He's a nice lad. But some of his pals tried to pick me up in the pub about three months ago. It started out as a bit of fun, then got out of hand. The bar staff had to call the police. Surprised you don't know about it.'

'I don't know everything that goes on.'

'That's not what I heard.'

Gilchrist ignored the compliment. 'So what did you do last night?'

'Stayed in. Ate a carryout Chinkie. Drank a few glasses of wine. Watched *Runaway Bride* for the nth time. Then crashed out at half ten.'

'That's early.'

'I need my beauty sleep.'

'Did you hear anything? See anything?'

She shook her head. 'I'm on medication. I don't sleep well. Popped a couple of pills last night, and that was that. Out like a light. On top of the wine, I wouldn't have heard a bomb go off in the kitchen.'

'I see. So you wouldn't have been out in the back garden last night after midnight?'

'No, of course not. Why?'

'Does anyone else have a key to your house?'

She shook her head.

Gilchrist moved to the back door by the side of the sink and asked, 'Mind if I look outside?'

'If you don't mind long grass. It's not been cut since the summer. Gardening's not my forte. As you will soon see.'

Gilchrist twisted the key, felt the old-fashioned lock turn over. He pulled the door towards him.

The grass lay flattened by rain. A worn trail from the window to the corner of the wall defined Pitter's route. A few slabs formed a pathway to a concrete coal bunker. Overhead, a lone seagull wheeled, and he followed its flight towards the sea. He heard the rush of waves over rocks.

Or maybe it was just the wind.

He looked up at the roof. He could not see Ian's bedroom window, and took three steps back before he caught the tip of a dormer.

'I see you still have a coal fire,' he said.

'It's wonderful, isn't it?'

'Do you light it often?'

'Not in the summer. In winter I have it on every night.'

'Did you have it on last night?'

'Yes.'

'Was it still burning when you went to bed?'

'Yes. Why?'

'Just asking.'

'I have a fireguard,' she protested. 'The fire was low.'

He lifted the bunker lid and peered inside. It was half-full of coal. 'What do you burn?'

'Coal. What else?'

The bite in her voice surprised him. 'Logs,' he offered.

She said nothing as he leaned over the edge of the bunker, then straightened. He closed the lid.

'You don't burn logs then?'

'No.'

He brushed past her, through to the lounge. 'You burn any wood at all?' he asked, and kneeled in front of the fireplace. The hearth was clean, the grate filled with ashes. He removed a pen from his pocket and poked at the ash.

'What are you looking for?'

'Nothing in particular.'

'I'm not sure I like what you're doing.'

'Want me to stop?'

She stood by his shoulder for several seconds before saying, 'Yes. I think so. I think I'd like you to stop.'

He stood up and smiled at her. 'It's what we do best,' he said. 'Poking and prodding.'

She frowned at the fireplace. 'Find anything?'

'Should I have?'

'I suppose it's too late to ask if you have a warrant?'

'It's never too late to ask,' he said. 'But anyway, I've no more questions.'

At the front door, he stopped. 'Oh, just the one,' he said. 'Lex. That's an unusual name.'

'For a woman, you mean?'

Gilchrist waited.

'It's short for Alexandra,' she explained.

He opened the door. 'Thank you,' he said. 'I appreciate your help.'

She did not return his smile.

CHAPTER 10

'PINT OF EIGHTY-SHILLING.'

'Rough day, Andy?' Fast Eddy nodded to the back corner. 'Old Willie's in. And by the look of him, he's thirsty.'

'Don't know if I'm up for him today.'

'Been asking for you.' Fast Eddy slid forward a pint mug filled with a creamy liquid that darkened from the bottom like a mulatto Guinness. 'There you go. One for Willie?'

'Why not?'

Fast Eddy turned to the optics on the wall and pressed a whisky glass to The Famous Grouse. 'Double?'

'Not yet.'

'He tells me it's worth at least a couple of doubles.'

'We'll see about that.'

Gilchrist slapped a fiver onto the bar then carried the drinks into the back area. He pulled a chair up to a table scratched from decades of heavy drinking. Tyke, Old Willie's Highland Terrier, lay curled on the floor and blinked tired-eyed at him.

Seated opposite, Old Willie barely glanced up. An empty glass and the dregs of a half-pint of Guinness circled with white rings reminded Gilchrist that Old Willie liked to take his time. He slid the half across the table.

'Eddy said you wanted to see me.'

Old Willie's rheumy eyes studied the whisky, his mouth open like a panting bird. A shaking hand moved towards the glass, and fingers as fine as a bird's claws gripped it. Lips slid over gums too old for false teeth.

'You'll have to dae better than this, son.'

'There's more, Willie.'

'There would have to be.'

'How about a half-pint?'

'That would do nicely. For starters.'

The glass shivered its way to a black hole of a mouth, and white lips wrapped the rim as if seeking support. A thimbleful tipped in, and Old Willie's eyes widened as if stunned that the whisky was real. Then the glass was returned to the table.

'So, what do you want to tell me?' Gilchrist tried.

Brown eyes, too large for the head, it seemed, sparkled to life. 'And here was me thinking you only wanted to ask how I was keeping.' A laugh rattled somewhere in his throat.

Gilchrist waited while the old man dabbed spittle from his chin. 'And how are you keeping, Willie?'

'How dae I look, son?'

'You look fine.'

'You're a bugger of a liar.' A bird claw lifted the glass to thin lips, and Gilchrist noted the shaking had all but gone. Another sip, larger this time. 'By God, son, you know how to reach a man's heart.'

'And his tongue?'

Willie's face creased into a smile. 'The doctor tells me I'll no see the end of the year. I asked him which one.' This time the rattle turned into a fit of coughing that brought a hint of colour to the grey cheeks.

Gilchrist leaned closer. 'Are you all right?'

'I'm fine, son. Just get me that half-pint. And another one of these.'

'In a minute.'

71

Old Willie's eyes glistened, wide as an eagle's. A tuft of grey hair that sprouted from the top of a tiny crown added to the avian image. 'You used to be a pushover, son.'

'I used to have a job, Willie.'

'Aye. I heard.'

Gilchrist took a mouthful of beer, then said, 'What else have you heard?'

'A bit of this. A bit of that.'

Gilchrist knew not to press. He pushed his chair back and stood. 'Double is it?'

Old Willie scowled. 'And make sure there's nae water in it.'

Gilchrist had known Willie Morrison for over twenty years and had learned never to undervalue the snippets he served up at little more than the cost of a couple of drinks. Once, when he had helped trap the mastermind of an illicit video distribution scheme, Gilchrist sent a bottle of Grouse to his home. Old Willie had never thanked him, it being accepted that payment for information did not merit gratitude.

But the last two years had seen Old Willie's health decline. Gilchrist had been unable to get a straight answer from him on his medical condition and, abusing his Constabulary powers, checked the hospital records to confirm the old man was dying and that last July, much to Gilchrist's surprise, he had hit eighty-nine.

At the bar, Fast Eddy was holding court over three young women. From the sparkle in his eyes, Gilchrist suspected that one, if not all, would fall victim to his infamous charm. 'A double and a half-pint, when you've got a minute, Eddy.'

'Here,' said one of the women, 'aren't you that Detective Inspector Wotsit on the telly?'

'That's him, ladies,' chirped Fast Eddy. 'And let me tell you that a finer Detective Inspector has never set foot in these premises.'

A shoulder nudged Gilchrist. 'Well, love, you're much better looking in the flesh.'

'Yeah, but what's he like in the buff?'

The three of them burst into laughter and slapped their hands on their knees like a choreographed circus act.

Gilchrist smiled in response as he picked up Old Willie's order and, turning from the bar, almost bumped into Maggie Hendren, one of Fast Eddy's bar staff.

'Oops,' he said, as he swayed the drinks to safety.

'Always in a hurry,' she snapped, with a flash from her eyes that Gilchrist had trouble interpreting. He followed her angry glance into the corner, where he noticed a dark-haired woman he had never seen before eyeing him through a fog of smoke. She tilted her head and exhaled with a twist of her mouth that he could have mistaken for a smile.

Back in his seat, Old Willie placed two hands around his whisky glass as if to thwart any attempts to snatch it back.

'So tell me, Willie. What about this and that?'

Shoulders, too narrow to take the grasp of a comforting hand, shuffled with discomfort. Tight lips moved, as if to speak, and Gilchrist realised the old man was having trouble catching his breath.

Silent, he waited.

With a rush of breath, Old Willie tilted his head to the side. 'Did you know that a certain manager of a certain bank was on the fiddle?'

'Was? That's past tense, Willie.'

'You're still as sharp as a razor.'

'Past tense because he's stopped fiddling? Or because he's dead?'

'If he's deid he cannae be fiddling, now, can he?'

'How much?'

Old Willie tackled his Guinness, mouth twisted against the bitter taste, then said, 'Rumour has it that this certain bank manager of a certain bank has fiddled about a quarter of a million.' He offered Gilchrist a black smile. 'That's pounds.'

'And where has all this money gone?'

'Here and there.'

When Old Willie offered nothing more, Gilchrist realised he had no idea where the money had gone, only that it had been fiddled. 'Does the bank know about the missing money?' he asked.

'Not yet. But if I was you, I'd watch Sam MacMillan.'

Gilchrist struggled to keep his surprise hidden. 'Why do you say that?'

Old Willie tapped his nose with a bony finger. The nail was long and cracked, the skin paper-thin, almost transparent. If Gilchrist looked hard enough, he could almost see the blood pulse its weak way through the old man's failing system. Old Willie wiped his lips with the back of his hand and from the way he then eyed his Guinness, Gilchrist knew he had said all he was going to say that day.

Gilchrist leaned forward, close enough to smell the old man's odour, a warm sourness that reminded him of milk gone off. 'Can I give you a lift home, Willie?'

'What for?'

'To save you the walk.'

'On you go, son. If you want to do anything for me, just put another one of these behind the bar.'

Gilchrist smiled. Old Willie had his priorities right, he supposed. At eighty plus, he was as well sitting in the pub drinking himself into oblivion as sitting at home waiting to die. Gilchrist pushed at his seat. He still had half his Eighty-Shilling to drink, and was on the verge of leaving it when Fast Eddy caught his eye.

Back at the bar he handed over a tenner to cover the rest of Old Willie's session.

'What's happening?' Fast Eddy whispered. 'You off the case?'

On the television above the bar, Gilchrist recognised the lecture theatre at headquarters in Glenrothes. He grimaced as the camera shifted and closed in on Patterson's pockmarked face.

'That guy's a wanker,' said Fast Eddy, and pointed a remote at the screen to turn the volume up.

'...sure that, with the able assistance of Detective Chief Inspector Christian DeFiore of the Scottish Crime Squad, significant progress will be made. We will of course continue to provide full co-operation.'

The camera shifted to DeFiore, dapper in a double-breasted suit, held for a second, then pulled back to capture the others in the group. At the far end ACC Archie McVicar looked calm and magisterial. The press conference must have gone well. DCS Billy Greaves sat next to McVicar, less relaxed. Shoulder to shoulder with Patterson, DeFiore sat clear-eyed and poker-faced.

'One last question,' Patterson announced.

Bertie McKinnon's voice rose discordant above the others. 'Detective Chief Inspector DeFiore,' he demanded, 'how do you intend to guarantee Prince William's safety and that of the citizens of St Andrews?'

The camera zoomed in for a close-up of DeFiore's white smile and polished skin. With his cropped black hair, red silk tie and crisp white collar, he looked more the City banker than Detective Chief Inspector. His Edinburgh accent purred with unchallenged authority as he spoke of teamwork, commitment and results. Then he brought the press conference to an unambiguous end with, 'Now if you'll excuse us, ladies and gentlemen,' and switched off the microphone.

The camera pulled back to capture a confounded Patterson before the screen switched to a woman with a microphone in her hand.

And that was that.

Gilchrist cleaned off his pint, tipped a finger to his forehead and said, 'Catch you later, Eddy.'

On his way out, he glanced at the corner table.

Maggie huddled close to her dark-haired friend, their lips frozen for the moment of his passing. Then he was out the pub, his mind playing out the ramifications of Old Willie's snippet.

CHAPTER 11

GILCHRIST CUT UP Logie's Lane to Market Street and remembered he should return Jack's call. He had not spoken to either of his children for almost two weeks, having managed to track Maureen to her mother's home a week last Saturday. Gail had answered, but she still had nothing to say after the needless acrimony of their divorce. He had hung on for a full minute before Maureen picked up, breathless and full of apologies for not keeping in contact more often. She sounded pleased to hear from him but was rushing for a date, couldn't talk, and promised to call back in a few days.

'Why don't you come up for a weekend?' he had offered. 'It's only an hour's drive. Bring Stephen with you.'

'I'd love to, dad. It's just, you know...'

'Pressure of work?'

'Yeah.'

That was eleven days ago and Gilchrist had rationalised her silence by telling himself she was busy, exams were close, boyfriends were hounding her, she was a gorgeous twenty-two year old with a life of her own. But deep in the heart of him he

76

knew if she really wanted to talk to him, all she had to do was pick up the phone. And that was what hurt the most.

But Jack was worse. Jack almost never called.

An artist, he spent much of his life hanging around the bars in the west end of Glasgow drinking beer. And pernod and ice, for God's sake. And throwing sloppy concrete at walls under the misnomer of art.

Gilchrist had seen some of Jack's art, splattered on the wall of one of the local pubs, an ugly mixture of hessian, wood and God knew what else, swilled in concrete that looked as if it had been plastered there by mistake.

'What do you think of the mural, Andy?' Jack had asked.

'Not quite sure yet,' Gilchrist had replied. 'Maybe if it was a little more colourful?'

'That's the whole point. Everybody thinks they have to see the world through rose-tinted glasses. Life isn't like that. Life is real. It's unattractive. It's dull. It's brutal. It forces us to look inside ourselves to find our own colour, our own reality. Outside, we're all the same. Grey, bland, uninteresting.'

Gilchrist nodded, asked for a pint, while Jack lit up.

'Hope that's all you smoke.'

Jack crossed his heart and hoped to die and swore he had never smoked dope. Gilchrist had simply prayed that his son was mature enough never to get hooked on the hard stuff.

He opened his mobile. After ten rings, he was about to disconnect when a woman answered.

'Hello?'

For an instant he thought he had dialled the wrong number. 'Is Jack there?'

'Who's calling?'

'His father. Returning his call.'

'Oh...' Then a voice whispered, 'The old man.'

A clatter like a dropping phone, then, 'Hey, Andy. Long time. How's it going?'

'Don't they have phones in Glasgow?' he replied, and listened to the infectious rush of Jack's laughter, a staccato chuckle that had stayed with him since he was a boy.

'Hey, I heard on the news that the Stabber struck again last night.'

'That's right,' said Gilchrist, remembering with a spurt of disappointment that the last time Jack had called was when the Stabber's third victim had been found.

'And the Scottish Crime Squad's been pulled in, too. Is that normal?'

'Yes and no.'

'So where does that put you?'

'Out the loop.'

'As in fired?'

'Not quite. Suspended. And don't sound so happy about it.'

'Shit, Andy. No, I'm not. Shit, man. That's a bummer.' A pause, then, 'Hey, listen. How about you come down for a visit? I've got a project on at the moment that'll blow your mind.'

'Maybe I'll take you up on that.' But Gilchrist knew he had no intention of travelling to Glasgow. 'Of course, you and, eh, what's her name...'

'Chloe.'

Chloe? 'You and Chloe could come up here for a weekend. It's been a while since we've had a few beers together. I'd love to meet her.'

'Sounds great, but I think you should come down here first.'

It was not like Jack to be so persistent to see his old man. Gilchrist shifted the phone to his other ear. 'What are you trying to tell me?'

The line hung in electronic silence for a long second, then Jack said, 'Has, uh, have you heard from Maureen?'

'No.' And it struck Gilchrist that this was the real reason Jack had called, the Stabber's most recent murder only an excuse to make contact. 'All right, cough it up.'

'It's Mum.'

'What about her?'

A pause, then, 'She's got cancer.'

Something tight clamped Gilchrist's chest. 'How bad is it?' he asked.

'It's bad.'

Gilchrist felt his lungs empty. When had he last talked to

Gail? What had she said? How had he felt? Had she been ill then? He took a deep breath, tried to keep his voice level. 'Has she had a second opinion?'

'And a third. And a fourth. You know what Mum's like.'

Gilchrist searched for something to say, but his mind seemed lost in a mental smog.

'It's the pancreas, Andy. There's no doubt. And no hope.'

'How long does she have?' he heard someone ask.

'Three months. Six at the max.'

'I can come down and...'

'That's why I'm calling.'

Gilchrist squeezed the phone.

'Mum doesn't want you to come.'

Jack's words reverberated in the depths of his brain, the cruel truth of his failed relationship with Gail. Mum doesn't want you to come. My God, did she hate him that much? What had happened between them? When had they changed? He could still remember her telling him she would love him forever, and later, when...

'I think you should.'

'Come again?'

'I don't agree with her. I think you should come down. You owe her that.'

It was on the tip of his tongue to remind Jack he owed Gail nothing. Instead, he tried to imagine giving Harry, her new husband, a hug of support when they met. But it was a bit like trying to imagine Bush hugging Bin Laden. 'What about Harry?' he asked.

'Harry? He's a wanker.'

'A wanker he might be, Jack, but he's still her husband.'

A quick snort, then, 'So what do you say?'

Gilchrist stared along Market Street. Images of Gail and him and their kids marching along that same cobbled street on their way to the East Sands stirred in his mind's eye. That I've failed you as a father? That I wished Gail had never left? That I still love her? 'What the hell do you expect me to say?' he grumbled.

'I take it that's a yes?'

79

'Yes.'

'Great. Hey, listen, Andy. Got to go.' Something rustled in the background and Gilchrist realised Jack was still in bed. 'I'll get back to you and let you know what'd be a good time to come down,' Jack added. 'All right?'

'Sure.'

They said their farewells, Gilchrist pleased he had at least forced a promise from Jack to call again. But images of Gail now flickered through his mind like an old movie. When she left six years ago, he had been devastated to the point of not wanting to live. Suicide seemed such an easy way to end the pain, but the thought of how that might affect Jack and Maureen had kept the lid on the pills. Then, when Gail left St Andrews, feelings of helplessness had risen inside him, reminding him of how he felt when his mother had told him his older brother, John, was not coming back.

Gilchrist had been twelve. John, eighteen.

She had pulled him to her, hugged him close.

'When, Mum? When?'

She never told him.

The police never traced the hit-and-run driver. Or the car. It hurt to know that his brother's killer had escaped justice for causing the death of a teenager, a young man who had the promise of the brightest of futures. Gilchrist had always wondered if it had been that single failure of the police that had driven him to join the Force in the first place. Now, the Force was the only thing he had to live for. Other than his kids, of course, whom he seldom saw—

Presents. He should take them presents.

He glanced at his watch. Almost six.

He retraced his steps.

Although quieter than Market Street, some of the shops on South Street remained open until six. This and That sometimes stayed open later. The shop's wooden sign hung on chains and swayed in the breeze, the name painted in red and gold swirls.

It had been a while since he had last visited, but the window display seemed oddly familiar to him. Would Jack like the Art

Deco CD rack? Probably not. How about the wooden marionette with the painted face for Maureen? He guessed not. She would likely see it as another instance of her father treating her like the child she no longer was.

He gripped the door handle and pushed inside.

The air smelled as thick and quiet as a library. Music murmured in the background. He recognised Sade, heard her husky voice whisper to him, ask if he thought she'd leave him when he was down on his knees. No, she wouldn't do that.

He walked to the counter and said to the top of a blonde head, 'I'm looking for a couple of great-to-see-you-again gifts for two troublesome youngsters.'

Beth looked up with a strained expression that made him think she was expecting someone else. Then she smiled. 'Andy. What a surprise.'

He smiled back. 'A pleasant one, I hope.'

'The less said about the past, the better.'

Gilchrist felt a flush creep to his cheeks. 'You look great,' he said, and meant it.

'Don't be fooled. Old Man Time is beginning to do his stuff.'

'If you ask me, I'd say he's passing you by.'

'Always the charmer,' she chuckled. 'Great-to-see-you-again gifts? Are Maureen and Jack coming up?'

He shook his head. 'I'm going down to visit.'

'Special occasion?'

'Not quite.'

Beth seemed to give his words some thought, then said, 'I heard about it, Andy. It's just awful.' For one confusing moment, Gilchrist wondered how she could know about Gail's cancer, until she said, 'That's six now. How many more people have to be murdered before they catch this killer? Are you any closer?'

Despite not wanting to, Gilchrist found himself telling her he was off the case. 'The powers that be thought it better if someone else led the investigation,' he added.

'Oh. Andy, I'm so sorry.'

He smiled, which he hoped hid the truth.

'Hi, Andy.'

'Hi, Cindy,' he said, and nodded at the pile of cardboard boxes balanced up to her chin.'Keeping you busy, is she?'

'Nought but a slave-master. Or is it slave-mistress?'

'Somehow that doesn't sound right,' said Gilchrist, but Cindy had stooped and was laying out the boxes on the floor behind the counter.

He turned back to Beth. 'You look troubled,' he said.

Her smile was as quick as a nervous tic. 'Can we talk?'

'Of course.'

'In private.'

'Your place or mine?'

Beth looked away, and Gilchrist felt annoyed at having made such a lame joke.

'We're going through to the back,' Beth called to Cindy. 'Can you get ready to lock up?'

'No problem.'

Gilchrist followed her into a tiny office that smelled of dust and flowers. A wooden desk and fabric chair seemed to choke the room. A tower computer hummed on the floor by the side of the desk, and a monitor squeezed in beside a keyboard doubled as a window onto outer space through which stars flashed past at the speed of light.

Beth backed onto the edge of the desk. Then off again. She locked her gaze on the monitor for a long moment, then gave an ugly grimace. 'Someone fouled the shop entrance today.'

'Fouled?'

'Masturbated over the door handle then ran away.' She pressed a hand to her lips. 'It dripped onto the tiles. It was on the glass. I had to clean it up. It was disgusting.'

Gilchrist kept his tone level. 'He ran away?'

She nodded.

'Did you see him?'

She nodded again.

'Did you report it to the police?'

'I just did.'

It took a full second for the meaning of her words to reach

him. 'So you've not filed a formal complaint?'

She shook her head.

'Have you told anyone else?'

'Only Cindy.' She lowered her eyes, then whispered, 'I think he came into my shop.'

Think? 'When was this?'

'Later in the morning.'

'He came back?'

'I think so.'

Gilchrist let his silence do the asking.

'He pretended to be interested in the model Harleys.'

'What do you mean, pretended?'

'He didn't look the collector type. Cheap clothes. Poor hygiene. Fingernails like, uh.' She shuddered. 'He knocked something over and swore out loud then almost ran from the shop when Cindy ordered him to leave.'

'Did you get a good look at him?'

'Just his hair and his filthy fingernails.' She shuddered again. 'And he had a cut on his arm.'

'What kind of cut?'

'A scratch, maybe.'

'Was it bleeding?'

'I don't think so.'

'No blood dripped on the floor?'

'No.'

'And Cindy ordered him to leave?'

'You know what she's like. She was in his face.'

Gilchrist nodded. Cindy might be able to give a good description. He made a mental note to talk to her, but not now, not while Beth was close to tears. He fought off the urge to reach for her hand. But it had been a while, and he was not sure how she would respond.

'Beth,' he said, and tried a smile of reassurance. 'From what you've told me, he sounds like one of those perverts who does it for shock value and nothing more.' Her lips tightened and he knew his words were having little effect. 'Is there something you're not telling me?'

She sniffed. 'It sounds stupid, I know, but I feel as if I'm being targeted or stalked or something.'

'After what's happened, that's normal.'

She shook her head. 'Why would he come into the shop? I keep asking myself. I don't know. It's just this feeling I have. Like a sixth sense, or something.'

Gilchrist knew all about sixth senses.

'I'm frightened, Andy. I can't help thinking something else is going to happen.' Her eyes welled with tears. 'I'm frightened he's going to come back.'

CHAPTER 12

AFTER LEAVING BETH'S shop, pangs of hunger reminded Gilchrist he had not eaten that day. He decided to have a beer and a bite in the Dunvegan Hotel, close to the Old Course.

But first, he had to call the Office.

He asked for Sa and declined to give his name, adding that it was a personal call. Being suspended meant no one was supposed to talk to him. Strictly speaking, of course. But as long as Patterson didn't find—

'This is Sa.'

'Andy here.'

'Are you trying to get me fired?'

'Whatever gave you that idea?' He heard Sa curse under her breath and added, 'I'd argue I'm on leave of absence.'

'Wouldn't work.'

'At the worst, I'm suspended.'

'That's not what Patterson's saying.'

Gilchrist gritted his teeth. Patterson was already greying the black and white of the truth. Another week and it would be set in stone that Gilchrist had handed in his notice.

'He's been sucking up to McVicar,' Sa continued. 'Rumour has it McVicar blew a fuse.'

Archie McVicar. Fife Constabulary's Assistant Chief Constable. If Patterson was successful in bending McVicar's ear, Gilchrist's career was over. 'Listen, Sa, I need your help.'

'I should've known.'

'Beth's had a bit of an incident at her shop.'

'I thought you two split up ages ago.'

'We did.'

'Is it back on?'

'Quit the interrogation for a minute, and just listen.'

'Uh-huh.'

Gilchrist told her what Beth had told him, but Sa could confirm only that his complaint was noted and would be looked into once manpower was freed from the Stabber's case. All as expected. For the time being, he could do no more.

He walked down Mercat Wynd, his thoughts on the reasons for his break-up with Beth. The magnitude of his sin had been blown out of all proportion. He worked too hard. Simple as that. They had talked about it, but he got snarled up in yet another case and failed to make a dinner engagement. It still hurt to think how readily she had replaced him with Tom Armstrong, a businessman whom Gilchrist never believed was her type.

In the Dunvegan a crowd of golfers, replete with beer and whisky, their weather-beaten faces ruddied from the cold November wind, hogged the space in front of the bar, forcing him to squeeze past and claim a seat at a table in the corner. He laid his gift-wrapped presents on the chair next to him and slipped off his jacket.

He ordered steak pie, chips and peas, and a chilled Guinness. A television set on the far wall showed blue lakes and tree-lined fairways, and he tried to work out which US PGA golf tournament was being played. It was only when he took a sip of his Guinness that he glanced over the rim and saw her.

Her short blonde hair stood tight in tufts that looked wet. A white blouse hung loose beneath a dark blue cardigan that could have been mistaken for a man's. Her muscle tone exuded a healthiness that seemed to make her gleam in the crowd. Lex Garvie was more than just attractive. But her companion intrigued him. The same woman he had seen with Maggie Hendren in Lafferty's.

He carried his glass across to their table and said, 'Can I buy you a drink?'

Garvie gave a smile as tight as a grimace.

'Is that a gin and tonic?' he asked the other woman.

She frowned, as if puzzling over his presence, or perhaps thinking as Gilchrist was, that they had met somewhere before. 'Vodka and tonic, actually.'

'Double?'

'Thank you.'

Gilchrist detected a masculine hardness about her. A crumpled packet of Camel cigarettes lay in an ashtray on the corner of the table.

'Ice and lime?' he asked her.

'Are you always this disarming?'

Gilchrist was not quite sure what to make of her comment. He turned to Garvie. 'I've ordered some food,' he said to her, and nodded to his table. 'I don't mean to interrupt your evening, just to offer a drink.'

'Glenfiddich then,' she said. 'No water. Plenty of ice.'

He ignored her coldness. 'Double?'

'What's the occasion?'

'It's my way of apologising.'

'For what?'

'For poking and prodding.'

'But not for thinking I could be involved?'

'We have to be thorough,' he said. 'But if it helps, yes, that too.'

Garvie looked away.

Her bitterness puzzled Gilchrist. He was about to turn from the table when the woman by her side leaned forward and held out her hand. Nicotine tanned her fingertips. 'We've never been introduced,' she said. The strength of her grip surprised him. 'Patsy,' she offered. 'Patsy Lynch.'

He nodded. 'Andy Gilchrist.'

'I know all about you, Andy.'

Hearing his first name spoken by a stranger sounded odd. He glanced at Garvie. Her eyes danced with anger. 'I can't help thinking we've met before,' he said to Patsy.

'You've probably seen me with Sa.'

'I didn't know you were friends.'

'And Maggie. As you know.'

Gilchrist nodded. 'Of course,' he said, then fished up an image of Patsy driving off with Sa as a passenger. 'Land Rover Discovery. Dark blue. Dent in the driver's door.'

'You'll be telling me the registration number next.'

'My memory's not that good.'

Patsy gave a wry grin. 'That's not what Sa tells me.'

'You still drive it?'

'Sold it. Why? Looking to buy one?'

'Just asking.'

'That's what he does,' Garvie cut in. 'Next thing you know he'll be digging through your rubbish bin.'

'Is that true, Inspector?'

'Why would I want to do that?'

'See?'

'Why don't I order your drinks?' he said.

'Good God. He even talks in questions.'

Gilchrist excused himself and pressed his way to the bar where he paid for their drinks.

When his steak pie arrived, he had to divert his eyes to avoid glancing over at Garvie. The attraction he felt towards her surprised him, and it puzzled him to hear that his visit to her home had upset her so much. He had been polite, not overly investigative, nor had he stayed too long.

So what was her problem?

On clearing his bill, he gathered his jacket and presents and stood up. A final glance towards Garvie and Patsy, faces fired with the heat of their conversation, had him thinking they would not survive the evening together.

Gilchrist walked up North Street to the Police Station and

told the desk sergeant that he was back to clear his desk.

The back office had an eerie quietness about it, as if he had arrived seconds after some party had ended and left its echo in the walls. He found Stan behind a grey divider, sifting through a pack of files.

'You look the way I feel,' said Gilchrist.

Stan started. 'Bloody hell, boss.'

'DeFiore giving you grief?'

'And then some.' Stan shook his head. 'You'd think we'd done bugger all for the last four months except sit on our arses and wait for the bloody Crime Squad to drive in and save our souls.' He slapped the files onto the desk as if he was throwing in a hand of cards. 'I tell you what, boss, you're well out of it.' Then he frowned. 'What are you doing here anyway? Patterson will have you.'

'I need to use your computer to check out a few things.'

'Tell me you're kidding.'

Gilchrist shrugged.

Stan stood. 'Well, I'm out of here. It's your head, not mine. I'll deny all knowledge. All right?'

'Sounds fair.'

Gilchrist waited until Stan closed the door before slipping behind the divider and taking his seat. He keyed in Stan's password and set about clearing some niggling thoughts. When he next looked at his watch, it was 11:20.

No one paid him any attention as he left the building.

Stars glittered in a black sky. The night was North wind cold.

Muttoes Lane led onto Market Street. A couple tottered arm in arm from the direction of the Central Bar, the man in short sleeves, drunk, oblivious to the cold, the woman grumbling beside him.

At PM's Fish and Chip Shop, the main thoroughfare narrowed to a lane wide enough for only one car. His footfall echoed off the walls on either side. He had almost purchased a house here, when he and Gail first married. But she had proclaimed the street too dingy, the house too dilapidated. As he recalled the ensuing arguments, he realised with a spurt of sadness how early he and

Gail had started growing apart.

He found himself slowing down as he came to the spot where the Stabber's fourth victim had been found. He cast his gaze into the darkness beneath the open pend and wondered for the umpteenth time what the victim, Johnny Gillespie, had been thinking as the Stabber attacked. Had his brain, sodden with whisky, worked out in those final seconds of life as the stave popped his left eyeball, always the left, and plunged deep through the soft mass of his brain, that he was about to die? And dead before his body thumped onto the cobbles. Had he let the Stabber walk up to him? And if so, why?

Again an image of the Stabber as a woman, muscles hidden beneath her feminine facade, flooded his mind's eye. And it livened him to see how well Lex Garvie fit the role.

Then he passed the spot, cut onto South Street, then left towards The Pends and Deans Court. As he neared the Roundel, the skeletal ruins of the Cathedral's spires braced the night sky like Siamese twin rockets waiting to be launched.

He checked his watch.

11:44. Plenty of time.

He sheltered behind the support column of the archway to The Pends. His breath puffed white in the frigid air as his thoughts drifted to Gail. It still surprised him how upset he'd been at losing not only his wife and lover of eighteen years, but his stone-built home in Windmill Road. Years ago, before their relationship soured beyond repair, he would often imagine the two of them walking the West Sands together, grandchildren in tow, an elderly couple still deeply in love.

What had marriage meant to him? Loyalty, he supposed. And understanding, too. Being a policeman's wife required considerable understanding. And trust. Definitely trust. But he had found out, almost by accident, that Gail was having an affair with an administrative manager in the hospital where she worked. Several days later, when he finally found the courage to challenge her, her response had been to file for divorce. Six months later, he lost his home, his furniture, his wife, both his children, and thirty-plus years of living in St Andrews. It seemed as if he had wakened one morning to find his past had evaporated.

The pain he now felt at the news of Gail's illness reminded him that their relationship had not always been bitter. Far from it. When he first met her, in the Whey Pat Tavern, drunk and loud on the second night of her summer break, up from Glasgow for the week, her libido surprised him. That first night, after a walk through the darkness of the West Sands, they crossed the first and eighteenth fairways of the Old Course. As they neared the last green the other side of midnight, Gail had said, 'I know all about golf. I've heard about this hole.' She tottered off to the side, pulling Gilchrist with her. 'There's a dip in the green called the Valley of Sin.'

She led him straight to it, and together they stood in its lowest spot, the night-lights of St Andrews twinkling all around them, it seemed. With the salty smell of the cold night air, they could have been on a ship at sea, looking at lights on the shore.

'The Valley of Sin,' she repeated, then dipped forward. One step, two steps, and her knickers were in her hand. 'Such an appropriate name,' she whispered, as she lay down on the grass, her right arm reaching up for him. Even now, the memory of that moment could bring a smile to his lips—

MacMillan came into view, walking past Deans Court. And sure enough, a pair of binoculars dangled from his left shoulder. Gilchrist waited until MacMillan was only a few yards from the corner of South Street, then crossed, unnoticed.

'Sam.'

MacMillan stiffened, almost backed away.

'DI Gilchrist,' he said, making sure his voice gave off the authority it had once possessed until Patterson emasculated it.

'Buggeration, son.' Sam slapped a thick hand onto his chest. 'For a nasty moment there, I thought it was my turn.'

Gilchrist stepped up to MacMillan, close enough to see the moisture in his eyes. 'I didn't mean to scare you.'

MacMillan's lips almost pouted. 'Well, you're going about it the wrong way.' He tightened his grip on the binoculars and Gilchrist had an image of Sam as a younger man, tough and tight and a fearsome adversary.

'Would you like to take a walk, Sam?'

'I've just had one.'

'It won't take long.'

'Where to?'

'This way.'

Down by the harbour, a stiff wind blew in from the sea, carrying the smell of salt and seaweed and the distant sound of surf crashing over rocks.

Gilchrist walked along the stone promontory that sheltered the entrance to the harbour from northerly gales. Spray, fine as mist, drifted on the air. He looked up at the sky.

'Sometimes I think Scotland's the most beautiful place in the world,' he said. 'Other times I wish I was any place else.' They reached the first of four breaks constructed in the wall, the stones inset to form a seating area. 'What do you think?' Gilchrist asked.

'About what?'

'About anything.'

'I think you're an odd sort.'

'In what way?'

'If you can't answer that, Mr Gilchrist, how do you expect me to?' His eyes narrowed and his stance widened, and again Gilchrist had the impression that MacMillan had once been a tough guy to face down.

He held out his hand. 'Binoculars?'

MacMillan slid them from his shoulder and handed them over. Gilchrist focused on the gable end of the building where Granton was killed.

'Did you spy on him from here?' he asked.

'On who?'

'Don't play buggerlugs with me, Sam.'

MacMillan inhaled, then let it out in a defeated rush. 'Next one back,' he grumbled.

Gilchrist walked towards the second cutback. 'Here?'

MacMillan nodded.

Gilchrist raised the binoculars and scanned the harbour, shifting his view along the harbour building, the entrance to The

Pends, the bridge, the black expanse of the East Sands, then back again. 'It's a bit far, Sam.'

Another grunt.

'I said, it's a bit far.'

'I didn't want anyone to see me.'

'No one would see you from here, I grant you that.' Gilchrist lowered the binoculars and handed them back. 'And even with these, you wouldn't see much of Bill. If you get my meaning.'

MacMillan retrieved his binoculars, flung the strap over his shoulder, and looked back at the harbour. Gilchrist did likewise, sensing that MacMillan was reliving events of the previous night.

Out here on the promontory, the waves would have crashed over the wall, the spindrift icy, the rain horizontal. MacMillan's binoculars would have been useless. What could he have seen? And it was easy to lose your footing and stumble into the harbour. Why would he have put his life in danger?

'What're you thinking, Sam?'

'Not a lot,' he growled. 'How about you?'

'I think you're in trouble, is what I think.'

MacMillan glared at him, and Gilchrist had a real sense of the brute strength of the man. All of a sudden, being alone with him out there at midnight did not seem a sensible place to be.

'Granton had two hundred quid on him,' Gilchrist said. 'All brand new notes.'

'So?'

'So what was he doing carrying that kind of money around with him at night in the middle of a storm.'

'How the fuck would I know?'

It was the first time Gilchrist had heard anger seep into MacMillan's voice, and he was aware of standing with his back to the harbour. It would not take much for MacMillan to push him over.

'We know Bill was embezzling the bank,' he said.

MacMillan pressed closer, as if willing Gilchrist to take a step back. But Gilchrist held his ground until MacMillan's face was inches from his own, the sour stench of whisky warm on his breath.

'What are you implying, son?'

'I'm asking if you knew about it.'

MacMillan's eyes flared for an instant. 'I know bugger all about that,' he growled, and adjusted the strap of his binoculars with an angry snap. 'You're fishing, son. You know nothing. I can read it in your eyes.'

'You think so?'

'I know so.' MacMillan straightened, as if readying to face the firing squad. 'Are you going to arrest me, or what?'

Surprised by the question, Gilchrist said nothing.

MacMillan snorted again. 'I thought so. Now if you've nothing more to say, sonny Jim, I'm going home to bed.'

Gilchrist stood silent as MacMillan's broad back slipped into the darkness and faded to a hulking shadow.

Then he faced the sea and took a deep breath. Air rushed into his lungs, as clean and clear as his thoughts. The faintest of ideas was manifesting in his brain. In all the years he had known Old Willie, his snippets were never wrong. If his latest snippet was correct, then Granton was an embezzler and sexual deviant who got his thrill from flashing his cock at an old friend for two hundred quid a pop. But what happened to the money once it was handed over? From his appearance, Sam's standard of living was far from extravagant.

So, what did he do with it?

Gilchrist stared into the dark expanse before him, his thoughts riding the wild waves, fighting the cold wind.

After another minute, he thought he knew.

Sebbie pushed through the shrubbery onto the pavement. He had wanted to use a kitchen knife, the black-handled one with the serrated blade that could cut through tin and still be sharp enough to slice tomatoes and slivers of paper. But he decided against that as being impossible to explain if he was stopped by the police. In the end, he chose a Swiss Army knife that doubled as a key ring.

He reached the car, knife out, blade open, pressed it along the side, from front to rear. Then blade folded, and into his pocket. He walked on and stopped at the corner by the mini-roundabout.

The street was deserted. He waited two minutes then retraced his steps, this time stopping at the boot. The knife bit into the polished paint and screeched like chalk on a blackboard. He dug deeper and finished off with an artistic flourish.

One minute later, he was jogging down Lade Braes Lane, a smile on his lips. His act of vandalism gave him a sense of power that cleared his mind and soothed his thoughts.

Already, he was thinking ahead.

Next time he would use the kitchen knife.

The big one.

CHAPTER 13

The total is six now. But six is not a lot.

Six is only the beginning. I have always known that.

What I hadn't known until now, was that my modus operandum would change. I had thought the killings would be controlled by the weather. Nothing else.

I am puzzled by this misplaced feeling, like a smile that tickles your lips at a funeral. Like the vagaries of life, the reasons for death are every bit as whimsical. Before each of the killings my libido peaked, and I wonder why I never noticed before. Are the storms nothing more than weather patterns that coincide with my increase in sexual desire?

I see now that the killings have changed me. I feel my hate swell, my anger rise, the need for release as relentless as a sexual stirring. Something grips me, and I hear a quiet hiss that repeats itself like a sibilant echo. I wonder where it is coming from, until I recognise it as a voice.

'Seven,' it whispers. 'Seven. Seven.'

Tomorrow night I will kill again.

Beth wakened to a dark morning, the streets black from a pre-dawn squall. She had not slept well and longed for another thirty minutes in bed. But she had a busy day ahead, stock-taking.

As she soaked in the bath, the previous day's events hung in her thoughts like smoke in wool. She had arrived at the West Port Café on time but had to wait half an hour before Tom turned up. She might have forgiven him his tardiness if her day had gone better, but not after everything that had happened. The man in her shop, Andy showing up, then Tom being late, had her thinking it all happened for a reason.

'Got held up,' Tom had said as he pulled out the seat opposite. 'You know what it's like.'

'No, I don't.'

'What's that, pet?'

'I don't know what it's like to get held up.'

He picked up the menu. 'Fancy a starter?' he asked, and flagged down a waitress. 'Double Grouse, miss. No ice. No water. And a bottle of Chianti.' He eyed the tight fit of her skirt as she walked away. 'What a day I've had. It's dog eat dog out there.'

Beth stared at him.

'How was your day?' he asked. 'Busy behind the counter?'

From his glazed look Beth could see he'd already had a few. Maybe more. 'Not good,' she said, and tried to catch the waitress's attention.

'Did you want something else, pet? Why didn't you say?'

'I'm saying now.'

'Same again?' He nodded to her glass. 'What's that?'

'The usual.'

'White wine?'

'Dry white wine. With soda. And a slice of lime. Not lemon.' The waitress caught her eye, and Beth tapped the rim of her glass and mouthed, Same again.

'Mind if I smoke?'

'We're in the non-smoking area.'

'Had a meeting with the bank this afternoon,' he said, lighting up. He took a deep draw then exhaled. 'Talk about tough.'

All of a sudden, the futility of it all overwhelmed Beth. 'I've had enough,' she said.

'What? You look fine. Have another wine.'

'No, Tom. I've had enough of us.'

He blinked, took another heavy pull.

'I'm sorry, Tom. It's not working.'

Smoke powered from his nostrils. 'Have another wine,' he said again. 'You'll feel better.'

Beth looked down at her handbag, stunned by the gap between them. She snapped the clasp shut then, as if seeing him for the first time, took in his ruddied face, his blotched skin, his shirt collar that seemed too tight for his thick neck.

'I don't want another wine,' she had said as she pushed back her chair. Her parting memory was of hairy fingers crumpling a long stub into the ashtray.

Refreshed from her bath, Beth had a bowl of bran flakes with home-made tropical fruit salad. The forecast was scattered showers, and she grabbed her umbrella from the stand in the entrance porch.

Outside, she took four steps and stopped.

At first she thought the scratch on her car was a chalk mark, then she placed her hand to her mouth and whispered, 'Oh, my God.'

Up close, she saw the cut had not just scraped the surface of the paint, but had gouged exposed metal. She read the writing scratched on the boot.

CUNT PIG

The hot sting of tears nipped her eyes as she dug into her bag for her mobile. It barely registered with her that she had not forgotten his number.

'Andy?'

'Beth? What's up?'

'He's come back.'

A frisson of ice ran the length of Gilchrist's spine.

'Where are you?'

He had his leather jacket over his sleeve and his car keys in his hand by the time she told him.

'I'll be there in ten minutes.'

He found Beth standing by her car, and was surprised when she hugged him. Her body shivered, from cold or fear, he could not say. 'Tell me what happened,' he whispered.

She did, then he called the Office and listened to Stan tell him that every man, woman and child who worked in Fife Constabulary and beyond, had been assigned to the Stabber case. All leave had been cancelled, and DeFiore was really a slave-master in disguise who loved to whip his staff to death.

And he'd been there only one day.

As Stan moaned on, Gilchrist studied the passers-by on either side of the road. They all seemed oblivious to the act of vandalism on Beth's car. In the end, all Stan could promise was to run a quick computer check on the Sexual Offenders Register.

Gilchrist slipped his mobile into his jacket and held Beth's hands. She seemed unable to hold his gaze.

'It's him,' she whispered. 'He's come back.'

He had nothing with which to contradict her. He did not believe in coincidence. If two seemingly disparate events occurred within a short period of time, they were connected. Simple as that. All he had to do was work out how, why, and who. But first, he had to help Beth.

'Give me your car keys,' he said, 'and I'll get an estimate for your insurance.' He took her by the arm and opened the Merc's passenger door. 'Come on. You've got a business to run.'

'I thought it was him,' she whispered to him. 'I thought he'd come back.'

Gilchrist shook his head. 'It's more likely an act of random vandalism,' he assured her, 'completely unrelated to the incident in your shop.' But as he said his silly words of comfort, he knew that her prediction had come true.

Gilchrist spent over an hour obtaining estimates for the repair to Beth's car, which ranged from twelve hundred pounds to a more reasonable four-fifty at a small garage next to a betting shop, then returned her car to the open area at the side of her flat. By the time he pulled up at Jack's it was two minutes before midday.

He stepped into the damp Glasgow air, overnight bag in hand. The sandstone tenement building stood timeworn grey in the dull city light. The front door had been painted since he'd last been there six, or was it nine? months ago. The wood shone black and wet. Grey city. Black door. No wonder Jack's art was morbid.

He buzzed the entrance intercom, and Jack's voice said in quick response, 'Hey, Andy. In you come.'

The door clicked, and he entered a cold stone close with green and red tiles like glossy wainscoting that ran all the way to the concrete staircase. His footsteps echoed like hammer hits in a tunnel.

Jack's flat was on the third floor. A shape as grey as a ghost moved beyond the frosted glass. Then the door opened.

'Andy, hey, man. In you come, in you come.'

Jack surprised him by giving him a hug that crushed the air from his lungs. Then Jack looked him up and down, arms out by his side. Gilchrist feared he was going to be crushed again.

'Hey, you look great, man. On a diet?' Jack stooped. 'Here. Let me take that.'

Gilchrist tightened his grip. 'I can manage.'

Jack chuckled. 'I see you haven't changed.'

Gilchrist frowned.

'Is the Pope a Catholic? Is my old man stubborn?'

Jack stood back to let Gilchrist enter, and shouted down the hall, 'Hey, Chloe, come and meet the old man.'

A slender figure dressed in black, with fair, shoulder-length hair, and a white face with a purple gash for a mouth, stepped out the first room on the left.

She held out her hand.

'Chloe Andy Andy Chloe.'

Gilchrist took hold of her hand. It felt thin and weak, and he kept his grip loose.

'Hi,' she said, and a smile lit up her eyes and told Gilchrist she could be attractive if she abandoned the grunge look.

'I'm the old man,' he said. 'But call me Andy. Everyone else seems to.'

She gave a nervous giggle. 'Call me Chloe.'

'This way, Andy.'

Gilchrist followed Jack into a bedroom that contained a king-sized bed with a cream duvet and an unusual headboard constructed of coloured pipes. A chest of drawers painted dark pink stood in the corner. White walls exhibited a number of unframed oil paintings, swirls of bold colours and twisted shapes that hinted of tortured eyes and screaming mouths.

Gilchrist lowered his bag to the floor. 'What happened to the grey look, Jack? Life is unattractive. It forces us to look inside ourselves to find our own colour. I think that's what you said.'

'A phase we all go through.'

'And the earring?'

Jack fingered his earlobe. 'Present from Chloe.'

'Talking about presents. Here,' Gilchrist said, and unzipped his bag. 'I got you this.'

Jack frowned at what looked like a gift-wrapped shoebox.

'What is it?'

'A present.'

'What for?'

'For you.' As Jack tore at the wrapping, Gilchrist's mind pulled up an image of Gail handing out Christmas presents from under the tree. Their lives had seemed full of so much promise then.

'Cool,' said Jack, and held up a model Harley Davidson.

'I couldn't afford a real one,' said Gilchrist.

'Hey, thanks, Andy.'

Gilchrist felt the warmth of a flush on his cheeks. 'Are the paintings yours?' he asked.

'Chloe's.'

From the whorled mass of yellows and greens, Gilchrist thought he could make out a skull with yellow whirlpools for eyes. He never claimed to be an art aficionado, but he saw a distinctive style to the painting, a precise pattern in the brush strokes, and an almost tactile sense of horror that both surprised and attracted him.

'What d'you think, Andy?'

Gilchrist nodded.

'She's good, Andy. I keep telling her.'

'All Chloe's?'

Jack nodded to the metal headboard. 'Except that.'

Gilchrist tried to hide his disappointment.

'You don't have to like it, Andy. The important thing in life is to keep learning, keep creating, keep trying out new ideas, new colours, new materials. Each of us has to keep experimenting in our lives. It's what makes the human species superior to... what?' Jack held out his hands in a gesture of helpless supplication. 'What?'

'Experimenting?'

Jack shook his head. 'Hey, Chloe?'

Chloe joined them, and Gilchrist realised she had stayed in the hallway, not wishing to hear criticism of her work.

'Andy thinks I'm smoking. Tell him.'

Chloe shook her head. 'He doesn't do drugs. Neither of us do.' She glanced up at Jack. 'I used to. But I don't anymore.'

'A close friend died of an overdose,' said Jack, and put his arm around Chloe's shoulder. 'And that did it.'

Gilchrist watched Chloe's eyes brim with tears, and her face lift up to Jack's. He kissed her dark lips, and Gilchrist saw how gentle he could be to a woman.

Jack lowered his arm. 'Beer?'

'A bit early for me.'

'Nonsense. We haven't been together since last February. That's as good an excuse as any.'

Jack's words cut. Last February. Had it been as long as that? Nine months? Why had they not seen each other sooner? If Jack had not called about his mother would it have been another nine months? 'A beer sounds great,' he heard himself say.

'We'll go to The Attic. I can show you my new mural.'

'I can hardly wait.' He caught Chloe's eye and nodded to the wall paintings. 'Are any of these for sale?'

She looked startled.

'I might be interested in this one,' he said, and brushed a finger over it, almost touching the image. It seemed a shade lighter than the others, the image less disturbing.

'Framed or unframed?' It was Jack.

'Unframed.'

'What do you think, Chloe?'

Chloe stared at the painting as if not comprehending that her work could have any monetary value at all. Then it struck Gilchrist that money was not an issue, that she was recalling her thoughts at the time of painting, remembering how damaged her mind must have been to have created a canvas so visually disturbing. A close friend died of an overdose, and that did it. Did what? Get her off drugs? Brand her memory with drug-induced horror so that all she could paint were tortured faces in swirling colours?

'Why don't you get back to me in your own time?' he said, 'and let me know how much.'

Chloe nodded.

He turned to Jack. 'Right, Jack the lad, how about that beer?'

CHAPTER 14

THE ATTIC WAS a bar in Ashton Lane off Byres Road, reached by a cold staircase that crept up the corner of the building. Windows on the sloped ceiling were covered by a cloth of sorts, and Gilchrist wondered why anyone would want to dull the natural light in a dull city.

They sat at a high table like a short plank of wood wide enough for only one glass. The window behind them was faced with a metal fence more suited to a garden than a pub.

'To prevent the drunks from toppling out?' he asked.

'To stop them from taking a flying runner. Apparently some nutter downed four doubles at the bar then did a header through the window.'

'How could he have run from there to here without wriggling past this table?'

'You've been a detective too long, Andy.'

Gilchrist frowned.

'Lighten up, Andy. Hey, what're you having? My treat.'

Gilchrist tried a smile. 'Well, in that case I'll have a Corona.'

Jack frowned. 'Off the hard stuff?'

Gilchrist shook his head. 'Don't want to turn up at Mum's reeking of beer.' Chloe's look saddened, and Gilchrist realised that although visiting Gail was the purpose of his visit, no one had mentioned her until now.

Jack returned with a Corona, a piece of lime jutting from the neck. Gilchrist poked it in with his finger, and watched the beer froth in response. Chloe took delivery of a tall glass of something that looked like watery milk, and Gilchrist made a decision not to ask. Jack had a pint of real ale that looked dark and flat, and a whisky with ice that looked like a double at the minimum.

They raised their glasses, or bottle in Gilchrist's case, and chinked. 'Cheers,' said Jack, and took a slug of his pint.

Gilchrist pressed the neck of his Corona to his lips and watched Chloe take a sip from her glass. For some odd reason, he found himself thinking of Beth and wondering if she could ever put up with Jack and his careless lifestyle and his punk-Bohemian mistresses. Maybe Chloe was different. Maybe she was the one. She had at least managed to put some colour into Jack's life.

'Can you spot it?' said Jack, and smiled at Chloe.

'Spot what?'

'The mural.'

'Oh, right.' Gilchrist searched the bar, looking for something concrete and grey, stuck to the walls like unpainted plaster. But the walls were mostly bare. 'I give up,' he said. 'Which one?'

Jack looked up at the ceiling.

Gilchrist followed his gaze, but all he saw were covered windows and wooden rafters. 'I don't see it.'

'The skylight windows,' Jack said. 'The coverings.' He sat back. 'Cool, don't you think?'

Gilchrist took a sip of beer. 'I thought mural meant it went on a wall.'

Jack laughed and reached for Chloe's hand. 'Andy's never going to like my stuff. But that's what's great about living in a democratic society. Freedom of speech. Freedom of expression. No one's going to drag me outside and shoot me because they don't like how I'm trying to express myself.'

'Not yet, they haven't,' said Gilchrist, and chuckled when Chloe burst out laughing.

By the time Gilchrist took a taxi to Gail's, he'd been persuaded by Jack to have one too many. Mum'll understand, Jack had told him. But from past experience, Gilchrist knew not to be convinced.

He stood alone on the front step and rang the doorbell. In the garden, he recognised plants that had been groomed to perfection in their front garden in St Andrews. Gail had not lost her green fingers. The lawn sported stripes from its last cut, and aeration holes dotted its surface in straight lines.

The door opened.

Gail had lost weight. As much as a stone, he thought. Maybe more. Her eyes looked tired and sunken, her hair light and short.

'Jack told me to expect you,' she said.

'Well, here I am.' He held a bunch of flowers out to her. 'Freesias. Your favourite.'

She took them from him. 'You've been drinking.'

'Liquid lunch with Jack and Chloe. It's been a while.'

'With who?' she snapped. 'With Jack and who?'

'Chloe.'

'Never heard of her. What's she like? If she's anything like the last one, the sooner he gets rid of her the better.' She turned away and retreated inside. 'Harry is in, so be nice,' then added over her shoulder, 'If you can.'

Although he had never set foot in Gail's house before, he was struck with an odd sense of familiarity. A framed photo at the end of the hall, Gail with the kids, pre-divorce, in a beach-front café in Marbella. Pre-Harry, too, he thought. Or was it? Had Gail been having her affair then?

In the lounge, he recognised his old mahogany television stand. And the maple coffee table, which still stood on his prized Persian rug. And his grandmother's crystal vase. It had always been full of flowers whose names he could never remember, although he did know that the white and burgundy arrangement now sprouting from it was carnations.

But no freesias. Maybe Gail had gone off them.

And Harry seemed strangely familiar, too, but smaller, as if being married to Gail had reduced him inch by inch, year by year. He eyed Gilchrist from behind the sofa, then left the room without a word.

Gail took a single chair by an ugly stone fireplace, and Gilchrist sat on the sofa without being asked. He felt regret at having succumbed to Jack's persistence, and thought he saw signs of Gail's illness. The corners of her mouth down-turned more than he remembered, and gave her scowl a permanence it never used to have.

'Chloe's nice,' he ventured.

'What a ridiculous name. Chloe.'

'It suits her.'

'What's that supposed to mean?'

'That once you meet her you'll—'

'God forbid.' She slapped invisible crumbs from her skirt.

Gilchrist gripped the arm of the sofa. 'You always said you would never have leather furniture. But this feels nice.'

'It grows on you.'

He nodded. 'I see you still love the garden.'

'It's a mess.'

Gilchrist pressed on. 'I don't hear too much from Jack and Maureen.'

'The phone works both ways.'

It doesn't where you and I are concerned, he wanted to say, but instead said, 'So, how is Maureen? I spoke with her last week,' he lied. 'She was going to call back.'

'As well as can be expected.'

'Jack phoned yesterday.'

'I know. He told me.'

'I had no idea,' he said, and lifted a hand, 'about...'

'No.'

He stared at his hands and realised he was twisting his fingers. Why did he always feel tense around Gail? Why would she never let him through to her? He flattened a hand on each knee and tried to keep his voice level. 'Are you being well looked after?'

'I have Harry.'

Hearing Harry's name being uttered by Gail in that way stabbed at his gut. He struggled to contain his frustration. 'What I meant was, is there anything I can do for you?'

'No.'

'Well, if you think of anything, anything at all, I'd—'

'I'm dying, Andy. Does that make you feel better?'

Her comment stunned him, and he struggled with the urge to just get up and leave. He bit his tongue for a few seconds to make sure he was in control, then said, 'Jack said you didn't want me to come.'

'That's right.'

'Why?'

'What's the point?' she clipped.

Gilchrist wondered if Harry could hear their discussion, and if so, was he proud of the way his wife was managing to diminish the feelings of her ex-husband?

'I still care for you, Gail.'

'Well, don't. I have Harry.'

Gilchrist felt his face colour. Gail had succeeded in doing what she always could. Smother any remnant of whatever feelings he had for her. All the support and sympathy he had wanted to offer her, all the kindness he had felt towards her, all of it vanished like steam in fog. Even his frustration at her coldness evaporated. He watched a frown creep across her forehead, and a tiny crease pucker her lips.

He stood. 'I'm sorry for troubling you. I thought, I thought...' He shook his head. 'I don't know what I thought. I'm sorry. I'll let myself out.'

'In six months I'll be nothing but a memory to you and the children.'

He refused to rise to the bait, did not have it in his heart to be cruel at that moment. 'We were happy once,' he said to her. 'That's how I would prefer to remember us. Not like this.' He thought he caught the glint of tears in her eyes and wanted to reach out to her and give her a hug.

As if sensing that possibility, she flapped a hand. 'Go away,

Andy. Please, will you do that for me? Just go away.'

Gilchrist shifted his stance as Harry stepped from the kitchen, a cup of tea in one hand, a plate of biscuits in the other. But Gilchrist ignored him and let himself out into air as damp and heavy as his heart.

He strode down the garden path telling himself he would not look back. He knew she would not stand at the window to give a parting wave. So when he closed the gate and glanced back, he was not surprised. Gail had thrown him out of her life. Why could he not discard her from his?

By the time he reached the road junction, despite all he had seen in his career, the decapitated bodies, the crushed skulls, the gruesome autopsies, the drug overdoses, despite seeing walls and ceilings and floorboards splattered with blood, and flesh slashed and sliced and gouged and rotting, despite having witnessed the cruellest and most evil of human depravities and becoming inured to it all, despite all of that, he found to his surprise that he could still cry.

CHAPTER 15

GILCHRIST SPENT THE rest of the afternoon in the city centre trying to put his visit to Gail behind him, as well as clearing his brain of the alcohol he had consumed with Jack and Chloe. He wanted his mind to be firing on all six when he tied up this particular loose end.

Cockburn? Granton? One and the same?

He purchased two books in Waterstone's and browsed a couple of hours in Slaters. At quarter past five the skies opened. Rainwater sluiced the streets in shimmering streams. Traffic shunted in stops and starts and pedestrians swelled through gaps in the flow. In the teeming rain, the city seemed stunned into sodden silence.

Gilchrist caught a taxi at Queen Street Station and gave the driver the address he had finagled through Stan's computer the night before. By the time he was dropped off in Newton Mearns the storm had passed, his hair had dried, and his trousers had lost their crease.

He stepped onto the leaf-covered pavement and watched the taxi turn at the end of the road, then sweep past him, its tyres hissing over the wet asphalt.

The driveway was fifty yards long, if it was an inch. Two stone pillars, chipped from careless driving and tilted from settlement, defined the entrance. A knee-high wall stretched off on both sides into the darkness. The night air smelled of an abandoned forest whose damp scent seemed to come at him from the ground at his feet.

He reached the covered vestibule and rang the doorbell.

Thirty seconds later, a flicker of light at eye level told Gilchrist he had just been spied on through a peephole. Another flicker, then a key clicked, and the heavy weather-door was pulled open with a crack like splintering wood.

'Alex,' said Gilchrist. 'Good to see you again.'

'Fuck do you want?'

'To come in, for starters.'

'Got a warrant?'

'Don't need one. Been suspended.' Gilchrist stepped into a hallway, rich with wood wainscoting. Intricate cornicing rimmed the high ceiling like frosting on a wedding cake. 'This is nice, Alex. You've done well for yourself. Must cost a lot to maintain.'

The door slammed shut.

Alex Granton, also known as Alex Cockburn, alias 'Fats' Cockburn to Strathclyde Police and law-enforcement agencies throughout the nation, stood with his back to the door. The buttons on his white shirt strained to contain his belly. Black eyes blazed.

'Bit far from home, Gilchrist. Take a wrong turn?'

'Like I said, I've been suspended.'

'Caught with your cock in someone's mouth?'

'This is a friendly call, Alex. Let's keep it that way.'

Granton glared at him.

'I didn't know they paid male nurses enough to maintain a mansion in Newton Mearns.'

'Fuck's it got to do with you?'

'Just asking.'

'If you must know, I day trade.'

'Expert with computers now, are we?'

'Know enough to get around.'

'I bet you do.'

'Fucking fortune last year.' Granton's mouth twisted into an ugly sneer, then he gave a beefy chuckle. 'Fuck did you take home?'

'A lot less than you, I'm sure.'

Gilchrist slipped his hand inside his leather jacket, and Granton stiffened, as if expecting to find a handgun aimed his way. 'Mind if I put this here?' said Gilchrist, and placed his plastic bag of books on a hall desk inset with coloured wood.

In the lounge, a silver tray with handles curled like leaves sat on a trolley in the corner. Crystal decanters that glowed with the warmth of their contents stacked its shining surface. Gilchrist removed the stopper from a ship's decanter. 'Mind if I have a drink?' he said, and poured himself a hefty measure. The fiery liquid salved his throat. 'Not bad.' He held the glass to the light. 'What is it?'

'Bruichladdich. 25-year-old Special Reserve.'

'Didn't know you were a whisky connoisseur. Real ale's more my style.' He poured another glass and handed it to Granton who downed half of it in one gulp. 'You're supposed to sip single malts, Alex.'

Granton finished it off, poured an even bigger measure, then eyed Gilchrist over the rim. 'Fuck do you want? I did my bit yesterday,' he said. 'ID'd the old man's body. Here to get me to sign off on more fucking paperwork?'

'Interesting choice of words.'

'What is?'

'I heard you didn't like Bill, so I was intrigued as to why you would elevate him to old man.'

'She tell you that?'

'She?'

'Liz.'

Gilchrist waited a beat, then said, 'Liz gave me the impression you loved her.'

'Fuck's that got to do with anything?'

'I must say I was surprised when your mother told me her maiden name.' Gilchrist took a sip of whisky, but kept his eyes on Granton. 'Cockburn.' He shook his head. 'Took me a while to make the connection, but once the old wheels start turning they take some stopping.' He looked down at the rug on which he stood, and flexed his legs. 'Feels nice, Alex. This expensive, too?'

Granton polished off his whisky and returned the glass to the tray with a metallic smack that should have cracked it. 'You've got ten seconds to tell me what the fuck you want,' he growled, 'then I'm calling the police.'

'I am the police.'

'Thought you were suspended.'

'Temporarily.'

'You always were a smarmy bastard, Gilchrist. Time's up.'

Gilchrist let Granton walk to the phone on the side table by the five-seater sofa and pick it up, before he waggled a finger and said, 'I wouldn't do that, Alex, if I were you.'

'You're not me.'

'No one knows I'm here.'

'Fuck off.'

'If you want the whole world to know where I am, just keep going.'

Granton slammed down the phone. 'Fuck do you want?'

'To talk about a couple of things.'

'Fuck should I answer anything you—'

'Let me ask the questions, Alex. All right?'

Granton's face flushed. 'Fuck don't I just tell you to take a shit in the Clyde?'

'Give it up, Alex. You're beginning to piss me off. I should have put you away years ago.'

'You had nothing on me.'

'You were only a petty thief back then. But despite your failings, you had a good upbringing and a father with friends in high places who could pull strings behind everyone's backs. Even mine.' Gilchrist tutted. 'Now he's gone, who's there to help you now?'

'I don't need help from anyone.'

'Oh yes you do Alex old son. Oh yes you do.'

Veins bulged beneath Granton's eyes like tiny worms.

'Liz knows nothing about what you do, of course. That's why she's proud of you. You can see it in her eyes. She even thought you stood up for her against your father.' Gilchrist shook his head. 'Bill beat her throughout their married life. You knew that, though.'

Granton's eyes looked like red slits.

'Not that it mattered one iota to you. As long as you received your regular payments from your old man you couldn't give a toss about Liz.'

'Fuck are you talking about?' snapped Granton. 'What regular payments?'

'Going to deny it, are we?'

'Fucking planet are you on?'

'Earth,' said Gilchrist. 'Same planet as you.' He fought off the urge to deck the fat slob, and took a sip to keep his distance.

Granton reached for the decanter and poured another measure, and something in that movement told Gilchrist all was not what it seemed.

'Should kick your fucking head in for what you just said.'

'That would be silly, Alex.'

Granton parted wet lips that revealed tiny teeth. 'Been sillier.'

Gilchrist finished his whisky with a gulp and held the glass, pleased at its empty weight. 'Since your father packed you out of St Andrews all those years ago,' he said, and returned an unpleased smile of his own, 'you've developed quite a career for yourself.' He shifted his glass to the flat of his hand, like a butcher guessing the weight of a cut of meat, and hoped Granton feared he might smash it into his face. 'Illegal video distribution. Credit card fraud. Counterfeit passports. Fiddling tax returns. Buying and selling shifty goods. Nothing much to write home about. But all of it breaking the law.'

'I'm clean now.'

'Are you?'

'Dead right.'

'Prepared to go to court on that statement?'

'Not a bit far from home to be making threats?'

'Like me to move down here?'

Gilchrist's question hung in the air. One of the crimes he had chosen not to mention was GBH. Granton had been charged in the past with grievous bodily harm against minors, the case against him being not proven in the end. Granton was a bully by nature and a coward by heart. But despite that, Gilchrist found his bulk intimidating.

Granton bristled. 'Fucking cheeky bastard,' he snarled. 'Got fuck all on me. Never had. Never will.'

It pleased Gilchrist to see his words were stinging home, like pepper in the eye. 'How about your latest venture?' he asked, and caught a stiffening of Granton's posture, a quick dunking of the Adam's apple.

'What venture?'

'Blackmail.'

Granton's fists clenched. 'Repeat that in public, you smarmy fucker, and I'll sue you for slander.'

'It's slander only if it's not true,' said Gilchrist. 'The law's a bit funny that way.' But even as he spoke, a pinprick of anxiety nipped him. Granton's reaction was not what he had anticipated. Did he have it all wrong? Or was Granton bluffing? Unsure of his reasoning all of a sudden, he took the top off another decanter. 'Mind if I try something else?'

'How about trying to fuck off?'

Gilchrist needed to keep the momentum going, see if he could confirm his theories. He poured a generous measure and slipped the stopper back into the decanter with a careless clatter. He took a slow sip, thought he caught a hint of peat and smoke. 'Think I prefer this,' he said. 'Don't you?'

'You're something else, Gilchrist.'

'If you say so.'

'Fuck am I supposed to have blackmailed?'

'Past tense, Alex.'

'Do what?'

'Which tells me you know damn well who you're supposed

to have blackmailed.' Gilchrist decided to dig deep. 'Sam told me,' he said.

Granton grimaced in disbelief. 'Sam MacMillan?'

'The very same.'

'Sam knows fuck all.'

'That's not what Sam tells me.'

Granton stared hard at Gilchrist, as if trying to read his thoughts, and for one awful moment, Gilchrist had the feeling he could see right through his bluff.

'Sam's ex-Army,' said Granton.

'Ex being the operative word.'

'Wouldn't be scared shitless talking to a skinny-arsed runt like you.'

'Why would Sam be scared shitless, Alex? Does he know something I'm not supposed to?'

'Stop twisting my words, you pompous prick. All the fucking same, you lot.'

'You think so?' said Gilchrist. But the discussion was not going at all as he had hoped. He tried his final bluff. 'How often did Sam deliver the money, Alex? Twice a month? Once a week?'

'What money?'

'Bill's been a bit naughty. Embezzling from the bank. Took me some time to work out why.'

'And you think he was passing it on to me?' Granton laughed, a belly-rumble that shuddered his jowls. 'Crack me up, so you do. Bill might have battered the old dear around a bit, but when it came to business he was as straight as they come.'

'You deny it, then?'

'Fucking right, I deny it. You've got the wrong bloke, Gilchrist.' Granton smirked. 'Fucking plonker. That the best you can do?'

Gilchrist turned away. Doubts about his hunch scalded his thoughts. He pretended to study an oil painting that had been mounted in an ornate gilt frame, then beyond, a tall vase that looked as if it was Ming. Surely not. His insides churned. He had it wrong. A good hunch, perhaps, but wrong. He worked through his logic once more, the memory of his conversation with MacMillan, the sound of Granton's simple response an echo of his mockery. That the best you can do?

He had convinced himself that Granton had been embezzling money, not to line his pockets, but to keep some secret that could destroy him. Gilchrist had figured homosexuality or domestic abuse. But as Granton's wife had refused to report him, Gilchrist had reckoned homosexuality. But Sam was homosexual, so how could he blackmail Granton? As he led such a modest lifestyle, the money had to be going somewhere else. But where? Then up popped Alex 'Fats' Cockburn, petty criminal with an eclectic record, including blackmail, who knew all about his father's physical abuse.

It sounded a complicated theory, but it wasn't really. And up until a few moments ago, it had been a theory in which Gilchrist believed. Now he knew he was wrong. Not about Bill Granton being blackmailed, perhaps, but about where the money was going.

Gilchrist stood by a grand piano near the bay window. An overgrown cheese plant reared up from the side, its leaves stooping over a gallery of framed photographs that littered the piano lid.

'Didn't know you were into photography, Alex.'

'Presents from the old dear.'

Gilchrist palmed the piano's polished surface, fingers sliding along wood as smooth as glass. 'You play?' he asked.

''S just furniture.'

Gilchrist pressed a finger to one of the keys, held it down as the note resonated then faded, leaving nothing but an echo imprinted on his senses. He tried another, then another, each time listening to the note evaporating as he studied the images before him.

A young Bill Granton in a short-sleeved shirt on the steps of the Sea Front Hotel, bespectacled, squinting against the sunlight. A woman verging on the skinny hooked to his arm, unsmiling. A photograph to the side showed the same couple, older this time, a row of shops in the background. Again, the same hooked arm, the same tense look. Gilchrist now understood that the look was not one of scorn but of repressed fear, the images a black and white reflection of how Granton had tyrannised his wife all their married life.

'No home to go to?'

'Not going to offer me another whisky?'

'Fuck that.'

Gilchrist pressed another key. A chubby Alex as a young man astride a bicycle, the Whyte-Melville Memorial Fountain in the background defining the locale as Market Street. Another of a fat child with a kite on the West Sands, the black and white image exaggerating whiter than white skin. Others, too, of the Grantons as a family group, or as individuals, ageing before his eyes. But as far as Gilchrist could see, none of the photographs showed Alex Granton with a woman.

Except one.

Gilchrist lifted his finger from the key. The note died.

He placed his whisky on the piano lid and picked up the framed photograph. 'Who's this?'

'Why don't you make yourself at home?'

'Who's this?' he repeated.

Granton glanced at it. 'Don't you recognise her?'

Familiar eyes stared back at Gilchrist, sharp and dark. The young girl faced the camera, a stale smile on her face. It was not the smile that had him pulling the image closer, but the pet she held in thin arms, thrust towards the camera like some sacrificial offering. 'Can't say that I do,' he said.

'Try Maggie.'

'Maggie Hendren? Works in Lafferty's?'

'Ten out of ten.'

'When was this taken?'

'Fuck knows?'

'How old were you?'

'Fucking deaf or what?'

'Have a guess, Alex, before I have to confiscate it.'

'You can't confiscate—'

'Don't play buggerlugs with me, Alex.'

Granton shrugged. 'Twenty-one, twenty-two, maybe.'

That would put Maggie at about eleven or twelve. He pulled

it closer. It was in good condition, the monochrome images still sharp.

'Whose cat's she holding?'

'Not mine. Hate the fuckers.'

'Hers?'

'Fuck knows. She used to keep rabbits, guinea pigs, all sorts of pets. None of them lasted long.'

'What do you mean?'

'Died. Ran away. Fuck should I know? Ask her.'

'What's wrong with its face?'

Granton gave the photograph a quick squint. 'Run over by a car or something. How would I know?'

Gilchrist flipped the frame over, slid the clips aside, removed the cardboard backing, and pulled out the photograph. He noticed the top edge had been cut off to centre the image in the frame. On the back, in weak pencil in the bottom right hand corner, were printed the words *Summer 1982*.

'Mind if I take it?'

'Fucking right I do.'

'Don't annoy me, Alex, or I might not give it back.' He slid the photograph into his jacket pocket and retrieved his whisky. 'Cheers,' he said, then downed it and held out his empty glass to Granton. 'I'll be in touch.'

'Don't make it any time soon.'

Gilchrist closed in on Granton so their eyes were level. Beads of perspiration dotted Granton's thick upper lip. An almost overwhelming surge of hatred flashed through Gilchrist. Alex Granton had been raised to be just like his father, a contemptible misogynist. He pressed closer, and Granton bumped against the piano, knocking over a photograph.

'Next time we meet,' Gilchrist snarled, and patted his pocket. 'I'll be slapping on a pair of these.'

Outside, the ground sparkled with frost. Gilchrist pulled his collar up, felt the photo tucked in his pocket. Used to keep rabbits, guinea pigs, all sorts of pets. None of them lasted long.

The cat's disfigured face intrigued him. Had it really been run over by a car? Arson and bed-wetting are two of the triad of predisposing characteristics of serial killers.

Cruelty to animals is the third.

CHAPTER 16

Beneath me, the body jerks. Then stills.

I stand, grab the wall for support, run a shaking hand across my chin. My breath pumps in hard gasps that tear cold air in and out my lungs with a force that scares me. My heart pounds as if something is caged in my chest.

I fight back the urge to run.

My mind screams at me to stay calm. But I am unable to obey and break into a trot, then I am running. And as I run, I struggle to fight back the panic, comprehend the twisted rationale of what is happening, why I am behaving the way I am.

But I know the answer.

I am decompensating. It is what happens when the defence mechanisms of the mind fail to prevent the onslaught of mental disorder, when the mind can no longer stand the strain of what it has to live with, then breaks down.

And that frightens me.

I always thought I would never be caught.

Now I am not so sure.

'Morning, Andy.'

White light exploded at the front of Gilchrist's brain. He squeezed his eyes shut. 'What's the time?'

'Eight o'clock.'

'In the morning?'

'It is indeed,' said Jack. Another burst of light, less bright, as the curtains were ripped open. 'Another beautiful day.'

'Not raining?'

'Of course it's raining. That's what makes Glasgow such an inspirational city. All that dreich and dreary weather brings out the morbid best in us.'

Gilchrist risked opening his eyes and gave a hollow cough, a reminder of his life as a forty-a-day smoker.

'Here,' said Jack. Something flapped onto the bed. 'You should read this.'

Gilchrist picked up the *Daily Record*. Two-inch high headlines, more suited for the declaration of World War III, announced STABBER'S TALLY HITS SEVEN. Gilchrist fired awake. 'The weather,' he snapped. 'What was it like?'

'Dry.'

What? 'No rain?'

'That's what's got everyone in such a tizzy,' said Jack. 'And that DeFiore guy, he's in the firing line. Thought that would bring a smile to your face.'

Gilchrist read on, barely breathing. Number seven was in conflict with the Stabber's M.O. The victim, Ronnie Turnbull, a professional caddy, had put up some resistance. Footprints were found close to the body, on the path that ran from the Scores to the beach. Moulds were being taken to identify the make and size of shoe. But Gilchrist felt a rush when he read that bloodstains had been found on the victim's face and on the wall, too. Got the bastard, he wanted to shout. DCI DeFiore was reported as saying that the post-mortem was still to be carried out, and until that time he could not rule out the possibility of a copycat murder.

Gilchrist slapped the back of his hand across a photo of DeFiore. He recognised the podium at the back of the Office. 'This guy's an idiot,' he said. 'The last thing the citizens of St

Andrews need to hear is that someone could be copying the Stabber.' He shook his head. 'You might think it. But you don't say it. Patterson would have my balls on a plate of fried rice if I'd let that slip.'

'Maybe DeFiore's balls are ready for the chop.'

'Not a chance. Patterson's made his choice. He has to stand behind DeFiore no matter what.' Gilchrist scowled. 'Is this the only paper you have?'

'Too far left for you? Welcome to the world of socialist Glasgow.'

'No, you daft plonker. I want to read more.'

'Who was it who once said that press conferences were only a hindrance to the investigation?'

Gilchrist knew Jack was right. How often had he withheld information from the press in order not to jeopardise his investigation? He was about to pull back the sheets when Chloe entered carrying two mugs of tea. A cream silk dressing gown did little to hide the curves of her slender figure, and from the loose sway of her breasts, Gilchrist could tell she was naked underneath.

She handed a mug to Jack then turned to Gilchrist. 'Good morning. Would you like a cup of tea?'

'Once I've had a shower,' he said.

Then she surprised him by sitting on the edge of his bed. She cocked her head at the canvases on the wall. 'The eyes are the window to the human psyche,' she said. 'They don't just speak about the painting, they reveal the inner soul of the artist.'

Gilchrist pushed his newspaper to the side.

Chloe leaned forward. As she did so, her dressing gown slipped open to reveal a tiny handful of perfect breast, the nipple wide and proud like a fleshy thimble. As if warding off a chill, she pulled at the material and covered herself with the casualness of someone adjusting a tie.

'I remember working on that one,' she said. 'I felt such anger at the needlessness of it all. And pain, too. It was not long after Kevin.'

Kevin? Gilchrist caught a flicker of concern flit across Jack's face, and wondered if Chloe was about to explain who Kevin was. But instead she said, 'All I could feel was this need to release my anger. Free my mind of the pain. I tried to put it into my work.' She shook her head. 'But I failed.'

'Why do you think you failed?' Gilchrist asked.

'Now, when I look at that painting, I don't feel pain. I see it, though. I see it in the eyes. They remind me of my pain. But I don't feel it.'

'Perhaps you've recovered from Kevin,' he offered.

Jack frowned, and Gilchrist regretted his statement. But Chloe seemed oblivious to Jack's discomfort. 'I still feel for Kevin,' she said. 'He still hurts.'

Gilchrist said nothing. Jack's hand moved to the nape of Chloe's neck and stroked it. She turned to Gilchrist as if an idea had just struck her. 'I think you need to be asking that,' she said to him.

'Asking what?'

'What the Stabber thinks of when he kills someone.'

Gilchrist shrugged. 'We have reams of psychobabble that supposedly answers that, ranging from the Stabber has one eye or knows someone with one eye, to the murders symbolising humanity's blindness against the evils of a cruel world. And everything in between.'

'But why the left eye?' said Jack.

Gilchrist smiled. 'Maybe the Stabber is a right wing extremist who hates socialists.'

'Maybe he's a Rangers supporter.' Jack dug his fingers into Chloe's shoulder. She laid her hand on his, and some unspoken message seemed to pass between them.

Gilchrist talked on. 'Out of all the mumbo-jumbo, the psychological evaluation, the printouts, the discussions, the endless theories...' He shook his head. 'No one even knows for sure if the Stabber's a man or a woman.'

Chloe frowned. 'What do you think?'

'Well,' he said, 'according to our one and only witness, the Stabber's a young man.'

'So what's the problem?' It was Jack.

'I'm not sure I believe him.'

'Why not?'

Why not, indeed? What could he say? That he thought MacMillan was too far away on too bad a night? That Maggie Hendren might have been cruel to animals? That something was niggling the back of his brain? He held the newspaper up. 'Maybe it's this,' he offered. 'Just when you think you have it sussed, the Stabber goes and does it differently.'

'If it is the Stabber,' said Chloe.

'Maybe Chloe's right,' said Jack. 'Why would the Stabber change his habit?'

'He's smart,' said Gilchrist.

'Maybe she's smart,' said Chloe.

Something seemed to settle in Gilchrist's mind at the sound of Chloe's words, as if the fact they had been spoken by someone unassociated with the crimes confirmed his suspicions. 'She knows we're closing in,' he said, pleased with the way the feminine pronoun slushed through his lips. 'She knows we're on to the meteorological service every hour of every day checking when the next storm is forecast for the east coast. And she knows that when it does, we'll be out on full alert, because we know that's when she kills.' He grimaced. 'But now she's done a flanker, I wonder what the profilers will make of that.'

'You sound convinced it is the Stabber,' added Jack.

'Oh, it's the Stabber, all right.' After the second murder, Gilchrist had known they had a serial killer on the loose. By the third, he was convinced the Stabber bore a grudge against men who abused women. That was when females hit the top of his list. But a female serial killer was a rarity, and when he presented his own criminal profile to Patterson, he had been all but laughed from his office.

'Do you think they'll catch her?' It was Chloe.

They? Not him. Gilchrist felt a stab of hurt at his exclusion, but nodded anyway. 'One day,' he said, and added, 'Sooner rather than later, I hope.' He felt another stab of uncertainty. They would catch the Stabber. Of that he was certain. It might take time. But they would prevail. And now when that day came,

Patterson would pile the glory onto DeFiore's head and revive his efforts to remove Gilchrist from the Force. Then what? It didn't bear thinking about.

'Right,' said Gilchrist, and slapped his hand on the bed. 'I'd better get up. I must see Maureen before I head back.'

'Maureen's in Edinburgh for a couple of days,' said Jack. 'Didn't mum tell you?'

'We never really spoke about you and Maureen.'

Jack nodded, as if understanding, and Gilchrist was pleased he did not press for details. 'What's she doing in Edinburgh?' he asked. 'Did you tell her I was coming?'

'It's her new boyfriend. Larry somebody-or-other. Total wanker. But you know Maureen. Head over heels in sixty seconds flat.'

Sixty seconds flat. Maureen's reaction to the opposite sex reminded him of his own relationship with Gail. He had sworn his undying love to her on their first date. Making love in the Valley of Sin had helped, but look where it got him. He dreaded Maureen being hurt the way he had, and made a silent promise to himself to talk to her the first—

'You can have it,' said Chloe.

'Sorry?'

'My painting. Jack and I would like you to have it.'

Gilchrist glanced at Jack.

'What can I say?' Jack's eyebrows shuffled. 'It's a gift.'

'I can't accept your work as a gift,' Gilchrist said.

'Please.' Chloe glanced at Jack as if seeking support, but from his silence she was on her own. 'I want you to have it,' she said to Gilchrist.

'Only if you let me pay.'

'It's a gift from Jack and me.'

'How much?'

'Nothing. Please.'

'I can't, Chloe.'

'Please?'

He realised that his obstinacy was hurting her, so he gave a smile of defeat and thanked her with a kiss and a hug.

After a light lunch of peppered haddock garnished with the

reddest tomatoes Gilchrist had seen since Gail divorced him, it was time to leave. Chloe covered the canvas with a paint-stained bedsheet and loaded it into the back of his Mercedes.

They shook hands and pecked cheeks and Jack promised to call about Gail. Chloe promised to try to persuade Jack to take a weekend in St Andrews over Christmas. Like a child going on holiday, Gilchrist tooted the car horn and waved out the window until Chloe and Jack slid from view behind the towering corner of their tenement building.

One night away from the job seemed to have worked wonders for his energy level, and he bustled through the Glasgow traffic like a teenager. He joined the M8 at Charing Cross and had moved into the outside lane when his mobile phone rang.

'You've fucked it up this time, Gilchrist.'

'What's the weather like in St Andrews?'

Patterson gave a forced laugh. 'You've heard the news, I gather.'

'Any results on the blood?'

'Listen to me, Gilchrist. When I say you're suspended, that means you're suspended from active duty until I reinstate you. Got that?'

'I don't remember reporting in—'

'I've received a formal complaint. Filed by Alexandra Garvie. Name ring a bell?'

'Sounds familiar.'

'She says you more or less forced your way into her house.'

'More or less? What does that mean?'

'You entered her house uninvited, Gilchrist. Good Lord, man, do you deny it?'

'Of course I do. I was polite. She was helpful—'

'What the hell were you doing asking her questions in the first place? You were suspended, for Christ's sake.'

'I was following up a hunch.'

'Are you listening to me? You were suspended. And you still are suspended. I'll be formally writing to the ACC with my personal recommendation that you be asked to submit your resignation forthwith. Do you understand, Gilchrist?'

'More or less.'

Patterson sighed, and Gilchrist caught an image of a pockmarked face bulging red. 'You really are an annoying piece of—'

'I'm losing you...' Gilchrist clicked off his mobile.

Damn it. If he ever had doubts about Patterson having it in for him, they were now history. It made little difference that others more senior liked Gilchrist. He had disobeyed a direct order. And with Garvie's complaint, and Patterson's recommendation, his career was finished.

He gripped the steering wheel. But what had he done to make Garvie complain? He thought back to his interview, to her cat on the window sill, to the coal bunker out the back, to the beads of sweat on her forehead when she had opened the door. Exercising, she had explained.

Now that was interesting.

One of the main objections raised to the Stabber being a woman was strength. She would need to be strong to overpower a man. Garvie looked strong. And fit. And she had invited Gilchrist in, walked away from the door and let him follow.

So why had she complained?

Gilchrist played over the possibilities, but came back to the same conclusion. His career was about to be terminated.

Which meant he had nothing to lose.

CHAPTER 17

'SA, ANDY HERE. I need you to do me a favour.'

'For God's sake. You can't keep calling.'

'You're beginning to sound paranoid. What's up?'

'Patterson's lost it. And DeFiore never had it. Is that clear enough for you?'

Gilchrist smiled. Sa's feistiness was refreshing. 'I need you to get me a copy of a report.'

'Let me guess. Garvie's complaint?'

'You know about it?'

'The whole office knows about it.'

'Can you get me a copy?'

'No can do.'

'No can do? Or no want to do?'

'No can do. Patterson's delivering it personally to McVicar this afternoon.'

Damn. Once McVicar received Patterson's report it would be only a matter of time until Gilchrist was called before him. 'Have you spoken to Garvie?' he asked.

'Are you crazy? She's off limits. That's a direct order from

Patterson.'

'Even for DeFiore?'

'Already interviewed her.'

'And?'

'And nothing.'

'You sure?'

'Sure I'm sure. What's so special about Lex anyway?'

'Nothing. Just a hunch.'

'About what?'

'Something doesn't fit.'

'Give it up, Andy. DeFiore interviewed her this morning. Your hunch is wrong. If you want my advice, which I'm sure you don't, but I'm going to give it to you anyway, stay away from her. Okay?'

'Okay.'

'I hear traffic,' said Sa. 'Where are you?'

'Passing through Cupar,' he lied. 'Any results on the blood samples yet?'

'You never give up, do you?'

'The job's my life,' he said, and felt a pang at the truth of his words.

'I'm sorry, Andy. I've got to go.' Sa disconnected.

Gilchrist had lied to Sa on impulse because of... what? Because she had called the complainant, Lex? He had never seen Sa and Garvie together. And Sa had given no indication that she had known Garvie. But Garvie had been with Patsy in the Dunvegan, and Patsy had given Sa a lift in her Land Rover.

Did that mean anything?

Now he had hung up, he could think of a dozen reasons why Sa would call Alexandra Garvie, Lex. But it wasn't the dozen reasons that intrigued him.

It was only the one.

Fast Eddy looked up from the pint he was pulling. 'Andy. It's your good self. Pint of Eighty?'

Gilchrist shook his head. 'Looking for Maggie Hendren,' he said. 'You seen her?'

'Expecting her in later this evening.'

'What time?'

'Six. But I wouldn't go holding your breath.'

'She doesn't look the unreliable type.'

'Looks have eff-all to do with it, mate. Treats this place like she's a part-timer.'

A quiet voice from behind said, 'Why all the interest in Maggie? You could make a woman jealous.'

Surprised, Gilchrist turned around.

Patsy faced him, cigarette in one hand, empty glass in the other. Without taking her eyes off Gilchrist, she said, 'Same again, Eddy.'

'With you in a sec, love,' said Fast Eddy, and carried a pint of lager to the far end of the bar.

'Going to join me for a drink, Andy?'

'Too early for me.'

'Eighty-Shilling, is it?'

'You'd be wasting your money.'

She caught Fast Eddy's eye. 'And the usual for Andy.'

'Gotcha.'

She drew on her cigarette, her cheeks pulling in with the effort, smooth and angular. Top fashion models would kill for a jawline like that. But it made Patsy's face look hard. In a downpour, from a distance, she might even be mistaken for a man.

Smoke spilled from the side of her mouth. 'I hear you're divorced,' she said.

'It's a small town.'

'I can't imagine someone with your looks being unattached for long.' Another pull at her cigarette, another cloud of smoke. 'But that's not what I'm hearing.'

'Put it down to pressure of work.'

'Too many villains to chase?'

'Something like that.'

'You're not dating?'

Gilchrist shrugged. 'Are you?'

'I'm working on it.'

'There you go,' Fast Eddy said. 'Ready for yours?'

Gilchrist raised his hand. 'Maybe later.'

'Put one in the pipes, Eddy. My tab. There's a good boy.'

'Gotcha.'

Patsy lifted her double vodka and tonic and stared into Gilchrist's eyes. 'You haven't answered my question.'

'Which one?'

'Why all the interest in Maggie?'

'Why would that make you jealous?'

Her smile widened. 'I'm not like the others.'

'The others?'

'Our little group.'

Patsy. Maggie. Lex. Our little group?

'In what way?' he asked her.

'You're the detective.'

Sa called Alexandra Garvie, Lex. Patsy knew Sa. All of a sudden the rumours of Sa's bisexuality seemed well-founded. Patsy, Maggie, Lex. And Sa?

Patsy took another pull at her cigarette. This time she inhaled and almost swallowed. Twin streams of smoke blew from her nostrils like an unspoken warning to back off.

But backing off was no longer on Gilchrist's agenda.

Sebbie flattened his hands to his ears to press out the sound of the hammering on the front door.

'Open this door, Mr Hamilton. We know you're in there.'

He pulled the quilt around his shoulders like a winter blanket. Spikes of pain shot through his stomach. He groaned and slipped a corner of the quilt into his mouth, the material soft between his teeth. The pain in his stomach drifted away for a blissful second.

'Open this door, Mr Hamilton. We will not leave until you open this door.' The wall by his ear gave a shiver, as if a sledgehammer had struck the framing. 'Open up.'

Another thud. A pause. Then again.

'Open the door. This is your landlord. I have a legal right to enter my property. Open this door.' The letterbox flapped, a tinny rattle against a booming background. 'I'm not leaving until you let me in to inspect my property. Open up, Mr Hamilton. Open—'

Sebbie let out a high-pitched shriek.

Silence.

He held his breath. Had they gone?

Four quick raps from a knuckled fist. 'Mr Hamilton?' The voice sounded quieter, as if the landlord was concerned over Sebbie's well-being. But he had met the landlord before, a bungling ape of a man with a bald head and hair like thin fur that protruded from the back of his shirt collar.

'Go away,' Sebbie shouted. 'Just go away.'

'Can't do that. Under the terms of your lease agreement, I have the right to carry out an inspection of my property once a year. I am exercising that right.'

Sebbie closed his eyes. 'Go away.'

'You have refused to acknowledge correspondence from my lawyers, and you are obliged to provide me access to inspect my property. Failure to do so will result in eviction proceedings being initiated against you.'

Sebbie blinked at the hot sting of tears. This was the house he had been raised in, the only home he had ever known. 'I pay my rent,' he shouted.

'That satisfies only one condition of your lease, Mr Hamilton. You need to satisfy other conditions by letting me perform my annual inspection.'

'My parents lived here.'

A burst of light lit the hallway as the letterbox opened, then darkened as a face lowered to it. Two dark eyes blinked then changed to a black hole of a mouth. 'I couldn't care less if the fucking Pope lived here,' the mouth growled. 'I own this property, and I'm coming in, even if I have to break this fucking door down.'

'You can't do that. I have rights.'

The letterbox closed with a clatter then reopened. A folded sheet of paper pushed through and fell to the floor. Sebbie did not have to look at it to know it was a copy of his lease agreement with the inspection clause highlighted.

The black hole returned. 'There's your rights. You have the right to pay me rent. That's what rights you have. And I have the right to get into my fucking property. Now open up.' The letterbox clattered again, followed by a dull thud like a muted explosion.

Sebbie covered his ears. 'Fuck off,' he screamed. 'Fuck off fuck off fuck off.'

Two eyes again. 'Oh, I'll fuck off all right, you little fucker. But I'll be back. You'd better believe it. And I'll be back to break this door down. So, sleep tight. And sweet dreams.'

The letterbox snapped shut. Someone laughed.

The door thudded. Once. Twice. Then silence.

Sebbie suckled the quilt. The landlord would keep his word. He would be evicted. Of that he had no doubt. Then where would he go? What would he do? He had squandered almost all the insurance money from his father's policy, and had not worked since being fired from Coulthart's Engineering for poor timekeeping.

Then it struck him. His life had been leading to this moment. His father's death. His mother's disappearance. His failure at university. His inability to hold down a job. His burgeoning hatred of life, of people, of all things beautiful.

Of her.

A low groan escaped his lips as he rocked back and forth.

If he was going to lose, then so was she.

Gilchrist realised he had switched off his mobile after talking to Sa. He powered it up and found he had missed two messages. One from Beth, thanking him for returning her car, and asking if he could drop the keys off at her shop. The other from McVicar, ordering him to call at his earliest convenience, and leaving a number Gilchrist did not recognise.

Gilchrist wondered if he should call McVicar right away. True to his word, Patterson had forwarded Garvie's complaint to him, accompanied by a scathing report, no doubt, and Assistant Chief Constable Archie McVicar had no option but to follow through.

Christ. It was really happening this time. He was about to be fired. Then what would he do? Take a part-time job at the driving range? Work the bar in Lafferty's? Or nights for some security firm out of town? The injustice he felt he had suffered at the hands of Patterson more than irked him.

He stared off along the street, seeing in the random movement of an unconcerned public the passing of the final hours of his own police career. His once promising sky's-the-limit career had peaked at Detective Inspector and was about to be terminated with the stroke of a pen. For one crazy moment, he wondered if McVicar had called for some other reason, then saw there would be no saving grace. He could almost hear Patterson tell it how it is.

After twenty-seven years with Fife Constabulary the stagnating career of Detective Inspector Andrew James Gilchrist, father of Jack and Maureen, ex-husband of Gail Gilchrist, née Jamieson, is herewith terminated.

He was finished. Just like that.

And that thought brought him to a decision. After twenty-seven years, they could bloody well suffer him for one more day. He switched off his mobile, stuffed it into his jacket pocket, and drove off to Beth's shop.

It always struck Gilchrist that This and That had the lazy ambience of a library reading room. The soulful sound of Kenny G filled the air. Beth looked up from sorting the shelves, her eyes seeming to dance with pleasure at his arrival. He handed over her keys and the envelopes with the repair estimates.

'Any good news?' she asked.

'Not as bad as it could be.'

It felt nice being close to her again and his frustration at the imminent loss of his career seemed to melt from his being. He breathed in her smell, a hint of familiar perfume, an altogether female fragrance that both pleased and aroused him.

When he finished telling her about his rounds of the garages, she asked, 'How did it go with Gail?'

'She's not handling it well,' he said. 'She's bitter, hurt, angry, confused. All of the above.'

'Is she in any pain?'

'Not according to Jack. But I never really had any conversation with her. I just can't...'

'Andy, I'm so sorry.'

He shook his head. Even though it had been Gail who had the affair, he felt as if he had let her down in some way. He cared for her, wanted to help her, but she would not let him near. 'Maybe I'm frustrated at my own failure,' he said. 'I know she's got Harry now, and the kids keep in touch with her. But Gail and I had a life together. We were happy once.' He shrugged. 'At least I thought we were.'

Beth seemed to give his words some thought, then said, 'Maybe she wants to let you in, Andy, but doesn't know how.'

'She seems to be way past that now. For whatever reason, she can't stand me. And as for Harry, well, what can I say?'

Dark smudges stained the skin under Beth's eyes like misapplied mascara. 'How are Jack and Maureen holding up?'

'Jack's hurting,' he said. 'But he'd have you believe he's taking it all in his stride. He talks to his mum every other day, and visits her twice a week. Alone,' he added, deciding not to divulge Gail's hurtful comment. 'God knows if he'll ever make it as an artist, though. But he keeps doing his own stuff and seems to be making some kind of living. I never saw Maureen. She was in Edinburgh for a couple of days. With her boyfriend. Don't ask which one.'

'She didn't get to see her wonderful present?'

'Afraid not.'

'Did Jack like his?'

'He liked it so much he said, Cool.'

Gilchrist loved the high pitch of Beth's laugh and the way her eyes creased with pleasure. It struck him that his life had been devoid of real happiness since they split up. On impulse, he said, 'Are you doing anything later?'

Her surprise deflated him.

'I'm not sure, Andy, I—'

'I mean, would you like a drink, or a bite to eat? Or even just a chat. To catch up.' He hoped his smile would resolve the doubt he caught shifting behind her eyes. 'If you're free, that is,' he added.

'I can't get out of here until six at the earliest.'

'I think I can survive until then.'

'And I was planning to take some paperwork home with me. Accounts.'

Gilchrist gave a quick shrug to hide his disappointment. 'If you're busy, that's okay. Why don't you give me a call if you can find the time? All right?'

She nodded and smiled.

But when Gilchrist glanced back as he left the shop, she had her back to him.

Robbie McRoberts reached across to the passenger's seat and dug his fingers into a fat thigh.

'Wakey wakey, Kev, old son.'

Kev groaned, tried to rub the pain from his leg. 'Fuck sake, Robbie, I've got a wife and kids, you know.' He pulled himself up on his seat.

'Keep that ugly coupon of yours out of sight. He'll see you.'

Kev slid back down into his seat. 'What's he at?'

Robbie scratched a podgy finger at his bald head. 'It looks like he's going for a walk, is what he's at.'

Kev tried to peer over the dashboard.

'Come to Daddy, you fucker.'

'Still see him?'

'I see him all right. But does he see me? is what I ask myself.' Robbie let out a laugh that formed spittle at the corners of his mouth. 'And do you know what the answer to that one is, Kev, old son? Boy wonder doesn't have a clue. Not a fucking clue.'

Kev pulled himself up. In the distance, he watched a skinny figure walk down the side of the house, hesitate at the street, then look left and right as if deciding whether or not to cross the road. 'What's he doing?' he asked.

'He's thinking we've gone, is what the fucker's doing,' said Robbie, his grin crushing his neck into folds of flesh. He slapped the steering wheel. 'I think we're in business.'

'Hang on,' said Kev. 'He's going back inside.'

'You know your problem, Kev? You're a worrier. That's what your problem is. You worry too much.'

Kev had nothing to say to that. Of course he worried. Battering their way into someone's home when they were out was against the law, no matter what the lease agreement said about annual inspections. But as usual, he said nothing, just slid down in his seat and tried to catch another forty winks before he was ordered to do his stuff.

Thirty minutes later, they stepped into the damp evening air. 'Ready to do the necessary?' Robbie asked, and cracked his knuckles.

'Fuck sake, Robbie. One of these days you're going to pull the lot off if you keep doing that.' Kev tucked the head of the sledgehammer under his donkey jacket. But he was short and the handle thudded against his thigh with each step as he followed his employer.

In the dark by the back door, an overgrown hedge offered some protection from the neighbours' eyes.

Robbie turned to Kev. 'Give it one.'

The first blow splintered the door frame and cracked the panel. The second buried the head of the sledgehammer into the wood. Kev struggled to pull it back out.

'The lock,' complained Robbie. 'How many times do I have to tell you? Hit the fucking lock.'

Kev gritted his teeth, lifted the sledgehammer, held it for a second, then swung it hard with a step to the side.

The frame splintered. The door burst open.

Robbie kicked his way inside and placed a hand over his nose and mouth. 'Fucking hell, Kev. Open a window. Get some air in here.'

Kev fought back the need to gag.

Robbie turned, eyes ablaze. 'Don't just stand there, Kev. Open the fucking windows. All of them. And the front door.'

Kev stomped along the hallway and opened the front door.

Back in the kitchen, strips of plaster showed where the wallpaper had peeled off. Tin cans, black toast and clotted baked beans littered the floor around an overflowing bin. In the sink, crusted plates lay in scum as thick as vomit. Kev toed a furred slice of green bread and stepped back as maggots crawled from beneath it.

'Fucking hell.'

Kev looked up. He had seen many a sight, but he had never before seen his boss on the verge of throwing up.

'I'm going to have that fucker's balls,' growled Robbie. 'What did I tell you? I knew something was up. And tomorrow morning I'm going to see my lawyer and charge that fucker with vandalism.'

Kev stared at the mess around his feet, pleased at least that they would probably not be charged with forcing their way into a private residence. 'Good on you, Robbie,' he tried, then stepped outside and threw up.

'We're going to get that fucker's stuff and toss it all out into the back. And d'you know what else we're going to do? We're going to have ourselves a bonfire, a right good fucking bonfire, Kev, old son. D'you hear?'

'I hear you,' Kev said, and threw up again.

CHAPTER 18

'I'M IN THE Central,' Gilchrist said. 'Fancy a pint?'

'Love to, boss. But that numbskull's got us working all hours. And besides, you're suspended. You know the rules.'

'No one'll miss you for five minutes.'

'Want a bet? DeFiore's got eyes in the back of his head. And there's more coming up from Edinburgh.'

'What about Sa?'

'Hang on. I'll go find her.'

Gilchrist sipped his Eighty-Shilling. The bar was already filling up, and he was squeezed into a seat just inside the main door. From the street, he heard the sound of a scuffle, voices rising. He was back on his feet as Sa came on the line.

'Some things'll never change,' she said.

'What's that?'

'You having a pint.'

'One of life's few pleasures.'

On the road, a small crowd stood in a haphazard circle. Two drunks were grappling with each other, swinging wild punches, misaligned hits that connected with dulled effect. 'Care to join me?' he asked Sa.

'I can't. I've got all this—'

'In that case I'd like to report a public disturbance,' he said. 'Market Street. Outside the Central.' He held his mobile towards the scuffle for a few seconds, then returned it to his ear. 'Did you hear that?'

'Can't you arrest—'

'Nope. Suspended.'

Gilchrist disconnected and slipped his phone into his pocket. Sa would be livid. But no matter how many hours DeFiore had them working, she would have to respond to a public disturbance.

He pushed past a heavy-set spectator and stepped into the tussle. He grabbed the nearest battler by the hair, pulled him off his opponent, twisted his arm up his back and marched him onto the pavement.

He shoved him hard against the wall.

Out with the handcuffs. Click once, twice, and the guy looked in drunken disbelief at his wrist locked to the pub door handle.

His opponent swayed, chest heaving, the tip of his nose skinned and bloodied. Clenched fists swung by his side, as if demanding something to hit. Gilchrist approached him and sidestepped an arm that whipped in front of his face. Then he grabbed the flailing limb and twisted, pushing high and hard against the shoulder blades. The drunk gave out a dulled scream and fell to the ground like a lump of meat.

Gilchrist followed him down and dug his knee into the small of his back. He fought the short kick of resistance then felt the slump of defeat as the fight went out of the guy. He grabbed a handful of hair and jerked the head to the side.

Spittle slavered from bloodied lips in angry gasps. 'My arm. You're breaking my—'

'Up.'

Gilchrist pulled the drunk to his feet and frog-marched him off the street. He thudded him against the pub wall and ordered him to stand. With only one set of handcuffs, it was not a good idea to lock the two together. So he waited.

The crowd began to move away, seemingly disappointed.

'You you and you,' snarled Gilchrist, pointing to three men who looked as if they had seen the bottom of a beer glass at breakfast and every hour since. 'You're witnesses.' He pointed to a spot near the door. 'Over there.'

Like trained dogs, they obeyed, and stood silent in their positions. A few minutes later, a police transit van drew up, and the gathering dispersed like leaves in the wind.

The two fighters, now subdued and both handcuffed, were bundled into the back with barely a murmur. Sa appeared from College Street, a hand-held radio at her ear. The witnesses were pointed out to her and she scribbled down their personal details and a brief witness summary. When she finished her preliminary interrogation, she instructed them to report to the Police Station to give a formal statement.

Approaching Gilchrist, she said, 'Citizen's arrest, was it?'

'Keeping in touch.' He nodded to the Central. 'Beer's getting warm,' and returned inside. His pint stood on the table where he'd left it.

Sa sat down beside him.

'Thirsty?' he offered.

'Can't. I'm on duty.'

'When did that ever stop you?'

'DeFiore's got us doing more door-to-door.'

'Hard taskmaster, is he?'

'Makes Patterson look like a clueless lump.'

'Nothing's changed then.'

Sa forced a smile.

'How about a coffee?' he asked.

'Why not?'

Gilchrist ordered Sa's coffee and carried it back to the table. As she took a sip, he was surprised to see her hands shake. The pressure to catch the Stabber had the entire East Coast Constabulary desperate for a breakthrough. And with the Scottish Crime Squad involved, others would be suffering likewise.

'What happened to your hand?' he asked her.

'What?'

'Your wrist. It's bruised.'

Sa lifted her left arm and turned it around.

'The other one.'

She studied two scrapes on the inside of her right wrist. 'Must have bruised it jumping over Granton's wall.'

'Next time use the front door. It's never locked.'

Sa's smile failed to reach her eyes.

'How long have you and Maggie been friends?' he asked.

Sa took a shaky sip of coffee. 'Why?'

'She knew Alex Granton as a child. Did you know that?'

'She grew up here.'

'And you must have known Alex, too.'

'Hardly at all. I never liked him.'

'But you must have seen him around, spoken to him.'

'Not for donkey's.'

'Remember when?'

'What's all this about?'

'Alex Granton is also known as Fats Cockburn. You knew that, too. Why didn't you tell me?'

'What's that got to do with the Stabber?'

Gilchrist pulled out Granton's photograph and slid it across the table.

Sa stiffened. 'Where did you get this?'

The venom in her voice surprised him. 'From Fats,' he said.

'You spoke to him?'

'Last night.'

'Where?'

'Glasgow.'

'You visited him?'

'Yes.'

A series of emotions shifted through Sa's eyes until they stilled in a cold look Gilchrist had never seen in her. Then she picked up the photograph, ripped it in two, and slapped it onto the table with a smack loud enough for the barman to raise an eyebrow.

'What do you think you're playing at?' she snapped.

Gilchrist pulled the two pieces of the photograph towards him and slid them together. Alex's left arm had been ripped from his shoulder. How appropriate, he thought. But a pre-teen Maggie and her pet cat remained intact.

'What happened to the cat's face?' he asked.

'I'm still waiting for an answer.'

'So am I.'

Sa glared at him. 'Why are you doing this?'

'I have an inquisitive nature.'

'And that gives you the right to look into the past lives of my friends?'

'Alex was your friend?'

'You're twisting my words, Andy. I won't have it.'

He tried to disassociate Sa's voice from his memories of irrational arguments with Gail. 'Has anyone figured out why Bill Granton was embezzling from the bank?'

'Who told you that?'

'Pub talk.'

'Name?'

'You know I can't give you names.'

'And you know I could have you arrested for interfering with an ongoing investigation.'

'But that would mean Granton's embezzlement is linked to the Stabber case.' He watched his rationale work its way through her mind, then leaned closer. 'Is that what you think?'

'I think you should stay out of it, is what I think.'

'Alex said the cat was Maggie's pet,' he pressed on.

'Don't push it, Andy.'

He brushed a finger over the photograph. 'So you don't know what happened to its face?'

Sa jumped to her feet. 'Stay out of my private life, Andy. You got that? Just stay the fuck out of it.'

The table wobbled as she stormed out.

Gilchrist pulled the photograph closer. What about it had made Sa react that way? The cat? Fats? Maggie? His snooping around? What? The image of the cat was too small, the quality too poor to scrutinise it in detail. But the sliver of an idea was shifting in his head.

'All things are possible,' he whispered to himself.

Beth locked the shop door.

Beside her, Cindy tightened her scarf around her neck and puffed her breath into gloved hands. 'Look at it,' she said. 'Ten past six, and it's pitch black.'

'Only four weeks to Christmas.'

'Don't say that, Beth. I haven't even thought about presents yet.'

'Don't worry. Neither have I.'

After the warm stuffiness of her novelty shop, the night air smelled fresh. Beth looked up at the dark skies. 'It's supposed to snow this evening,' she said.

'You're full of good news, and I must say,' moaned Cindy. 'I'm missing the summer nights already. I hope it warms up for the weekend. Stewart's driving down from Inverness.'

'Again?'

'He says he loves me. But I know he's only after my body.' Cindy giggled. 'I can hardly wait.'

'How long has that been now?'

'Two years come January.'

'Isn't it about time you proposed?'

'No way, José.'

Cindy was in her early twenties, a former student at St Andrews University who decided to take a year out. Three years ago. Since then, she had shown no desire to return to the penury of full-time study, preferring instead to work and date a string of well-to-do young men.

'Talking about proposals,' said Cindy. 'That was a surprise seeing Andy again. Is it back on?'

Beth gave a tight smile. Cindy was broaching a subject that was out of bounds. Her affair with Andy had lasted almost two years, but she could acknowledge only now that she had loved him. And for the duration, they had each lived on their own, Beth in her luxury flat in St Andrews, Andy in his restored fisherman's cottage in Crail. Perhaps if he had moved in they would still be together—

'Did you tell Andy about that creep?'

'He said he would look into it.' Beth felt her skin crawl. 'Just the thought of it—'

'Forget about it.'

'That's easy to say.'

'Did you see the way he ran? He couldn't leave quick enough. He was scared we were going to call the police.'

'Maybe he won't be so scared next time.'

Cindy grabbed Beth's arm. 'What next time?'

Beth pulled her arm free and kept walking.

'You think he's going to come back?' Cindy asked.

'I don't want to talk about it.'

They reached the entrance to Crail Lane, a narrow alley that connected South Street to Market Street. Beth halted as Cindy stepped into it.

'Aren't you coming?' Cindy asked her.

Beth stared towards Market Street. The stone walls cast shadows like waiting figures.

She shook her head. 'I'm going to take the long way.'

Cindy glanced behind her then retreated.

As the echo of their departing voices died in the wind, out of the walled shadows stepped a man. Without a backward glance, he walked along the lane, stepped into the brightness and strode across Market Street like a single-minded madman. Two couples stepped to the side as he stalked past. One of the girls turned to watch and tapped a finger to her head.

But the man never noticed.

He crossed onto Union Street, then left onto North, and marched down the shallow incline towards the sand dunes and the dark expanse of the West Sands.

In the cold darkness he faced the sea, erect penis in hand. The only way to appease his pain was to have her. He knew that now. And as his sperm spurted into the wind like thin strips of white ribbon, he whispered to the surf, 'Yes, mother. I'll do as you say.'

CHAPTER 19

CINDY WAVED GOODNIGHT at the corner of Bell Street then set off with brisk steps to prepare for her date with Stewart. As Beth watched her leave, the thought of going home to an empty flat sent a shiver through her. She felt an overpowering need to talk to someone and, on impulse, pulled out her mobile phone.

She smiled when she heard his voice. 'Is that offer still on?' she asked.

'You look stunning,' Gilchrist said as Beth took the seat beside him, then gave her a peck on the cheek. 'And that perfume. It's familiar. What is it?'

'Men.'

'Never heard of that one before.'

'No, Andy. You bought it for me. Way back.'

'Ah, yes, so I did.'

'What's it called, then?'

'The name eludes me.'

She gave his arm a playful slap. 'Ysatis.'

'I was about to say that.'

'You have such a way with words.' She slipped off her jacket and folded it over the back of her seat.

'Would you like a drink?' he asked.

She nodded. 'I'd love a drink.'

'The usual?'

'Does that elude you, too?'

'Dry white wine. Chilled. Splash of soda. Slice of lime. Not lemon.'

'I'm impressed.'

While he stood at the bar, he watched Beth dig into her leather satchel for her mobile. By the time he returned, it was back in her bag. She frowned and rubbed her upper arms, as if cold.

'Problems?' he asked her.

Beth reached for her wine and took a large sip.

'Want to talk about it?' he tried.

She held her glass for a long moment, deep in thought, twirling the stem. Then she sat back. 'That was Cindy,' she said. 'She just called me from home.'

'Is she all right?'

'She's fine. It's just... Cindy's got a great memory.'

Gilchrist took a sip of his beer, not sure where this was leading. 'Give her time,' he joked.

'Do you remember the body on the beach? Some years ago?'

Gilchrist was not sure which body on which beach Beth was referring to. He had seen seven, as best he could recall, but he nodded anyway.

'Cindy was a student at the time. She used to jog along the West Sands every morning. She was there.'

Gilchrist leaned closer. 'Go on.'

'She remembered the boy. She remembered thinking how awful it must have been for him. It was his father.'

Gilchrist remembered, too. The body she was talking about was the bloodless corpse with the gash on the neck.

'What about the boy?' he asked.

'It wasn't until Cindy got home that it hit her. The boy on the beach. That creep in the shop...'

'The same person?'

'She's not sure. It only flashed into her head.'

Beth looked frightened, and he resisted putting his arm around her. Instead, he changed the subject. 'Leave it with me. I'll check it out. In the meantime, you once had a friend who was big into computers.'

'Terry Leighton?'

'That's the one. Still see him?'

'From time to time.'

'If you asked him, would he do me a favour?'

'Depends what you want me to ask.'

He removed the two pieces of Granton's photograph from his pocket and laid them on the table. He slid them together and positioned them in front of Beth. 'I need some digital enhancement done on this.'

'What is it?'

'A photograph.'

'I see that, you idiot, but doesn't the police lab—'

'I've been suspended.'

'Oh, yes. I forgot. How many times is that now?'

'I'd rather not get into it.'

Beth fingered the photograph. 'And you don't want anyone to know what you're doing. Right?'

'Right.'

She leaned closer. 'It looks old. Anyone I know?'

'Could be.'

'Keeping secrets, are we?'

'Will you ask for me?'

'Is this to do with the Stabber case?'

'Could be.' He shrugged. 'It's just a hunch.'

'And we know all about your hunches, don't we?' she said, slipping her hand into her leather satchel and pulling out her mobile phone.

Gilchrist took a sip of beer as Beth called Leighton, and thought about his hunches. Beth had been referring to an earlier case of his in which he had chosen to ignore the usual line of questioning and go with his sixth sense. Trust it, he had told himself. It always works for you.

And it had.

His hunch and his inquisitive persistence had uncovered the murder weapon, a twelve-inch butcher's knife buried in the soil by the victim's headstone. The last place anyone would look. Anyone, that is, except Gilchrist. He had become the reluctant local hero after that, even portrayed as a genius by the Editor-in-Chief of the local newspaper, the one who had almost married Beth and whose article was the catalyst that sparked the beginning of Gilchrist's relationship with her. Now his instinct was being piqued once again, this time by an unclear image of a cat on a twenty-year-old photograph.

Why? How could he continue to investigate on hunches? What if this time he was wrong? Would that convince him that Patterson was right and it really was time to hang up his boots? Despite his doubts, the image of the cat still niggled.

Beth disconnected. 'Terry's driving to London for a week,' she said. 'He's leaving first thing in the morning. If you want him to work on the photograph while he's there, he needs to have it this evening.'

'Do you have an address for him?'

'I pass his street on the way home. I'll drop it off.'

'Oh. Okay.' Gilchrist lifted his pint.

Beth surprised him by taking hold of his hand and squeezing it. 'Terry's bald and grey and twenty-stone,' she said.

It irked Gilchrist that she could read him with such apparent ease, but with the digital enhancement now arranged, and concern over the creep in the shop seemingly behind them for the evening, he found them both relaxing as they ordered food and drinks and chatted about old times.

He liked how comfortable he felt with her, and how talk ebbed and flowed between them with no effort, and how her fingers would touch his, or her hand graze his thigh, if their conversation hinted at their past intimacy. And when her face lit up with a smile, he had to remind himself of his earlier invitation to her, and resist the urge to lean over and press his lips to hers.

After another two pints of Eighty and an unfinished glass of white wine, they left the bar at nine and walked arm in arm to the end of Market Street where Beth surprised him once again by giving him a quick kiss and ordering him to call her tomorrow. He wondered if her kiss was an invitation to respond, but by the time his mind had worked out that it had been nothing more than a parting peck, she already had her back to him and was heading off to Leighton's.

He pulled his jacket collar tight and set off towards the Cathedral. In the cold night air, his breath rushed like steam and his mind cast up an image of the bloodless corpse on the beach, a white mass that had lain at the water's edge like an abandoned lump of meat.

It had been cold that morning, too, and drizzling as he walked over the rippled beach of the West Sands, a uniformed policeman by his side. Five or six early morning beach strollers parted as they approached.

The body was naked, the skin flawless white in the cold light, drained of blood from a cut that ran across the throat from ear to ear and grinned at them like a clown's misplaced smile. The drizzle was thickening, gathering into teardrops that trickled over the skin like beads of sweat.

'Anyone here recognise him?' Gilchrist had asked.

'I do.'

A long-haired youth stepped forward, with skin as pale and smooth as that of a young boy. He would later be found to be in his mid-twenties.

'You know his name?' Gilchrist asked.

'He's my father.'

And Gilchrist saw that face now, the eyes more dark and dangerous looking, the hair longer, scruffier than it had been that day on the beach three years earlier.

He took out his mobile and asked to speak to PC Norris.

He was connected almost in the next breath.

'Andy Gilchrist here,' he said. 'Can you talk?'

'I don't know if this is a good idea,' said Norris.

'My lips are sealed,' said Gilchrist. 'So should yours be. That body on the beach three years ago,' he pressed on before Norris could object. 'You remember it?'

'Yes.'

'Who was it?'

A moment's pause, then, 'Jimmy Hamilton.'

Gilchrist smiled. Now he remembered. 'And the son is Sebastian. Right?'

'Yes,' said Norris. 'And a right weirdo.'

'Whatever happened to him?'

'Couldn't say, sir.'

'Got an address?'

'Way ahead of you, sir. I've got it up on the screen right now. You got a pen and paper?'

Gilchrist assigned the address to memory as Norris read it out to him. Hamilton lived on the other side of town. 'Do me another favour, can you? Get hold of Stan and tell him to take Nance and bring Hamilton in for questioning.'

'On what charge, sir?'

'Indecent exposure. And if he has any problems with that, tell him to call me on my mobile.'

When Gilchrist reached the Cathedral cemetery he walked towards the narrow entrance of Gregory Lane. To his right, the Cathedral ruins rose into the night sky like massive wraiths. Ahead, the lane beckoned like a cave.

He hesitated. His thoughts conjured up an image of the Stabber's first victim, Donald McLeish, killed in a lane not dissimilar to this. In his mind's eye, he watched a woman in denim jeans step from the deepest shadows and plunge a stave into Donald's left eye. Had Donald known her? Had he been abusive to her in a past relationship? Gilchrist would never know, not until he came face to face with the Stabber and asked outright.

He stuffed his hands deep into his pockets and entered the lane. His footfall reverberated as darkness enveloped him and he found himself taking comfort from the dim glow of penumbral light that spilled from the rear courtyard of St Gregory's.

He emerged at the opposite end with a shiver and crossed the path that paralleled the cliff face. He stood with his back against the metal railing. The sea wind was picking up, cold as ice.

To his left, the path rose, then spilled, black as the River Styx, down towards Kirkhill. To his right, it ran off like some spectral invitation to the castle ruins. From where he stood, he could just make out Garvie's bedroom window, a grey rectangle on a black roof. Through the McLaren's lighted window, he noticed young Ian slink around his bedroom.

Forty minutes later, a weak light spilled from Garvie's dormer, and a woman stepped forward to pull down the blinds. He thought he recognised Garvie's features, but from that distance could not be sure.

He waited another ten minutes before making a move.

Back in Gregory Lane he pulled himself up and over the stone wall and landed in a garden as dank and cold as an abandoned forest. He pushed his way through a tangle of bushes and uncut grass until he came to what he worked out had to be Garvie's perimeter wall.

He peered over.

Yellow light glowed from an upper window, soft and misted by the blinds. Through the fine material, he caught a flicker of movement. He imagined Garvie exercising, and an image of black Spandex shorts and blonde hair, short and damp, reared up in his mind.

He was about to move closer, when he stopped.

Had his eyes deceived him? Had someone else walked into the room? He kept his gaze glued to the window. Garvie lived alone, did she not? Did she have a visitor? And if so, who? And why upstairs? But ten minutes later, Gilchrist made out no other movement and decided the shadows must have tricked his eyes.

The luminous hands on his watch stood at 10:33. Nothing moved in the darkness around him. Cliff surf rushed in the distance like leaves in an autumn wind. Garvie had told him she took sleeping pills, so he crouched, deep enough in shadow to be invisible to all except the keenest of observers, and waited another fifteen minutes before he peered over the wall once more.

Garvie's house lay in darkness. Several lights still brightened the McLarens' ground floor, and through the light blue sheen of a fabric roll-blind he saw the silhouetted form of someone by the sink. All the lights were out on the house on the other side of Garvie's, grey windows dulled by drawn curtains. He toyed with the idea of entering Garvie's garden from that side, but doing so would still leave him with an exposed climb over the dividing wall.

Decision made, he placed his hands on top of the wall, gripped the stone, and pulled himself up and over.

He dropped onto damp grass as thick as wet straw.

He was in.

CHAPTER 20

KEV OPENED THE door with a 'Yeah?'

Nance gave one of her gentler smiles. 'We're looking for Sebastian Hamilton,' she said to him.

Kev's gaze slid to Stan by her side, then back again. 'It's a bit much calling round people's houses at this time of night is it not?'

'We like to work late,' said Nance. 'Is Mr Hamilton in?'

'He's gone.'

'Out for the evening?'

'Gone tattie bye-byes. Doesn't live here anymore.'

'Moved, has he?'

'You could say.'

Nance's smile thinned. 'Where's he moved to?'

'How would I know?'

'We need to talk to him.'

'Well, when you find him, tell him he owes Robbie for the mess in here.'

'Robbie?'

'The punter who owns this dump.'

'What's Robbie's surname?'

'His what?'

'His last name.'

Kev sniffed. 'McRoberts.'

'Robbie McRoberts?'

'That's him.'

'So, this Robbie McRoberts, he's the landlord, is he?'

'That's what I said.'

'So who are you?'

'Assistant landlord.'

'And your name?'

'Am I being interrogated, or what?'

'Not yet,' said Nance, and let her smile go. 'Name?'

'Kev.'

'Short for Kevin, is it?'

'That's right.'

'Kevin what?'

'It's Kev.'

Nance waited.

'Morris,' said Kev.

Nance glanced to her side. 'Like blood from a stone, Stan.' She gave a sliver of a smile, and said, 'That wasn't too hard now, was it, Mr Morris?'

Silence.

'You live here, do you?'

Kev's face shifted with indecision. 'Yes and no.'

'Which is it? Yes? Or no?'

'No.'

'So why are you here?'

'Clearing up the mess.'

Nance pushed past Kev's stubby bulk and into the hallway.

'Oh, that's great, that is,' complained Kev. 'Why don't you come in and make yourself at home?'

'Thanks,' said Stan, and followed Nance inside.

Bare floorboards stretched the length of the short hall and spread into the kitchen and living room. Two doors either side were closed, suggesting cupboards. The place smelled of stale food and sweat, the air thick with dust.

'Quite a mess.'

'You should've seen it before we kicked him out.'

Nance pushed through to the kitchen.

Black plastic bags lay stacked against the wall in one corner. Cracked linoleum had been ripped up to expose boards blackened with rot. A sledgehammer stood on its head by the sink. Nance lifted it up and turned to Kev. 'Kicked out, you said?'

'That's right. Evicted.'

'When?'

'This afternoon.'

'Why?'

''Cause we couldn't kick him out in the morning.'

'Fancy yourself as a comedian, do you?' Nance shifted her stance as if preparing to thud the sledgehammer onto the sink.

Kev stared at her.

'Just answer the question.'

'What one?'

Nance sighed. 'We've got a right comic here, Stan. Wouldn't you say?'

'Regular laugh a minute,' Stan replied. 'Should be on the telly.'

'Do stand-up, do you?' Nance sniffed. 'Something stinks in here. And it isn't the floor, Kev.'

Kev eyed the sledgehammer.

'I'll ask the question again,' offered Nance. 'Why was Mr Hamilton evicted?'

''Cause he wasn't paying his rent.'

'That sounds like a fair comment. Evicted because he wasn't paying his rent. Don't you think that's a fair comment, Stan?'

'Very fair.'

'How many months behind was he?' Nance continued.

'Dunno.'

'And here was me believing you really are the assistant landlord.'

'Yeah, well, I don't know everything.'

'Do you know anything?' Nance shifted her grip on the sledgehammer. 'Is this the same sledgehammer that knocked the hole in the back door?' she asked.

Kev scratched his head with his little finger.

'I take it that's a yes.'

Kev shuffled his feet.

'Where can I get hold of this Robbie McRoberts?'

Kev shrugged.

Nance stepped closer. 'We can do this the easy way,' she said, 'or we can take you down to the Station and do it my way.'

'Got his mobile number. That do?'

'Only if we get through.' Nance placed the sledgehammer on the floor then picked up the kitchen phone. The receiver had not been cleaned for years, she guessed, but she had seen worse.

'That costs money that does.'

'Keep the comedy routine for the stage,' she said, 'and give me the number.'

After ten rings, she hung up.

'Mr McRoberts wasn't in,' she said to Kev.

'He's a busy man is our Robbie.'

'Own a lot of property, does he?'

'He's got a few bob.'

'Enough to get you bail?'

Kev's gaze darted to Stan, then back to Nance.

'You're booked,' said Nance.

'You can't do that. I've done nothing—'

'Breaking and entering,' she snapped. 'Loitering with intent. Vandalism.' She glanced around the kitchen. 'Loot anything, did you?'

'Now wait a fucking—'

'Public nuisance, too, Stan. Got that?'

'Nuisance? I'm not annoying anyone.'

'You're annoying me,' she said. 'Oh, and violation of the Landlords Act.' She was making it up, but she couldn't care less. 'Like me to think of anything else while we're at it?'

'I'm not the landlord,' cried Kev. 'Robbie is.'

'Well, you'd better get Robbie's arse over here pronto,' she said, handing Kev the phone. 'Right now.'

Garvie's kitchen window lay straight ahead, the lounge window

157

to the side, its polished glass reflecting the crescent of a cold moon. Garvie had not drawn the curtains and from the glow of a night light by the television, he could see through into the dining room and beyond to the heavy velvet curtains that offered privacy from the lane.

He slipped his hand inside his leather jacket and removed his pencil-torch. Its thin beam danced by his feet where the grass lay flattened. He moved towards the kitchen door, his steps long and light in an effort to minimise his trail.

The window by the door had no strips of metal tape or electric wire stapled to it, making him conclude that Garvie had no alarm system installed on her property. A glance at the catch confirmed the window was locked. He shone the beam at the coal bunker then pointed behind it, into a six-inch gap wide enough for a cat to hide, illuminating yellowed pages of a sodden newspaper, a blue bottle cap, a plastic yogurt carton.

On the off-chance Garvie had forgotten to lock her door, Gilchrist gripped the weather-worn metal handle and gave a firm twist.

The mechanism squeaked until metal bit metal.

Locked.

He faced the garden area, his sixth sense telling him he was not alone. He scanned the open space, let the torch beam settle on a narrow strip of flattened grass, Pitter's feline pathway to the rest of the world. In the corner, two beads of light stared back at him, steady as twin moons. He could just make out Pitter, hunched on top of the wall.

Gilchrist swept his beam around and found another trail that led to the far edge of the lounge window. Someone had walked to the window within the last day or so. Garvie had said Gardening's not my forte, but the fresh trail confirmed that she, or someone else, had been outside.

Doing what? Cleaning windows?

A quick glance confirmed the windows could be cleaned from indoors by flipping the frame up and over a central swivel pin. So, why come out to her garden?

Then he saw it. At first, he thought it was a shadow on the

building's stonework. From another angle, he realised it was a ventilation grille, close to the ground, with one of the stone blocks that formed the opening not flush with the others.

He crept along the side of the house until he reached the grille and kneeled on the grass. Damp soaked through his jeans. The grille was constructed of precast concrete, no more than two bricks in size, with square holes for ventilation. Chicken-mesh was fixed over the face to keep out small rodents. But the mesh was loose, and bent up at one corner. Pencil-torch gripped between his teeth, he squeezed a hand under the mesh, gripped the grille, and pulled.

It slid from its slot.

He placed it on the ground and shone the beam into the hole. The light danced over grey joists that resembled the ribbing of a ship. The dirt area at ground level looked dry and tidy and flat as a beach. But why was the grille loose?

He shoved an arm through the opening and patted the earth. Nothing.

He tried scanning his pencil-torch in a wide arc that took in the underfloor void from one side of the house to the other. Again, nothing.

The space was dry and clear.

He was missing something. He was sure of that.

Why was the grille loose? And why had Garvie come over this way? He touched the opening and noticed a stain on one of the stones that formed the joint between the grille and the structural stonework. He scraped it with a fingernail. A crusted piece cracked free. Dried blood? Dirt? He put his finger to his nose. Nothing. He rubbed his fingers, watched whatever it was crumble to dust and realised that was all it was. Dirt. Not blood. But dirt from where? From the soil under the floor? From the garden area? Wherever the dirt had originated, it had to have found its way onto the exposed joint only by someone putting it there.

He thrust his hand through the opening again and felt the bottom of the wall beneath the grille, that area of underfloor void his pencil light could not reach and he could not see.

This time, he dug.

His fingers scratched the dirt, cold from its proximity to the outside wall. He scraped to the left, then back to the right. Tried closer to the wall. Then stopped.

He felt something.

He scrabbled at the earth, his fingers fumbling, found it, touched it. Something thin. Pointed. He clasped it.

Then dropped it.

He fumbled again, caught it, and pulled it out.

A nail. About two inches in length. Orange with rust.

He held it between his thumb and forefinger and rubbed its discoloured surface. He shone his light on it. The nail glinted with a metallic sheen where his fingers had—

Something moved.

From behind.

He spun around, his breath locked in his throat.

The sudden movement stopped Pitter dead in her tracks, her body settling low to the grass. Amber eyes glowed at him from the dark.

'Jesus,' whispered Gilchrist. 'You little rascal.'

Pitter's glowing eyes vanished in a long blink, then she high-pawed it over the long grass, tinkling in the dark like fairy music and leapt onto the coal bunker, then the kitchen window sill, where she settled on her haunches, as if waiting for the window to be opened in the morning.

Gilchrist switched off his torch and dropped the nail into his pocket. His watch read 11:17. He slid the grille back into its slot, crimped the chicken wire into place. From the window ledge, Pitter eyed him with feline indifference.

Gilchrist retraced his steps.

At the rear wall, he eyed the scene.

The unkempt grass looked flattened where he had trodden through it. Dark patches lay like whorled love-nests. In the morning, evidence of his prying might be noticeable.

But he could do nothing about that now.

He pulled himself back over the wall and crept through the neighbouring gardens until he reached Gregory Lane. Seconds later he was back on North Street, shoes and jeans soaked through. Icy dampness at his knees worked its way to his feet. A hot shower was what he needed.

He walked quickly, for warmth, his thoughts firing with possibilities. The trail to the ventilation grille could be important. McLaren's son had seen Garvie in her back garden around midnight. But she had denied that, saying she was on sleeping pills. Out like a light. Wouldn't have heard a bomb go off in the kitchen. But the trail looked no more than a day or two old. If not Garvie, then who? Was she lying?

Gilchrist thought he had a knack for reading guilt. If Garvie had been hiding something from him, he felt certain he would have known. He had seen it before in a thousand faces, the fear of being caught, but he had seen nothing in Garvie's manner to persuade him she was burdened with the secrets of a serial killer.

The east end of Market Street was not much more than a cobbled alley bordered by centuries-old homes. This was a popular route of Gilchrist's, a historical part of the town that conjured up images of beggars and thieves and horse-drawn carts, women with babies wrapped in shawls, town skies thick with the grey murk of damp smoke.

His route took him past the spot where they had found the Stabber's fourth victim, Johnny Gillespie. Less than thirty feet ahead, two women strolled shoulder to shoulder. As he approached, they parted, their hands slipping away to touch with only the tips of their fingers, then drift apart until a gap separated them.

They were younger than he had first imagined. Maybe early twenties. Probably students out for an evening stroll. He mumbled good evening as he overtook them and thought he caught a smile from one of them.

He reached the end of the lane where Market Street widened into a thoroughfare, and looked back. The girls were shoulder to shoulder once again, the press of their bodies suggesting more than just friends on a midnight stroll.

Lex Garvie was a lesbian. Did that make any difference as to how she would be profiled as a serial killer? Probably not. But it could provide him an answer to the question that was haunting him. Ian McLaren had seen her in her back garden the night of Granton's murder. Or to be more precise, he had seen a woman in the garden. What if the woman had not been Garvie, but a friend of hers? Someone with whom she might have had a close relationship? A relationship so close that her friend had ready access to her home? Even when she was upstairs, drugged asleep by sleeping pills?

Had young Ian unknowingly seen the Stabber?

And if so, what had the Stabber been doing in Garvie's back garden?

CHAPTER 21

My sense of panic has passed. I have regained control of my emotions. But something has changed. I feel it. And it makes me shiver, not from fear, but from the certain knowledge of what it is.

My needs have changed.

My need to kill has risen. My need to feed this burning hunger inside me has become more urgent, more relentless, more gripping, as if my mind can think only of my next victim and of ending his abusive existence. My need to kill is driving me, controlling me, and I can no longer wait for the weather to turn foul.

I need to kill soon. I need to kill now.

I think of my next victim and feel relief calm me, as if my murderous thoughts alone are enough to satiate my hunger, like a prisoner calmed on the dawning of the day of his release by the certain knowledge he is about to be freed.

That is how I feel. Soon, my needs will be freed. Soon my hunger will be satisfied. Soon, I will strike again.

I read his name on my list and smile.

Taking this man's life will give me great pleasure.

Sebbie needed to change his plans. He needed a place to stay, needed someone to look after him, someone who would love him the way his mother had. And he knew that soon everything would be all right. Soon he would be home.

He gripped the knife tight, took hold of the door handle with his free hand. He puzzled at the tremor in his fingers and told himself he was not afraid. Only cold. That was all.

He entered a small room barely warmer than the street outside. A smoked-glass-panelled inner door separated the hall from the entrance vestibule. He took hold of the lever handle, eased it down.

The door cracked open.

The stupid bitch. Now he was going to show her why she should keep her door locked. Oh, he would show her all right. She was going to wish she had never known him. The bitch.

Voices drifted from an open door at the end of the long hallway, making him pause for a moment at the thought of how to handle her visitors. Then he heard a gun go off and an engine rev, and he realised she must be watching television.

He crept forward, his new trainers silent on the thick carpet. His fingers brushed wallpaper that smelled of fresh emulsion. A fragrance of flowers and lemon reminded him of the sickening air freshener his mother used to keep in their bathroom.

The bitch. She thinks she has come up in the world. But she does not belong here. She is way above her real station in life.

He reached the end of the hallway and stood in the open doorway, the knife secure in his grip. She was alone, watching television. As he was watching her now. Her hair looked thicker than he remembered, her face fuller. Yes, she had been living the good life, while he suffered. He eased closer, silent as a ghost, and closer still, until he could almost reach out and touch her, close enough to see the steady tick of her lifeblood pulse beneath the skin of her white neck.

'Hello, Alice.'

Her body jerked to the side as she spun round, her eyes wide with shock. In the stunned silence, time ceased to exist, as if her physical image was frozen and framed in space.

Then her lips moved, but no words came.

'Switch the television off,' he ordered.

She looked as if he had spoken in a foreign language, but she picked up the remote from the arm of the settee and the picture disappeared.

Rain whispered against the window.

'I've come for something,' he said.

'What?'

He stepped closer.

'Stop.' She held up her hand.

'You never used to tell me to stop, Alice.'

'Dieter'll be back soon,' she said, her voice rising. 'He won't like you being here.'

'Dieter?' Sebbie let out a forced laugh.

Then her mouth twisted in a thin grimace of disgust. 'What have you done?' she said. 'You look awful. Your hair.' She screwed up her face and eyed the length of him. 'You've lost so much weight. And your clothes. Oh, my God.'

Sebbie reached for her.

'Stay away,' she shouted. 'I mean it, Sebbie. Stay away from me.' She placed her hands over her mouth. 'Oh, my God,' she said. 'What's that smell? Oh, my God.' She closed her eyes.

'Look at me.'

She shook her head.

'Look at me.'

'Go away, Sebbie. Just go away.' Then she peered at him through half-opened eyes. 'Oh, my God. You're disgusting. Just look at yourself.'

It may have been her hurtful words that did it. Or her ugly look. Or the pain in his gut that had returned and now burned like a raging fire. But things seemed to happen then, almost out of body, as if he was watching some other person walk forward and take hold of her hair and pull her head back so that he could see the bobble of her throat as she tried to swallow her fear. And it puzzled him that he felt no anger towards her, despite her comments. He had loved her once. A long time ago, it seemed. When things were different. But he felt no love for her now. No anger. No love.

Nothing.

Her gaze transfixed on something by his waist, and he looked down at the black-handled knife in his hand and wondered how it had got there.

'Don't, Sebbie.' She shook her head. 'Please don't.'

She was begging him. She, who lived in this house with that poncy prick, Dieter, was begging him not to hurt her. Something surged through him then, and he pulled her head farther back so the sinews on her neck stuck out in thin cords. Her hands were no longer over her mouth, but raised by the side of her face, as if wanting to tear his grip free but somehow unable to do so.

'Please don't, please don't, please.'

He leaned towards her, and her eyes closed, as if she could not bear the sight of him.

'Open your eyes.'

Her head shivered.

'Open them.'

She opened her eyes and stared at the knife in his hand.

He squeezed her hair, jerked her head. 'Look at me.'

She peered at him from behind the pain. 'I'll scream,' she tried. 'I will. I'll scream.' But her words came out in a strangled choke.

'You won't,' Sebbie said. 'You never scream. You like it too much. You've always liked it. Haven't you?'

He watched realisation shift across her face with the slowness of a vanishing smile, pleased that she seemed no longer concerned with his looks or personal hygiene.

He brandished the serrated blade by her throat, swishing it left then right. Her eyes followed, tried not to lose it, then widened as he brought the blade closer and pressed it against her skin. Tears trickled down her cheeks.

'Please don't,' she whispered.

'If I don't, will you tell anyone about me?'

'No.'

'Not even Dieter?'

'No.'

'Don't lie to me.'

'I'm not lying honest I'm not.' Her voice livened with the glimmer of hope.

'You used to lie to me, bitch.' He paused, to see if his words triggered her memory. 'Do you remember?'

'I won't tell anyone. Cross my heart and hope to die.'

He turned the knife so that the blade lay flat against her skin. Her carotid artery pulsed with fear. He slid the gleaming metal across her neck and raised a drop of blood from the tiniest of nicks.

'Cross your heart and hope to die?'

'Please. Sebbie. Please.'

'You lied to me about Dieter.' He ran the blade up her neck and across her jawline so that her tears found their way onto the shining metal.

'I'm sorry—'

'What are you sorry for?'

'I'm sorry for... for, lying.'

'You lied to me?'

She hesitated, as if trapped by his question, knowing that any response would only worsen her predicament.

Then she whispered, 'Yes.'

'Why tell me now, bitch? Why tell me now that you're sorry? You weren't sorry then. Were you?'

'I didn't mean it, Sebbie. I'm sorry now. Truly I am.'

'If I couldn't trust you then, bitch, why should I trust you now?'

'I won't tell Dieter. I won't tell anyone. Please. Sebbie. Please. Let me go.'

He pulled the knife from her skin and stood back. She opened her eyes. With a suddenness that made her start, he reached forward, grabbed her hair, pulled her head back, and lifted the knife high.

'I know you won't tell anyone, Alice. Not this time.'

He flashed the knife down to her neck.

Her scream never surfaced, locked in her throat.

He released her hair, the point of his blade millimetres from the pale skin of her neck. She held her head still, as if waiting for the pain to hit. Then the tiniest of tremors took hold of her hands, spread to her arms, her shoulders, her chest, until her entire body trembled.

'Look at me,' he said.

'Oh, my God. Please don't.'

'Look at me, bitch.'

She looked at him.

'Will you tell anyone?'

'No.'

'Promise?'

She squeezed her eyes shut, spilling tears down her face, and nodded.

'You won't tell anyone?'

She shook her head.

'Say it.'

'I won't tell anyone.'

'Say it.'

'I promise I won't tell anyone.'

'That's better,' he said, and cupped her left breast. She opened her eyes. Her breast felt full, supple and soft, and his arousal sent a rush of urgency through his system.

'Take off your clothes.'

'Please. Don't do this.'

He ran the flat of his blade over her throat. 'Take them off.'

Her fingers trembled as she fumbled with the top button of her blouse, then the next.

Sebbie watched her slow unveiling in silence, and could do nothing to prevent the stirring in his crotch. It had been a long time, such a long time. With insolent reluctance, it seemed, Alice slipped off her blouse, twisted her arms behind her back, and removed her bra.

Sebbie's breath caught at the sight of her nakedness. She looked more full than he remembered, no longer a teenage girl, but a mature woman. Her breasts were white where her tan ended, making her nipples seem large and dark. She looked up at him, cheeks glittering, eyes pleading.

He pointed the knife at her. 'Get up.'

She stood, arms drooped by her side as if exhausted from the effort.

'Everything.'

'Please.'

He held the knife up. 'Don't make me have to ask again.'

She twisted to the side, unzipped her skirt, let it slip to the carpet. Then she hooked her thumbs over the top of her tights and eased them down her thighs. 'Please,' she said. 'I don't want to do this.'

He watched the uncovering of the white meat of her thighs as she undressed to her knees, then down and onto the carpet where she kicked her feet free. His gaze locked on tiny silk panties that seemed wrongly sized for her thighs. He gave an involuntary swallow as he eyed her pubic mound and tried to remember what her bush felt like, how he used to bury his face into her and search for her wetness.

He fingered his zipper and pulled out his erection and watched her eyes darken with the knowledge of what was about to happen. Somewhere in the dark chasms of his broken mind he heard a voice whisper to him, urging him on. His head tilted to the side like a curious dog, as if to confirm he was hearing her instructions correctly.

And it felt good knowing his mother approved.

'Yes,' he whispered back to her. 'Yes, I will.'

Then he faced Alice. 'On your knees, bitch.'

CHAPTER 22

GILCHRIST LAY STILL, trying to figure out where he was. Then he caught the cold reflection of a glass moon and realised he was looking at the Velux window on the sloped ceiling of his own bedroom.

Something had wakened him.

On the floor beside his cupboard door he caught the shadow of Chloe's painting, its vortices even more wild in the dim light, as if the image had a mind of its own and was trying to cry out to him. He had a vague recollection of bringing it in from his car last night and placing it there before crashing out. And dreaming.

That's what had wakened him. A dream.

A dream about Chloe's painting. Images came to him, as faint as wisps of cloud. A shape closed in. Then vanished.

With a spurt of dismay, he realised he was still wearing his shirt and underpants. He swung his legs to the floor and peered at his digital alarm clock. 6:33. He switched on his bedside lamp, pulled open the drawer, slammed it shut. Why did he always search for a cigarette first thing? He had not smoked in twelve years. Surely his brain should have adjusted by now.

His dream floated by. Shifting shadows. He almost had it. Then lost it. It was as if he held something then laid it down, only to find moments later he could not locate it and the memory of what he had held, where he had put it, vanished like a morning haar.

He tottered through to the bathroom on stiff legs that felt cramped, as if he had over-exercised. He straightened his back, then remembered pulling himself up and over stone walls, and lying on damp grass. Then the walk to his car with icy feet, shoes and socks sodden.

He stripped off his shirt and underpants and stood naked. The bathroom was heated by an oversized radiator on the back wall, over which hung four bath-towels. He removed one and wrapped it around his waist like a sarong, loving its soft warmth against his skin. He ran his tongue over the fur on his teeth and reached for his toothbrush, its bristles splayed and clogged. Time to buy a new one. He squeezed out a dollop of toothpaste and scrubbed hard and fast, forcing his thoughts into gear.

Chloe's painting. Faded dreams. What did it all mean?

He almost caught his dream again, watched something slink away from him like a frightened animal, then evaporate in the neural mist. He rinsed out his mouth, swabbed the sink, and returned to his bedroom.

He lifted Chloe's painting and held it at arm's length. What had been going on in her head when she had painted that image? He twisted it to the side, focused on the hole for a mouth...

The mouth. That's what he had dreamed of. A mouth. An open mouth. But more than just an open mouth.

He had dreamed of lips.

And through the haze in his mind, his dream came back to him. And in his dream, he was back where it had happened.

Glasgow. Fifteen years earlier.

Assisting with a routine investigation in Blackhill, a ruin of a residential development on the city outskirts. How anyone could live there defied the imagination. Ground-floor windows were bricked over. Rusted hulks of stripped cars dotted derelict streets. Back gardens lay hard and bare of grass. Graffiti slashed grey walls.

Gilchrist had been standing at the back of a tenement block when a young girl approached him. No more than twelve. Maybe eleven. Lipstick. He remembered her lipstick.

Bright red. And smudged, as if she had been kissed.

She told him her boyfriend had been hit over the head with an axe. He remembered feeling more surprised at hearing she had a boyfriend, than by the alleged attack. And he kept looking at her lips, fascinated by this eleven-year-old woman. His peripheral vision caught movement in the brown dirt behind and to the side of her. A skulking cat. Once domesticated, now abandoned and wild and living in fear of human predators. The cat had slipped under a concrete slab before Gilchrist had time to have a close look. But he had seen its lips.

And that's what he had been dreaming about.

The cat's lips. And Alex Granton's photograph.

He remembered asking the Glasgow detective what was wrong with the cat. It was a game the kids played, he'd been told. Like scalping. They caught cats and sliced off their lips. It was something to do. The residents didn't complain. It was better that the kids cut up cats rather than each other.

Gilchrist picked up his mobile. After a couple of rings, a sleepy voice grumbled, 'Hello?'

'Sorry to waken you.'

'Don't tell me it's you, Andy.'

'Okay, it's not me.'

'What time is it?'

'Almost seven.' He listened to some ruffling on the line, imagined Beth shifting her body, coming to, fluffing her pillow, and an image of her naked body seared into his mind.

'Did you see Terry Leighton last night?' he asked.

She let out a heavy breath, as if disappointed, and said, 'Yes, Andy, I saw Terry last night, and yes, I gave him the photograph, and yes, he said he would work on it as soon as he could. Anything else?'

'Do you have his telephone number?'

'Not trust me?'

'Implicitly.'

'Liar,' she grumbled. 'His mobile number. That do?'

'Perfect.' He jotted down the number as Beth read it out. 'Thanks. Try to catch another hour.'

'Oh, great. You waken me up to tell me to sleep?'

'Wish I was there.'

The words were out before he could stop himself. For several seconds the line remained silent, then Beth said, 'I enjoyed last night,' her voice soft. 'It was nice.'

'Me too.'

'Let's not rush anything, Andy. You hurt me. I don't want to be hurt again.' A pause, then, 'Why don't you call later and let me know how you got on with Terry?'

'I'll do that.'

'Talk to you later.'

He replayed their conversation in his mind and felt almost afraid of believing he could have resurrected their relationship. He had fallen for Beth hard, taken their break-up even harder. So how had he hurt her? Had it not been the other way round? And what had become of Tom Armstrong, the man with whom she had appeared to replace him so easily? He could ask these questions later. First, he had some facts to uncover. But Leighton's number rang out, connecting to voicemail, and he left a message.

Back in the bathroom, Gilchrist turned the shower up to hot. He flexed his muscles for a full five minutes under a roasting stream, feeling the heat work its magic.

By 7:30 the skies hung dull and dark with banks of raincloud. Outside, Gilchrist almost shivered. Cold enough for snow, he thought. Or was it too cold for snow? Was that not what his father used to say on days like this? And Old Willie, too? He could come up with the most peculiar phrase from time to time. Priceless information, too. Which had Gilchrist puzzling over his comment in Lafferty's. If I was you I'd watch Sam MacMillan.

Why MacMillan? What did Old Willie know about him?

Gilchrist's hunch about MacMillan had been proven wrong by Fats. Fucking plonker. That the best you can do?

It seemed to make no sense, but somehow a painter and decorator was mixed up in all of this. How? And why?

Gilchrist knew of only one way to find out.

The Merc started with a healthy growl. He cut through the miles to St Andrews in short order, parked by the harbour front and walked to where MacMillan had watched Granton being murdered. He was struck with the sudden thought that perhaps MacMillan was not homosexual but was hiding behind that misconception. Why would he do that? Because if the police believed he had an overt homosexual relationship with Granton, they would not ask the question he dreaded. Why was he extorting money from Bill Granton? Was that it?

Gilchrist removed his mobile from his leather jacket.

Directory Enquiries gave him the number.

MacMillan answered on the second ring.

'Morning, Sam. Andy Gilchrist here.'

'What do you want now, Mr Gilchrist?'

'Honest answers to some honest questions, Sam.'

'I've told you the truth.'

'That's today's first lie.'

'No it's not.'

'That's the second.'

'You really are an aggressive bugger.'

'I've been called worse.'

'Aye, son, I'm sure you have.'

'Ready to talk?'

'About what?'

'Honesty being the best policy.'

Silence.

'What did you do with all that money?'

'What money?'

'The money Bill gave you for flashing his cock at you.'

Silence.

'That's all it was, Sam. Wasn't it? There never was a homosexual relationship between you and Bill, was there? Bill had a fetish. He needed to expose himself in public. He got his thrill from knowing someone was looking. But he couldn't afford to be found out. He couldn't walk up to just anyone and open his coat and flash his cock. Not in a town the size of St Andrews. He'd lose his position at the bank before he had time to zip it up.'

Gilchrist paused to let MacMillan embellish his theory or deny it, but heard only silence.

'Every once in a while Bill would flash his cock at you, Sam,' he went on. 'Maybe even shoot a load or two in your direction. That way, his perversion was safe. You were friends from way back. He knew you would keep your mouth shut. As long as he gave you money. Make you both guilty in a manner of speaking. And you took the money, Sam. And kept quiet.'

Silence.

'I've checked the marriage register, Sam. You were married—'

'So was Bill.'

'But his wife didn't desert him.'

Silence.

'She left you for a reason—'

'She buggered off, is what she did.'

'And left you holding the baby, so to speak.'

'Fuck you, you wee shite.'

'She left you with Louise,' Gilchrist said. 'Louise Samantha MacMillan. Your daughter.' From the fumbling on the other end, he sensed MacMillan was struggling with his emotions. After several seconds, Gilchrist said, 'I'm sorry, Sam. I'm truly sorry.'

'So,' MacMillan said with a defeated sigh, 'you know all about her, what happened to her. To Louise, I mean.'

'Yes,' said Gilchrist. 'I do.'

'So, tell me, Mr Gilchrist. What would you have done in my situation?'

What indeed? But it was not Gilchrist who had broken the law. 'I think we should talk, Sam. Face to face.'

'When?'

Gilchrist was about to press for a meeting later that morning, but instead said, 'At your convenience.'

'Let me think about it.'

Gilchrist was not sure he liked where this was going.

MacMillan was in his sixties. Facing the consequences of the law catching up with him might be more than he could bear. Before he could stop himself, he said, 'Don't do anything silly now, Sam.'

'Like what?'

'Like running away.'

Sam growled, long and low, which Gilchrist thought was a stirring of anger. Then he realised with a smile of his own that he had never heard the old man laugh before.

'You crack me up, Mr Gilchrist, so you do. Aye, son, you crack me up.'

'Get back to me soon. Alright?'

'Aye, son, I will.'

Gilchrist stared off to the Eden Estuary and beyond across the Firth of Tay to the distant shores of Buddon Ness and Carnoustie. Sunlight burst through the clouds at that moment and painted the grey landscape with greens and yellows. He listened to the echo of MacMillan's voice ask him what he would have done in his situation. But he had no ready answer for that. He wouldn't have liked to have been there in the first place. But it had not been MacMillan's choice either. He had been dealt a bad hand. And life seemed to have a habit of dealing bad hands.

As Gilchrist strode back to his car, he passed the spot where Granton had been murdered, and his mind conjured up an image of Sa standing back from the body. Why had she not told him she had known Granton? Why had she not said she knew his son, Alex? And why was she so defensive about her past?

Maybe the answer lay in her childhood.

Or in the photograph of a wounded cat.

Sebbie opened the American-sized fridge.

Its shelves were stuffed with food, not like the tiny model in his own kitchen. He found a six-pack of Miller Genuine Draft and twisted the top off a bottle, took a swig, and strolled back into the living room.

Alice's skin had discoloured in shades of yellow and blue. Dieter's face had fixed in a stiffened grimace of pain and surprise. Sebbie tipped beer into Dieter's opened eyes. 'Up yours,' he said, then laughed, a crazed cackle that seemed to crack through the room—

He looked up at the ceiling.

Who lived upstairs? Had they heard him?

He stepped over Dieter's body and leaned into the window. The glass felt cold against his skin. Through the windows of the flat opposite he saw someone walking around the room. He pulled back, pressed himself against the wall. Had he been seen?

Without daring another glance, he closed the curtains.

The room fell into darkness. If he was going to live in Alice's flat, he would have to stay quiet, creep around in his stockinged soles, keep the television on low, maybe even Mute.

In the dimmed light, the bodies on the floor looked out of place, like nameless corpses waiting to be carted off by the undertaker. He caught a whiff of something foul, fetid, like rotting eggs.

He pressed a foot onto Dieter's stomach. The whisper of flatulence was followed by a stench so powerful he had to press a hand to his mouth. He cursed and rushed from the room.

A few minutes later, he returned, face wrapped in a dish towel, hands covered with a pair of yellow rubber gloves he had found beneath the sink. Under his arm, he held two cotton sheets stripped from a double bed.

Dieter's body was less bloodied. Sebbie had stabbed him as he kneeled over Alice. He rolled Dieter's body onto the sheet then dragged it from the living room, down and across the hall, and into a back bedroom.

Alice presented more of a problem. He had stabbed her in the chest and she had bled like a slaughtered pig. He smiled as he looked down at her. The irony had not struck him until that moment. Alice stabbed through her heart, the same way she had stabbed him through his. Dieter stabbed in the back, the same way he had stabbed Sebbie by screwing Alice while they were still dating.

He grabbed Alice's bare legs and twisted her body so that it rolled over onto the sheet, face down. Thick lumps of dark red slime like bloodied slugs slipped over her ribs and dripped onto the sheet. In a rush of disgust, he grabbed the corners of the sheet and threw it over the body, then dragged it from the room to join Dieter.

Back in the living room, he spent ten minutes scrubbing the worst of Alice's blood off the carpet. Not perfect, but by evening it would have dried, and he would—

The telephone rang.

He froze.

On the sixth ring, the answering machine kicked in, and Alice's annoying voice told the caller to leave a message after the long beep and have a great day. Bitch.

'Alice. This is Margo. You never called, and I wondered if you needed me to bring anything over this evening. If I don't hear from you, Jim and I will be round at eight. We're looking forward to it. See you then. Byeee.'

Sebbie stared at the phone. This evening? At eight?

What was she coming round for? Dinner? A party? Was that what the food in the fridge was for? Were friends expected?

Sebbie paced the room. His perfect hideaway was about to be ruined on day one. He could not afford to lose this flat. He could not let that happen. But if he stayed, he would be discovered.

He would need to find somewhere else. But where?

He stared at the dried blood on the floor as the seed of an idea sprouted in his mind.

He knew just the place.

CHAPTER 23

GILCHRIST WALKED UP the hill towards Kirkhill, the Cathedral ruins on his left, on his right the black craggy cliffs that separated the West Sands from the East. By the time he stood outside Garvie's front door it was after eight.

He pressed the bell.

Lex Garvie seemed not in the least surprised to see him.

'Up bright and early, I see. I take it this is a personal call.'

'Been expecting me?'

'Rumour has it you're suspended.' She stepped to the side. 'So in that case, you can come in.'

'Word travels fast,' he said.

'It's a small town. And small town people love small town gossip.'

'Got any for me?'

'Gossip?' she said. 'Or tea?'

'A bit of both,' he said. 'If you've got it.'

'I can give you tea. But no gossip.'

Lex Garvie was showing another side to him, a side unlikely to belong to someone who had filed a complaint against him. He followed her through to the kitchen, pleased to find Pitter seated on her spot by the sink. He stroked her chin and felt the press of her neck as she searched for maximum pleasure. He looked out of the window, relieved to see his trail through the back garden was not noticeable. He stepped to the side as Garvie put on the kettle and popped two teabags into a silver teapot.

As Garvie pottered about in silence, it struck Gilchrist that she seemed strangely unfazed by his presence. Her light-tanned skin and short blonde hair shone with a healthy glow and gave off a fragrance that reminded him of his father's hair oil. She was bare-footed, in black spandex shorts and a white T-shirt with the sleeves cut off, so he could see her firm muscle tone and run of smooth skin almost all the way to her bra-free nipples.

'Do you mind if I ask a few questions?' he said. 'Off the record, of course.'

'If you must.'

'Force of habit, I suppose.'

'I've already told that inspector whatsisname...'

'DeFiore?'

'That's him. I've already told him all I know.'

'It won't take long.'

'That's what DeFiore said.'

'Did he stay for a cuppa, too?'

She laughed and lifted her hand to run it through her spiked hair. Her upper arms flexed with sinewed ease. 'Care for a biscuit?' she asked, and removed a plastic container from the cupboard above the kettle. 'KitKat. Toffeepops. Happy Faces. Got them in for my sister's kids. Or just plain old suggestive digestive?'

'Whatever you're having.'

'I don't take chocolate.'

'Plain old suggestive digestive sounds fine, then.'

She giggled, which seemed out of character. But the ring of her laugh triggered something in his brain. He had heard a giggle like that somewhere before, but could not place it.

Garvie collected a couple of mugs and a side plate from the dishwasher, then opened the fridge and removed a crockery ramekin from the second shelf. 'Homemade pâté?' she asked. 'It's vegetarian.'

'No thanks.'

'Well, seeing as how you're here, let's have it.'

Gilchrist waited until she spread two knife loads of pâté onto her side plate and returned the ramekin to the fridge before he said, 'Your complaint.'

'Complaint?'

'Your complaint against me.'

She hesitated, then said, 'No idea what you're talking about.'

Undecided if she was telling the truth or not, Gilchrist chose not to press. 'Must have picked it up wrong,' he said.

'Must have.'

He waited while she dabbed a damp cloth over the work surface by the sink, then hung it over the stainless steel taps. It was only then that he noticed a small ashtray in the corner of the work surface by the side of the fridge. 'How did you sleep last night?' he asked her.

She lifted the teapot, and Gilchrist suspected he was about to hear the beginnings of a lie. 'Never heard a thing,' she said.

'Sleeping pills?'

'Where would I be without my pills? Sugar? Milk?'

'Milk only.'

'I sometimes worry about taking too many pills. But for the life of me I can't seem to sleep any more without them.'

'Guilty conscience?'

'Never miss a trick, do you?' She poured milk from an opened carton. 'Skimmed. It's all I've got.'

'Perfect.'

She split the wrapper off a packet of digestive biscuits and spilled half a dozen onto a plate. 'With or without butter?' she said, breaking one into several pieces and placing them on Pitter's tea towel.

'Without is fine,' said Gilchrist, and added, 'I've never seen a cat eat biscuits before.'

'She'd eat the food from your plate, given half a chance.'

He watched Pitter crunch one of the broken pieces then shake her head with a quick movement that spread crumbs across the sink. He could not resist stroking her, and smiled when she started purring. 'She has lovely colours,' he said. 'The whitest white. The blackest black. Nothing in between. Such a distinctive coat.'

'You like cats?'

'Never had one. But yes, I suppose I do.' He stopped scratching Pitter, then reached for the soap on a dish by the window. He washed his hands and removed a paper towel from a roll by the oven. 'You never gave me an answer,' he said.

'To what?'

'About the guilty conscience.'

She held out the biscuits. He took one. She shook the plate and he obliged her by taking another.

'I don't sleep because I spend a lot of time on the computer in the late afternoon and early evening. My work is creative and demanding. But it's stimulating. Once my brain is fired up, it keeps me awake.'

'Why not work during the day?'

'I'm not a morning person when it comes to brainpower. I prefer to exercise in the morning.'

'Had any work done on your home recently?'

She frowned, puzzled by his non sequitur. 'Like what?' She dabbed a biscuit into the pâté then took a bite.

'Roof tiles,' he said. 'New doors. That sort of thing.'

She shook her head, sipped her tea.

He tried a bit closer to the bone 'Replacement windows? Underfloor ventilation?'

'All that was done by the previous owners. That's why I bought the place.' She eyed the rear garden. 'Although that mess out there needs fixing. But I'm getting it landscaped in the spring. Grass out. Slabs and gravel and shrubs in. All mulched. No grass to cut. No weeds to pull. Efficient.'

'Just like you.'

She looked at him, as if not sure how to take his remark, then smiled. 'You should hear some of my clients complain about how long I take to construct their websites.' She shook her head.

'Efficient is not in their vocabulary. Another?' She shoved the plate at him.

'No, thank you.' He watched Pitter slip through the gap in the kitchen window. 'Last time we spoke, you said you were gay.'

'That's right. Nothing's changed.'

He did not fail to catch the bite in her reply, nor the steely haze that settled behind her eyes. 'Do you have friends stay over from time to time?' he asked.

'That's an odd question to ask.'

'Why do you say that?'

She tutted. 'One question after another. You really must break that habit of yours.'

He took a sip of tea. It tasted a tad on the weak side. But it was hot.

'Like a refill?'

'I'm fine, thank you.' He waited while she returned the biscuits to the cupboard and wiped the work surface with a damp cloth, then said, 'About those friends of yours.'

'Which ones?'

'The ones that might or might not stay over.'

'What about them?'

He kept his voice level and repeated, 'Do any of them stay over from time to time?'

'As in, Do I have sex with any of my girlfriends?'

'Not quite what I had in mind,' he said, surprised by the ease with which anger lit her eyes.

'What did you have in mind?'

'Did anyone stay over last night?'

'None of your damned business.'

'Any of your friends have a house key?'

'Why?'

'Just asking.'

'I know you're just asking. But why?'

'I'm curious.'

'You can say that again. You're becoming curiouser and curiouser.'

'I take it that's a Yes.'

'That's a Mind your own bloody business is what it is.'

He placed his mug of tea on the work surface. 'I'm sorry,' he said. 'I seem to have upset you.'

'I wouldn't go as far as that.'

'How far would you go, then?'

'My private life is just that. Private.' She replaced the cloth over the tap and turned to face him. 'Look, I've got some work to get on with.'

'Thought you weren't a morning person.'

'Exercising, then. Is that better?'

Gilchrist poured out what was left of his tea, rinsed his mug and placed it on the drip-tray. Then he picked up the last of the digestive biscuits and took a bite, but dropped a piece onto the floor.

'Sorry,' he said, and picked it up. He flipped open the metallic bin, dropped the crumbs into it, and closed the lid. But not before he noticed an empty packet of Camel lying in the rubbish.

'Thank you,' he said to Garvie, and patted his stomach. 'Just what the doctor ordered.'

At the front door, he paused. 'You could make my job a lot easier by just telling me which of your friends stayed over last night.'

'It's none of your business.'

'It could be.'

'What does that mean?'

'That I could have you come down to the Office.'

'Don't you have to be un-suspended to do that?'

The logic behind her earlier comment had not struck him until then. 'You knew I was suspended,' he said.

'Is that a trick question?'

'Who told you?'

Sunlight toyed with the blue specks in her eyes.

'It's not common knowledge,' he added.

She pressed a hand to his back. 'As I said, my private life is private. Please don't come back. Suspended or otherwise.' And with that, she closed the door.

He thought it odd how hard some people fight to keep certain parts of their lives to themselves. Which was the wrong thing to do where he was concerned.

He cut along South Castle Street onto Market Street, avoiding the Police Station. Beth often had breakfast in the Victoria Café. If he was quick, he might just catch her.

He reached the café as a cloudburst raked the street with liquid bullets. By the time he took a seat by the window, the worst of the storm had passed. He ordered coffee and a bacon sandwich. No garnish, bacon not too crisp, and bring the pepper.

The room was empty and he wondered if he had missed Beth, or if she had forgone breakfast and headed straight to her shop. Before his own breakfast was served, he decided to call Maureen and stared out the window while he waited for her to pick up.

'Hello?'

'Maureen?'

'Who's this?'

'How about Hello Dad.'

'Dad? Is that you?'

'The one and only,' he said, his gaze drawn to a scruffy man shambling along the pavement on the other side of the road. New trainers and filthy jeans tattered at the heel, and scrawny shoulders covered by a tidy casual jacket, looked out of place.

'This is a surprise, Dad.'

'Pleasant one, I hope.'

'Of course.'

'It's been a while.' The young man stepped into the traffic, forcing cars to swerve out of his way. He looked pale, almost drugged. But something seemed oddly familiar about him. 'How are things?' he asked.

'Mum said you visited her.'

Gilchrist turned from the window. Maureen had this annoying habit of evading questions. 'I said, how are things?'

A pause, as if she was trying to calculate the depth of his annoyance. Then, 'Sorry, Dad. I've been busy. You know how it is. Exams and stuff. And then with Mum not keeping well. I've got a lot on my mind. Sorry.'

And an equally annoying habit of making him feel a fool after he'd made his point. The waiter came with his order, and Gilchrist nodded for him to place it on the side.

'How's she keeping?' he asked.

'Same as yesterday. Terrible pain. Just waiting to die.'

He shifted the phone to his other ear. Of his two children, Maureen was closer to their mother and possessed an uncanny ability to rile him with nothing more than the flick of her tongue. The way Gail used to.

'Jack told me she was on medication.'

'Yeah, well, you know what Mum's like.'

No, he wanted to say. No, I don't know what Mum's like any more. She's changed. She won't let me near her. And you won't tell me what's going on. He took a deep breath, let the moment pass, then his need to know overpowered him. He hated himself for asking, but Maureen was closer to Gail than anyone. Even Harry.

'What did she say?' he asked.

'About what?'

'About my visit.'

'You don't want to know.'

'Yes,' he said. 'I think I do.'

Maureen took a second to respond, as if deciding whether or not to tell him. When she finally spoke, her voice sounded flat and dead. Gail at her worst.

'She said you didn't stay. That you never said a word to Harry. That you couldn't stand being in the same room as her. That you'd been drinking.' She hesitated, as if waiting for feedback. But Gilchrist was damned if he was going to play along. 'Would you like to hear more?'

'Sure.'

'She said you never even asked how she was keeping, Dad.'

Gilchrist caught the rise in her voice, and felt his teeth grit. 'That's not true—'

'If it's not, then why would Mum say it?'

'Because she hates me—'

'No she doesn't.'

'She wants to hurt me, Mo.'

'She wants you to feel some of the pain she felt, Dad.'

Gilchrist felt his fingers tighten around his mobile.

'Did you know Mum cried every day for two months after you split up?'

'I wasn't exactly doing backward somersaults with joy myself, you know.'

'It still didn't stop you from splitting up.'

'In case it's slipped your mind, your mother left me. Not the other way around.'

'It takes two to tango, Dad. Have you ever asked yourself why she found someone else?'

'I know why she found someone else.'

'Do you?'

'Yes.'

'Let's hear it.'

Gilchrist hated that Maureen had finagled the argument around to this topic. He felt there were certain things in life that children should not know about their parents. Or maybe he was just being old-fashioned.

'I'm waiting.'

'Your mother fell out of love with me, Mo.'

'Oh, no, Dad. You're not getting away as easy as that. Mum loved you. Mum's always loved you. She still loves you. Don't you see that?'

'Are we talking about the same Gail Gilchrist, here? The same woman who told me she was glad to have found Harry because at long last she had someone who cared for her? And sexually satisfied her?' He regretted his last comment the instant the words left his mouth.

'How can you say that?'

'It's the truth.'

'No it's not. It's bullshit. It's fucking bullshit.'

'Watch your language, young woman.'

'Oh, piss off, Dad.'

Gilchrist rubbed his forehead, waiting for the burring on the line to announce they had been disconnected. He could never win an argument with Maureen. Ever since the age of twelve, when she had shouted at him on the beach and accused him of favouring Jack over her, she had known then how to skip her way around him. Rationally, or otherwise.

'You still there?' he asked.

'Barely.'

He heard her sniff. 'Listen, Mo. I'm sorry.' He took a deep breath, then let it out. 'Your mum and me, we loved each other once. Some parts of us still do. I believe that. But after a while, it just, we just drifted apart.' He held onto the phone, praying for some response. But it was Maureen's turn to say nothing. 'These things happen, Mo. People change. Families split up.'

'But why did it have to happen to our family, Dad? Why did we all have to split up? Can you tell me that?'

He pressed the phone to his mouth, wished it was his lips to her hair, the way he used to when he came home from work and crept upstairs to her bedroom and kissed her sleeping face. He had no answer for her. He had no answer for himself.

'I have to go, Dad.' She gave a sniff.

'Listen, Mo, I—'

The line disconnected.

Silent, Gilchrist lowered his mobile. He felt abandoned. He felt as if he had just taken Maureen to the station and was watching her train depart, listening to the sound of its wheels on the tracks fade from his senses, knowing that when it did, when he could no longer hear its metallic rattle, then that would be the last sound he would ever hear of her.

He switched the power off. He worried that he might never hear from Maureen again.

But her voice echoed in his mind. Why did it have to happen to our family, Dad? Why did we all have to split up? Can you tell me that?

It happened because, because...

Because I had a job. Because I put that job before my family. Because I made no effort to spend time with my wife, or watch my children grow up.

Because, because...

'Because I failed you,' he whispered. 'Because I failed all of you.'

CHAPTER 24

HE REACHED THIS and That around 9:40. The tinny rattle of the overhead bell and the fragrance of potpourri put him at ease with its sense of familiarity. The shop was deserted, except for Cindy.

She looked up. 'Hi, Andy.'

'Is Beth in?'

'No-oh.' Cindy frowned. 'I haven't heard from her. It's so not like her.'

Gilchrist pulled out his mobile.

'I've already tried calling her,' Cindy said. 'And left two messages. I even tried your number, but I couldn't get through.'

'Switched off,' said Gilchrist. He placed a hand on Cindy's shoulder and squeezed. Beth's phone rang six times, then her recorded message cut in.

He slapped his mobile shut.

'Do you think she's all right?' asked Cindy.

'I'm sure there's a simple explanation,' he said. 'Probably just overslept.'

'I hope so,' Cindy said, and put her hand to her mouth. 'I've been so worried about her, what with that creep in here the other day. You read about these things, but you don't think they're ever going to happen to you.'

'Cindy. I'll check it out. Okay?'

She seemed to collect herself. 'Hang on,' she said. 'I've got a spare key to her flat.'

Outside, he ran down South Street, his mind clattering in time with his feet. In the two years he had dated Beth, she had never missed a day, was never sick, never late, always arrived at her shop at least five minutes early.

When he reached her apartment, he stabbed Cindy's spare key into the lock.

The flat was redolent of wood polish, its perfume warm from the central heating.

Heavy silence stilled the rush of his breathing.

'Hello?'

Nothing. Only the steady ticking of the grandfather clock at the end of the hall, a wedding present to Beth's parents from her Uncle Alex.

'Beth?'

The pendulum swung like an inverted metronome.

'Hello?'

Then Gilchrist caught it, a hint of something out of place, an undercurrent of something sour, a tainted smell that reminded him of a school gymnasium. Stale sweat. His right hand slid to his chest and he wished he had a gun.

He eased forward. The floor creaked.

He stopped, listened, was about to take another step when the floor creaked again. Was someone in the living room?

The door lay open. Not there. Beth's bedroom?

He cocked his head, straining to hear. On full alert now. If the creak had been caused by Beth, she would have heard him calling, she would have called back. He passed the spare bedroom door on his left. Ahead, Beth's bedroom door lay ajar, just a fraction.

He reached for the handle, heard the rush of movement behind him, lifted his arm in time to deflect the blow to back of his head.

Another blow, this time to his shoulder.

He stumbled against the wall, saw a lump of wood flash at him, felt something explode against his side. He swung his arms for balance, scattering ornaments off an antique table, then fell to the floor.

He lay there, stunned.

Legs. Jeans. Tattered and frayed. New trainers.

He twisted to his side, caught a leg as it swung past his face. He gripped hard, heard a cry, felt the floorboards shudder as a body landed by his side. He fought to hold on but something crunched against his mouth and he lost his grip. Then another hit to his head as hard as wood.

His fingers clawed, clutched for some grip, found it.

Then arms flailing at a casual jacket. Shit. The body moved away from him.

He followed it up, dropped the jacket.

A hit to his ribs stole his breath and almost felled him. He saw the next blow coming. A cricket bat. Christ.

Ducked. It hit the wall by his ear.

Ducked again. Glass exploded as the mirror shattered.

And again. Ducked lower. Skimmed off his back.

He fell to the floor, rolled to his side. The bat thudded the carpet, once, twice.

He bumped against the wall. Nowhere to go. Lifted his legs. Hard wood cracked against his calves.

He gasped with the pain, shouted, 'You're under arrest.'

The bat hesitated. But long enough.

He rolled the opposite way, into the far wall, pulled his legs up and over in a backward roll, and jumped to his feet as the bat clattered against the radiator then dropped to the floor. It had been thrown.

Escaping. Oh no you're not.

He dived at departing legs in scruffy jeans that slipped through the doorway and back-heeled the door shut, missed catching his fingers by a hair.

He pulled himself to his feet, stumbled against the wall,

struggled to stay upright. He stuck a hand out, palmed the wall as the world steadied, then staggered into Beth's bedroom.

Empty.

His breath tore in and out of his lungs in fiery bursts that seemed to pierce his ribs. 'Beth?'

Back in the hallway, he kicked at the spare bedroom door.

'Oh, God, Beth.'

She lay on the bed. Naked. Ankles and wrists tied to the four corners. Mouth gagged. Eyes bruised. Her body heaved with the effort of trying to free herself.

Gilchrist ripped the gag from her mouth.

'I'm okay I'm okay don't let him get away catch—'

'Beth—'

'Catch him catch the bastard don't let him get away catch him catch the bastard.' She gulped for air, then screamed, 'Catch the bastard, Andy.'

Gilchrist slipped her right hand free then stumbled from the room.

Outside, he looked left, right.

Shoppers, pedestrians.

He ran across the road.

Tyres screeched. A horn blared. 'You fucking blind?'

'Did you see someone running?' he asked a woman.

She backed away from him, almost bumped against the wall.

'I'm with Fife Constabulary,' he said. 'I've just been attacked. The man who hit me came out of that building.' He pointed at Beth's door, saw a scowling face and a finger tap a temple with the power of hammering a nail.

'That'd be thon young man then, so it would,' she said, looking at him with distress.

Gilchrist wiped sweat from his brow, surprised to see his fingers smeared with blood.

'Which way?'

'Down by the West Port.'

At school, Gilchrist had been useless as a sprinter. Too gangly and no muscle mass to fight the lactic acid, his gym teacher had told him. But he was a natural distance-runner, with long limbs, light frame and a pain threshold way above the norm.

He reached the roundabout in front of the West Port and stopped a man walking his Highland Terrier. The man's face reddened and he backed off. When the terrier started to bark, Gilchrist cursed and ran to the next pedestrian.

Same response. A stunned look that turned to fear, then relief as he moved on. He knew he looked a mess, but he ran on, hands at his ribs where something hotter than a burning poker dug into his side.

For Christ's sake. Someone must have seen something.

'That way, mister.'

Gilchrist spun around, grabbed the youth by his arms, saw he was frightening him, and let go. 'What did you say?'

'That way.' The youth's voice was less enthusiastic. 'I seen him go that way—'

'Where?'

'Down Lade Braes—'

'Who?'

The youth seemed puzzled. 'The man you're chasing, mister.'

'What did he look like?'

'Don't know.'

'Young old thin fat what?'

The youth shrugged. 'Skinny,' he said. 'Skinny as a rake. Wi' long hair, like.'

'Jeans?'

The youth nodded. 'And nae jacket.'

Gilchrist sprinted down Bridge Street but had to pull to a halt at the entrance to Lade Braes Lane. Pain as sharp as shards of glass gouged into his ribs and he concentrated on keeping his breathing shallow. He gripped the back of his neck. His hair felt damp and sticky. He looked at his clothes, the first time he had done so since the attack. His shirt hung out, smeared with blood. He pulled at his shirt collar, felt the material stick to his skin. When he looked at his hands they were as bloodied as a slaughterer's.

He clenched his teeth and eased into a jog.

Every step drove a six-inch nail into his head, twisted the broken bottle deep into his ribs. He groaned for breath. His attacker could have gone anywhere, could have jumped over any of several high walls that bordered the lane, could be running to places unknown.

He passed the end of Louden's Close, but his sixth sense forced him on, and he jumped down a set of concrete steps that opened up to a steep lane on his right. A short bridge at the foot of the lane crossed the Kinness Burn.

Where now? Left? Right?

His sixth sense took him left.

He stumbled along a muddy track at the edge of the burn, hands pressed to his side, fingers prodding and testing his ribcage for breaks. But his ribs were in the right place and seemed to spring back when he let go. Maybe torn cartilage. That could take months to heal.

The track ended at Kinnessburn Road and he turned left again, but had to stop at the bend.

His lungs burned, his head pounded and his left knee throbbed where the cricket bat had tried to reconfigure his kneecap. He leaned forward, gripped his leg, and through his jeans felt the swelling to the side of his knee. His world spun again, and he had to cling to the metal railing. He eased the weight off his left leg and at that moment heard something scuffle behind him.

Claws gripped his ankles. Heaved up. And over.

He was flying through the air before he understood that his grip had been torn from the railings.

He thumped onto his back.

He lay there, winded, mouthing for air like a landed fish, his peripheral senses aware only of a hard fluttering, raucous quacking, the feathered panic of flapping wings and slapping feet.

He had been lucky. His fall had missed the shallow water with its hard stony bed. Mud from a sodden mudflat squelched through his fingers as he struggled to fight off the darkness.

Before he slipped into unconsciousness, he was aware only of a white face peering down at him.

CHAPTER 25

I think of the killing place. I think of his home.

I have studied the layout of his drive, the way the hedge overhangs the slabbed path to the front door, how the gate is hidden from the living room window. I know where he will park his car. And I know where I will hide. He will be surprised when he sees me. But he will trust me as I walk up to him.

I know that from experience. They all do.

That is their fatal mistake. It will be his, too.

Heavy rain is forecast for tonight, worsening to sleet that may turn to snow, early for this time of year. Tomorrow, it will be December. But tonight Mark Patterson will lose his life.

Tonight Mark Patterson will become Number Eight.

I have never killed in the snow. I smile.

Perhaps we will have a white Christmas after all.

Gilchrist came to seconds later. He knew it was only seconds later, because several ducks were still paddling away from him with that neck-forward action, as if undecided whether to fly or swim.

He looked up at the railings. The black bars fluttered like wings. Then steadied. The white face was gone.

He took a long blink, not sure if he felt disappointed or relieved. He tried to sit up. Fire scorched his ribcage. He slumped back, took a few shallow breaths and decided he felt relieved. He pushed to his feet, felt his legs buckle, and sank to his knees. He tried to stop from toppling by throwing both arms forward, but splashed face-first into the shallow waters.

He lay there, head twisted to the side. The water by his face felt refreshing. He swabbed the bloodied gunk from his hair, then thought of all the wild life fornicating and crapping, and pushed himself upright.

This time, he managed not to fall, and slumped against the stone wall at the opposite side of the burn. The top of the wall lay at shoulder level and he wondered how he would pull himself out. But he reached up, tried a leap, slipped a leg onto the flat and heaved himself up.

He lay there, gasping for air, and realised with stunning clarity that the job was becoming too much for him. That is, if he still had a job. He remembered his phone and cursed for not calling earlier. He rolled onto his back and retrieved his mobile from his jacket. He pressed Connect, and the light came on. A small miracle. He dialled 999, requested police and ambulance, provided a brief description of what had happened, and gave Beth's name and address. Then he eased himself to his feet and stumbled along Dempster Terrace.

It never failed to amaze him how quiet the side streets could be, despite the busy town centre no more than a couple of rows of houses distant. Back gardens spilled down the hill to congregate their bushes and shrubs behind low walls like dams that prevented them from pouring into the burn. Windows glittered in the sunlight. He thought he saw movement at an upper window on the house two along, but could not be sure. Maybe someone in one of those houses had seen his attack. But that was a job for others.

By the time he reached Beth's, two police cars, with blue and yellow Battenberg checks, were parked on the pavement, lights flashing.

Gilchrist pushed towards the front door.

'Excuse me, sir?'

Gilchrist watched the young constable's face shift from surprise to concern then on to puzzled recognition as he pushed past him.

Entering the hall, Gilchrist was struck by how filthy he was. The rancid smell of the burn clung to him like sour body odour. He slipped off his shoes and dumped his jacket on the floor. His jeans were caked with mud, his shirt bloodied. But other than strip to the skin, he would have to live with it for the time being.

Beth was seated on the living room sofa. A policewoman Gilchrist recognised as PC Jane Browning sat next to her, police jacket and cap off, starched blouse laundered white. Browning glanced at Gilchrist as he stepped into the room. She seemed unfazed by his appearance and the nod she gave him was one of recognition rather than permission to come closer. Then her legs turned in towards Beth, and her fingers twiddled with the patterned quilt that covered Beth's shivering body.

Beth looked up at him then, her eyes seeking an answer to her unspoken question, and all of a sudden Gilchrist felt out of place, as if he was violating some private moment. He gave a tiny shake of his head, telling her he had failed, then watched in utter helplessness as she buried her face in her hands and her shoulders heaved in short silent sobs. Browning pulled Beth into her and gave Gilchrist a glance that told him she would take it from there.

Defeated, he left the room.

'Boss.'

Stan emerged from Beth's bedroom, Sa behind him.

'Holy shit, boss.' Something swept across Stan's face, the beginnings of a joke, perhaps. 'Want to step outside?' he offered. 'It's less...'

'Smelly?'

'You said it.'

Standing on the pavement, with no jacket or shoes, a shiver gripped Gilchrist's body.

'I'd invite you into my car, boss. But under the circumstances...' Stan's gaze roamed over his face. 'Jesus, boss. He's made a real mess of you.'

'He?'

Stan gave a twisted smile. 'You called it in.'

Gilchrist nodded. He'd forgotten he'd mentioned Beth's assailant as being a man. Maybe the blow to his head was worse than he thought.

'Let's have a look,' said Stan, and probed his fingers at the base of Gilchrist's skull. 'I wondered whose hair was on the cricket bat. Now I know—'

Gilchrist gasped, almost pulled away.

'Sorry, boss. Just pressing.'

'Well, press lighter, will you?'

'You're going to need stitches, I'm afraid. Best guess, ten or so. Quite a gash you've got back there.'

Stan came round to the front again, and Gilchrist had the oddest sensation that fingers were still pressing and prodding and fiddling with his wound, as if Stan were in two places at the one time.

Then Sa was facing him, her face pale. 'She says she wasn't raped, Andy. She says nothing happened.' The words were spoken almost as if Sa was disappointed. 'I don't believe her. She's hiding something. Can you give a description of the sick bastard?'

Gilchrist shook his head. 'I saw his shoes.'

'His shoes?'

'Trainers. White.'

'Is that it?'

Gilchrist nodded, ashamed by his failure to catch the man. 'Have you asked Beth?' he tried.

'As I said, she's hiding something.'

All of a sudden, Gilchrist felt leaden, as if his limbs had lost their power to support his body. He turned to Stan, but the pavement seemed to shift then tilt up at him. Stan's hand slapped hard under his armpit. 'Steady, boss.'

'Stan...'

'Looks like I'm going to have to seat you in my car after all.'

'I think...'

'Sa,' Stan shouted. 'Give me a hand.'

Together they manhandled Gilchrist into Stan's car and strapped him in. Sa threw in Gilchrist's jacket and shoes and slammed the door as Stan floored the pedal. Gilchrist fought off the almost irresistible urge to close his eyes and go to sleep. But halfway along South Street, he slapped the window.

'Stop the car.'

'Steady on, boss, you've had a right—'

'Stop the car, Stan. Stop the car.'

Stan pulled his Ford Mondeo over and ratcheted the handbrake like a learner driver. 'You going to throw up?'

Gilchrist fumbled for the door lock, but his fingers felt as if they belonged to someone else. He twisted around in his seat and stared behind him. He had caught something, some innocent action or movement, some thing that had flashed like a bolt of lightning deep into his mind. He looked back at the passers-by, struggling to see what had triggered his thoughts. But his mind was leaden now, conscious only of Stan's hand on his shoulder, tugging, his peripheral vision tunnelling, darkness swelling. He heard humming in his ears, like a whistling wind.

Then Stan's voice came back to him...

'...to the hospital, boss.'

'The man,' said Gilchrist. 'The old man.'

'What old man?'

Stan was spinning before him, whirling out of focus, like one of Chloe's paintings. 'Beth,' he tried.

'Beth's okay, boss. She's had a fright.'

Gilchrist hung his head. Images of Beth swamped him, her eyes beseeching in silence. He had failed again. Failing seemed to be what he was best at. He had failed Gail. He had failed Jack. He had failed Maureen, too. It seemed as if he'd gone through life failing those who depended on him until it culminated in the Stabber investigation and his failure to bring that case to closure. Patterson was doing his damnedest to kick him out because he had failed him, too. He had failed his team, failed the men and women who worked with him on the case, failed the townspeople of St Andrews who looked to him to bring an end to the reign of terror.

And now Beth. He had failed her, let the sick pervert escape. Surely his life was not going to be measured by the tally of his failures. Surely to God no one person could be expected to go through life—

The car shuddered, snapping him back to the present. Then they were moving again, and a dizzying sensation hit him in thick waves that threatened to topple him.

'Stan,' he whispered. 'I think, I'm...'

'Hang on, boss.'

A grip as tight as a steel claw thudded onto Gilchrist's arm, and he stared at the hand, wondered how it had landed there, who it belonged to.

'Nearly there.'

The car took a swing to the right that had Gilchrist pawing the window. Then it surged upward, like a fishing vessel riding a breaking wave, and drew to a halt.

A door opened. Frigid air brushed his face.

Twin wooden rods slipped under his arms and pulled him out. He tried to stand, felt his legs sweep out from under him and a rush of breath by his ear.

'Just as well you're not twenty stone, boss.'

Darkening clouds spun as they negotiated the entrance, then changed to speckled tiles and silver lights in a white sky. Gilchrist felt his back thud against a hard mattress, heard rattling and a steady squeak that seemed to keep time with the wobbling of his head. Overhead lights drifted by like flotsam in a milky sea that turned to grey and darkened with every struggling beat of his heart until it sank into a cold blackness that whistled like a cruel wind.

CHAPTER 26

'I'M DOCTOR MACKIE.'

Beth watched the doctor's baggy-eyed gaze take in PC Browning then settle on her.

'How do you feel?' he asked her.

She pulled the quilt tighter around her shoulders.

'We should perform a forensics examination.'

'But nothing happened. I've already told them.'

'I know,' he sympathised. 'But whoever did this may have left something, some evidence, or something.'

She was not sure what the doctor was saying, sure only that she would not let him touch her.

'He never had time to, to, to do anything,' she said, conscious of PC Browning's hand tightening on her shoulder.

'We can have Mary Girvan perform the examination,' said Browning. 'She's a trained nurse with the Procurator Fiscal's office in Dundee. If you think you're up for it.'

Beth lowered her head.

Browning gave the tiniest of frowns at Mackie, and he turned and left the room.

'I'll make us some tea,' Browning said. 'Shall I?' Beth felt PC Browning's fingers massage her shoulder then slip away.

From the kitchen, came the drumming rush of a kettle being filled. If Beth strained, she could catch the whisper of people talking in another room, the hallway, or her bedroom, perhaps, and she imagined them opening her wardrobe, her chest of drawers, and fingering her clothes.

The violation of her privacy was nothing compared to the violation of her person, of the fabric of her memory. She wished she could wipe that morning clean from the blackboard of her life. She regretted not having had the strength or the courage to fight.

Most of all, she regretted what she had not done.

She squeezed her eyes tight shut and held back a choke of disgust as she saw how she should have fought him rather than succumb to his sick demands. But he had a knife, slashed it wildly across her throat, close enough for her to feel the draught of its passing.

She had waited for the pain to hit, the spurt of arterial blood as her life erupted from the hack in her neck.

But the pain never came. Nor the blood.

And that was when she wanted to live.

More than anything, she wanted to take one more breath, live one more second, then more until she could breathe in the fresh air of a new day, smell the raw dampness of a new morning, see the orange rising of a new sun.

Dear God, just one more time.

So she had done as he had demanded.

She had taken off her clothes, folded them and laid them in a neat pile on the chaise longue by the window. Then, with solemn deliberation, lay on top of her continental quilt, naked. She watched him place his knife on her dresser and come to her. She fought back the urge to retch from his sour smell that told her he had not bathed for days, even weeks. He crammed a silk scarf over her mouth, his filthy fingernails almost touching her tongue, then pulled it so tight that it cut into the corners of her lips. His smell was in her nostrils, his taste in the silk, and she forced her thoughts away from his stench, knowing that if she threw up he was cruel enough to watch her choke to death on her own vomit.

But once tied down, she watched him study her spread-eagled genitalia in uninhibited closeness, felt the warm brush of his foul breath, saw his eyes light with desire at the knowledge of what was to come, and realised the fatal error of her surrender. With a force that almost stopped her heart, the reason he had made no effort to conceal his face struck her.

He was going to kill her anyway.

Panic set in then, and as she struggled against the bondage she realised she had been tied with slip knots that tightened the more she fought.

Then he took himself out.

She held still then, afraid that struggling would only excite him more, and tried to pull her knees together in a vain attempt to hide her nakedness.

His head jerked to the side.

Beth heard it, too.

The dull crack of a door opening. Then a call.

She had tried to scream, but it came out in a whimper. A sweaty hand smothered her mouth, the hand that had held his penis, and she thought she was going to choke when his hair fell into her eyes, dark clumps, thick and clotted. He swore at her, pushed himself to his feet, and rushed to the dresser. He reached for his knife, fumbled it off the edge, and failed to catch it as it fell down the back.

Beth could not interpret the gamut of emotions that twisted his features then set into a look of cruel determination. He moved towards her and she felt certain he was going to strangle her. Then he reached for her father's old cricket bat that hung above the headboard—

'Here we go, love,' said Browning. 'I've made us both a cuppa,' pouring weak tea from the teapot. She stopped midstream, gave the pot a swirl. 'Milk and sugar?'

'The knife,' whispered Beth.

Browning puzzled at the tray. 'What knife?'

'The one he used to threaten me. It fell down the back. Behind the chest of drawers. Next to the wardrobe.'

Without another word, Browning stood and left the room.

Beth stared after her. The knife would give the police fingerprints. But what if that was not enough to convict? What if they needed more? She closed her eyes and felt tears spill down her cheeks. She had almost convinced herself that nothing had happened, had almost convinced Browning, too. But an examination would reveal the truth.

Saliva.

They would find his saliva. They would find his saliva on her. They would find his saliva on her when they swabbed her vagina. She could no longer hold back the sobs and felt her head roll into her hands, as if her neck was no longer capable of supporting its weight. A low groan escaped her lips as she recalled black eyes looking up at her, then closing in sick ecstasy as his mouth rested upon her and his tongue pressed and flicked and entered her, slurping and sucking like a starved dog.

Doctor Matthews studied the x-rays and frowned. 'You're extremely lucky, Mr Gilchrist. If this man had not brought you here when he did, you could have slipped into a coma.' He glanced at Stan who returned a wry smile. 'As it is, you've suffered severe concussion. But nothing seems to be broken.' He grimaced down at Gilchrist. 'How do you feel?'

Gilchrist patted the back of his head where his hair felt short and spiky from being shaved. He fiddled with a plaster of sorts that seemed lumpy and hard. 'How many stitches did you say?'

'I didn't. But you've got eighteen at the back. And six behind your left ear. We'll have these out in a week or so.'

Gilchrist touched his ear.

'You've been doped up. You won't feel much until it wears off. When it does, it'll hurt. Take one of these in the morning with food.' Doctor Matthews shook a brown bottle in front of him. 'Another one at night. You should get by without too much discomfort. They're powerful. So be careful.'

Gilchrist took the bottle and slid from the gurney. His feet landed on the tiled floor with a thump that sent a stab of pain across his chest, despite the painkillers.

'Oh,' said Doctor Matthews, 'as best we can tell, you have at least two fractured ribs. Once the bruising settles down, the x-rays might show up some more. I'm afraid there's not a lot we can do for these except tell you not to play scrum-half for six weeks.'

'How about full-back?'

Matthews shook his head in mock dismay. 'That, too. And no alcohol with these, my man. D'you hear?'

Gilchrist put the brown bottle into his pocket and left the consulting room, Stan by his side, ready to give physical support. But Gilchrist grumbled, 'I can manage,' then grimaced as he opened the main doors.

'Does it hurt, boss?'

'Only when I laugh.'

'Well in that case, you won't feel a thing.'

Gilchrist almost stopped, but followed Stan to the car and waited until Stan put the key into the ignition before he leaned across and gripped the steering wheel.

Stan looked at him. 'Desperate to drive, are we?'

'You never could play dumb with me, Stan. What won't make me laugh?'

'It's nothing. It's just a joke. Okay?'

'Why don't I believe you?'

'You've been a detective too long, boss. You hear people coughing up crap all day long, day in, day out. All the lies. All the shite.' He shrugged. 'After a while you believe the whole world's a lying sack of shite.'

'Good try. But I'm not buying it.'

Stan glared at Gilchrist's hands on the steering wheel. 'Are we going to sit here all day like this?'

'If we have to.'

'Anyone ever told you you can be a right pain in the arse?'

'Plenty.'

Stan shook his head as if at the futility of it all, then dropped his voice. 'You didn't hear this from me. Okay?'

'Anything you say.'

'No, I mean it. Patterson'll boil my balls if he finds out.'

To show his sincerity, Gilchrist removed his hands from the steering wheel.

'Patterson doesn't want you back. He's talking to Archie McVicar to get you removed from the Force.'

Gilchrist gave a dry chuckle, felt a stab of pain at his side. 'Shit, Stan. I thought you said this wasn't going to make me laugh. I know all about McVicar. Patterson threatened me with it yesterday morning.'

'I'm not talking about yesterday, boss. I'm talking about this morning?'

This morning? Gilchrist waited.

'You visited Garvie against his specific instructions—'

'I'm suspended, Stan. Remember? Patterson's specific instructions don't include me.'

'You're splitting hairs.'

'That's not what McVicar'll think.'

'Patterson'll convince him.'

'Trust me, Stan. He won't.'

'That's not the problem.'

'Go on,' encouraged Gilchrist.

Stan shifted in his seat to face Gilchrist. 'Patterson's preparing a warrant for your arrest, boss. He's going to have you arrested tomorrow morning. First thing.'

Gilchrist clenched his jaw. He could kick himself for not returning McVicar's message. But he had been scared of being forced to retire, terrified of losing the one thing in his life that kept him going.

'What's Patterson going to have me arrested for?'

'Garvie says you sexually assaulted her.'

'And Patterson believes her?' Gilchrist gave out a gasp of disgust. 'The man's a bigger fool than I took him for.'

'I'm sorry, Andy.'

'For what? The whole thing stinks. It's a setup.'

'That's not what Garvie says.'

'Garvie says nothing.'

Stan stared at him. 'What do you mean?'

'The complaint that was allegedly filed against me,' said

Gilchrist. 'Garvie knew nothing about it.'

Stan gave Gilchrist's words some thought, then said, 'She has a witness.'

Gilchrist felt a hand of ice stroke his spine. He forced himself to keep his voice level. 'Who?'

'Maggie Hendren.'

An image of Maggie almost bumping into him in Lafferty's rushed into his mind. Our little group. 'Have you interviewed her?'

'No.'

'Has Patterson?'

'No.'

'DeFiore?'

'Look, boss—'

'Anybody?'

Silence.

'Does that not tell you something, Stan?'

'It tells me I don't want anything to do with it, is what it tells me.'

Gilchrist turned away, watched an old woman being helped from an ambulance and led into the hospital, her steps short, unsteady. Not like Garvie. He pictured her short-sleeved sweatshirt, her supple body tone. Sexual assault? If it wasn't so serious, it would be funny. He turned back to Stan. 'Where the hell does Maggie live?'

Panic flashed across Stan's eyes. 'Don't do this to me, Andy. Patterson'll know it's me. He'll have me.'

'Patterson doesn't know a thing.'

'He knows I'm with you.'

'How the hell does he know that?'

Stan lowered his gaze.

'Well, you're not with me any more,' said Gilchrist. He opened the door, the move so sudden that a flock of starlings fluttered over the wall in iridescent panic. 'You dropped me off at the hospital, Stan. I slipped out the back door. And that's the last you've seen of me.'

Stan shook his head. 'I never should have told you.'

'Stick to the story and it'll be fine. Trust me.'

From the dark weight around Stan's eyes, Gilchrist could see that he was near the edge of some mental precipice. Exhausted. The Stabber and Patterson and DeFiore and eighty-hour working weeks were finally taking their toll.

'I can't do it, boss. I'm going to have to call it in.'

'Give me until this time tomorrow.' Gilchrist slammed the door before Stan could tell him where to get off.

CHAPTER 27

This town, these streets, these buildings, have seen centuries of human creatures come and go, evidenced the worst of mankind's inhumanity against man. The Reformation started here seven hundred years ago. Heretics were burned at the stake, some famous enough to have cobbled stones built into thoroughfares to mark their spot of execution and monuments erected in their memory. Medieval cruelties were performed in Market Street in the square next to the fountain. Pillories, hangings, burnings, all for the supposed expurgation of human sins, but in reality depravities to satisfy sick individuals. Cruelties almost beyond imagination.

I now know that the Stabber will have a place among the ranks of the most vile perpetrators of cruelty this town has ever seen. That is how I will be remembered.

And that thought makes me smile.

Gilchrist towelled himself down and examined the damage in the mirror. He looked a mess.

Bruising on his thighs, his back, both upper arms, and an

ugly purplish tinge on his left side about the size of a football. He pressed his ribs, felt them give, but no pain, so the painkillers must be working. Doctor Matthews had told him to keep his head wounds dry, which was difficult in the shower, but he had done his best. His left ear had swollen and the hair behind it looked as if it had been torn from his head, not trimmed. He touched the hypoallergenic tape that covered the six stitches. It felt hard and tight to his skin.

The other stitches seemed to be a different matter.

He held up his shaving mirror behind his head, shoulder high. In the double reflection, he ran his fingers over an inch-wide strip shaved either side of the wound. The micropore surgical tape covering the eighteen stitches was stained dark from seeping blood.

Not good, but not too bad.

He dressed carefully, choosing something loose, a black ribbed Ralph Lauren sweater over a starched Hugo Boss shirt. If he was going to visit Maggie Hendren with a head like a half-finished Frankenstein, at least he could look and smell clean.

He pulled on his new black leather jacket and before leaving phoned Beth. But her mobile phone was switched off. Her home number rang out until her answering machine kicked in and he left a short message asking her to give him a call.

Next, Archie McVicar.

As he waited for the connection to be made, he stared out his window. The rockery garden needed some work. On the bright side, if McVicar discharged him, then that would be first on his list of things to tackle.

'McVicar.'

The booming voice almost threw him, then he heard himself say, 'Detective Inspector Andrew Gilchrist, sir. Returning your call.'

'You're a hard man to track down, Andy.'

'I was out of town, sir. Visiting family.'

McVicar mulled over Gilchrist's excuse for a few seconds, before saying, 'Gail?'

Gilchrist was not sure whether McVicar was asking if he had

visited Gail, or how her health was. He chose the former. 'Yes, sir. Jack and Maureen, too.'

'How's Gail faring?'

'Not good, sir.'

'Prognosis?'

'A year at the outside.'

'Pain?'

'She's on medication for that, sir.'

'Hmm.' A pause. 'I'm sorry to hear you say that, Andy. Next time you see her, if she's well enough, perhaps you could let her know Rhona and I are asking after her and praying for her every night.'

It was on the tip of Gilchrist's tongue to say there might never be a next time, but instead he said, 'Thank you, sir. Gail will be pleased to hear that.'

'Tragic,' McVicar said. 'Absolutely tragic.'

'It is indeed, sir.' Gilchrist heard McVicar take a deep breath then let it out in a gust of resignation. For Gail? he wondered. Or for himself? He felt his grip tighten on the phone. McVicar might be a sensitive man where family matters were concerned but when push came to shove, nothing stood in his way.

'Right, Andy. This to-do with Patterson. What the hell's it all about?'

'He believes I'm not the man for the investig—'

'Yes yes I know all that, but why the devil does he want you out? Sometimes I wonder if the man's not a liability. I would never have let you go at a time like this.'

'Define let go, sir.'

'Pushed off the Stabber case. By all means bring in the Scottish Crime Squad, or anyone else who could help bring this maniac to justice. But Lord above us, now's not the time to rack up the score in some personal vendetta.'

'I agree, sir.'

'We need every man we can lay our hands on. And more.'

Gilchrist listened to McVicar air his grievances. He knew McVicar on a personal level, knew him to be fair, but a tough codger. And a good man to have on your side. His wife, Rhona, had hit it off with Gail after they joined the same gardening club. But following their divorce they had barely kept in touch.

'...which brings me to my next point.'

Gilchrist stared down at his garden. He would start by levelling and relaying the slabs.

'This Alexandra Garvie. What's your interest there?'

Gilchrist let the loaded question filter through his mind. Just how much did McVicar know? Did he know of his suspicions of her? Did he know of Patterson's plans to have him charged with sexual assault? Smart? Or dumb? He chose dumb. 'My interest, sir?'

'Yes. Interest. Why are you always nosing around her home?'

Always? So, McVicar knew. 'I've spoken to her twice—'

'Yes yes I know. But why?'

'A hunch,' he said. 'Nothing more at this stage.'

'A hunch?' McVicar made the word sound like the world's filthiest disease. 'Nothing more than just a hunch?'

'No, sir.'

'No hard evidence?'

'No, sir.'

'Hmm.' Gilchrist caught an image of McVicar frowning, looking up to the sky in that thoughtful pose of his when his mind was churning over some facts. 'You think she's got something to do with the killings?' McVicar asked.

'I'm still fishing, sir.'

'Any nibbles?'

For a split second, Gilchrist wondered if McVicar knew about his searching Garvie's ventilation grille. Then just as quickly decided he did not. 'Not yet,' he replied.

'But you're not through with her. Are you?'

'No, sir.'

'Patterson disagrees.'

'He would, sir. If I said white, he'd say black.'

'He's instructed all personnel to stay away from Garvie's residence. You are aware of that order, I presume.'

'I am, sir.'

'So why do you continue to defy the man?'

'I thought being suspended from service provided me the rights of any other citizen in the United Kingdom. One of them being the freedom to talk to whoever I choose. Sir.'

McVicar chuckled. 'Quite.'

'Do you mind if I ask you a question, sir?'

'Not at all. Shoot.'

'Have you asked yourself, Why?'

'Why?'

'Why does DCI Patterson want no one to talk to Garvie?'

'The Scottish Crime Squad's already taken her statement. The Chief Inspector's well within his rights to direct the investigation as he sees fit.'

'And if he's wrong?'

'Then he'll have a great deal to answer for.'

'One other question, sir?'

'I'm listening.'

'Why did you ask me to call?'

'When I first got wind of this, I had intended to coerce your compliance with a demand for your resignation.'

'Why didn't you?'

'I feared you might be stubborn enough to tender it.'

Gilchrist turned away from the window. Repairs to the rockery were on hold. 'Thank you, sir.'

'Before you thank me, Andy, I should warn you that Chief Inspector Patterson has applied for a warrant for your arrest on the grounds of sexual assault against Alexandra Garvie.'

'I have heard, sir.'

'Lord above us, is nothing sacred?' Another pause, then, 'I'm assuming there's nothing in it, Andy.'

'That's correct, sir.'

'I'll be keeping a close eye on it, Andy. But I have to tell you I won't be stopping the charge.'

Something sank to the pit of Gilchrist's stomach. 'Sir?'

'I can't be seen to stand above the law. If the Chief Inspector believes he has sufficient evidence to charge you, then charge you he must. Let the chips rest where they fall.'

Gilchrist held onto the phone. 'I see, sir.'

'Good luck, Andy. And do give our regards to Gail.'

And with that, McVicar disconnected.

Gilchrist looked at his mobile and depressed the Power button. For what he was about to do, he could not afford to be interrupted. He had until tomorrow morning to clear his name.

Sebbie looked down at Alice.

Her naked body lay spread-eagled on the bloodied sheet. He eyed the slit of her vagina and tried to recall what he had felt when he pushed his penis into her.

But he felt nothing. Not a thing.

Not even the anger that had boiled from deep within him when she had first stepped out of her panties. That was gone, too. He kneeled, ran the palm of his hand over what was left of her pubic hair, nothing more than a thin strip shaved to satisfy Dieter's sexual longings.

He stared at her closed eyes. 'Why did you shave it off?' he asked, and poked a finger into the hard skin of her inner thigh. 'Huh? Can you tell me?'

Silence.

'Cat caught your tongue?'

He stood and pulled down his zip, took out his flaccid penis and pointed it at her stomach, his spray splashing off her hard skin. Midstream, he turned to Dieter's body and sprayed his face. Yellow urine splashed into his open eyes and the black hole of his mouth.

'Cat caught your tongue, too?' Sebbie laughed.

CHAPTER 28

GILCHRIST WALKED UP to the bar. 'I'm looking for a favour.'

Fast Eddy frowned at him. 'Easy there, big feller. What's the other guy like?'

'All my own work,' said Gilchrist, not wanting to get into it. 'Had a fight with a cricket bat.'

'Try to hit it for six?'

'Something like that.'

'Well, take my advice, mate.' Fast Eddy shoved a pint tumbler under the tap. 'Drink plenty of beer to ease the pain. This one's on me.'

'Can't,' said Gilchrist. 'I'm on medication.'

'Perfect. Twice the bang for half the price.' Fast Eddy continued pouring. 'Haven't seen Old Willie since you were here last. You heard from him?'

Gilchrist shook his head. 'Anyone call his home?'

'Couldn't tell you, mate. There you go, Andy. That should top you up.'

Gilchrist stared at his beer, its smooth head spilling down the side of the glass. It looked good enough to eat. He clasped the glass. He felt fine, a bit stiff, perhaps, but the pain had all but gone. He lifted the pint to his lips, took a mouthful, and returned it to the bar.

'Now, was that not worth waiting for?'

'Bloody marvellous,' said Gilchrist.

Someone called out and Fast Eddy glanced to the end of the bar. 'Two Bloody Marys, darling? That what you're after? One of them a Virgin? Not many of those around.' He gave one of his infamous chuckles and said, 'Gotcha, darling. Coming right up,' and jammed a glass under the vodka optics, removed two sticks of celery from the fridge and turned back to the bar. 'You were saying something about a favour, Andy. What can I do you for?'

Gilchrist leaned closer. 'I'm looking for Maggie. She still work here?'

Fast Eddy chopped one of the celery sticks. 'Not for much longer,' he growled. 'Stuck her head in here first thing and told me she was chucking it.'

'Handing in her notice?'

'What notice?'

'Do you know where's she going?'

'Do I look like I give a toss? Left me in a right old stink, so she did. Had to promise her time and a half just to persuade her to stay on for two more nights while I try to find new staff.' He sprinkled several drops of Worcestershire Sauce into each glass. 'What about your week's notice? I asked her. What about it? she said. I'm not a happy camper, Andy, let me tell you. There you go, darling. One Bloody. One Virgin. Now let me guess which one is for you.' Another chuckle, accompanied by a high-pitched giggle.

Gilchrist sipped his beer, while Fast Eddy wrapped up the order with some more banter.

'Maggie's supposed to be coming in tonight, Andy, but I'm not holding my breath. Donno what the world's coming to. Nobody gives a toss any more.'

'She have a new job?'

'Don't think so. Said she was moving off south.'

'Come into some money?'

'Couldn't say, mate.'

'Know where she lives?'

'Sure.'

Gilchrist made a mental note of Maggie's address and left his pint unfinished.

'Catch you later, Eddy.'

'Gotcha.'

The door paint was dull as rust and flaked around the trim. Gilchrist pressed the bell. Sing-along chimes rose and fell like a musical echo, then died.

He tried again.

A crack from an upstairs sash window startled him. The window slid up, then Maggie's head squeezed through the gap.

'I'm in the shower,' she said. Then her face deadpanned. 'Oh, it's you.'

'I'd like to talk to you.'

'I don't think that's a good idea.'

'You work in Lafferty's. We could talk there.'

'I've left.'

'I heard you had two more nights.'

'What d'you want?'

'A word.'

'Not interested.'

'We can talk from here, if you like.'

'You heard.'

Gilchrist watched her head withdraw back into the room. 'I know you lied,' he shouted up to her. 'What I don't know is, why?'

The window slammed shut.

Gilchrist knew then that Maggie had no intention of returning to Lafferty's. And being suspended, he could not force her to talk to him. He strode onto Market Street and ran through his mind what little he knew of her. She seemed nice enough. Attractive, too, but on the heavy side. One of those women who had a problem keeping her weight down. Seldom smiled, as if she had trouble finding pleasure in life. And a friend of Sa's. Although Sa offered nothing of her private side. And that was about it.

Ten minutes later, he turned into Alfred Place, stopped at the fourth door, and tried the handle. Locked. He rang the doorbell twice without any response, then took out his mobile and phoned Old Willie's number.

Again, no answer.

He crossed the road for a better angle.

The second-floor curtains were open. On the window ledge sat Tyke, Old Willie's black Highland Terrier, looking down at him, unperturbed. Without wasting any more time, Gilchrist rang emergency services.

Then waited.

Beth opened the front door to her flat, flapped her umbrella and poked it into the old wooden umbrella rack in the vestibule. Then she opened the inner door.

Her olfactory senses took in the subtle changes to the smell of her home. Something chemical tainted the air, a faint antiseptic aroma. And the stale smell of sweat. She shivered at the thought of the sanctity of her home being violated and wondered if she would ever again feel safe and comfortable here.

The gold-framed wall mirror, the one she had inherited from her mother and had reframed, hung at an angle, the glass shattered. She looked at the carpet, but someone had cleaned up the mess. She righted the mirror and noticed a tear on the wallpaper where the corner of the frame had caught it. The hall would need to be stripped and the wallpaper replaced.

Ornaments on the shelf above the radiator had been moved. She tried to return them to their original positions, but the head of her Lladro clown figurine toppled to the carpet. She kneeled, noticed blood smears on the pile, a missed shard of glass, biscuit crumbs. She stood and placed the figurine's head on the shelf.

Outside her bedroom, she felt loathing shudder through her. She would have to replace the sheets, the pillows, the quilt, maybe even the bed itself, the curtains, and wallpaper, too. But even that might not be enough.

Her mind flashed up an image of dark eyes looking at her from between her parted thighs and she strode to the kitchen and over to the sink where she filled the kettle. Although she had eaten little that day, she did not feel hungry. After her examination by Mary Girvan, she had been offered biscuits and tea, but the police niceties had done nothing to diminish the feeling of personal violation that clung to her. Under the even-toned spell of Girvan's voice, she had been asked to strip, her pubic hair combed and samples clipped off. Her vagina had been swabbed, as had her mouth, and it was then that she had broken down.

She tried to force the memory from her mind and put a slice of wholemeal bread into the toaster, removed a tub of hummus from the fridge. She pulled a bottle from the wine rack and filled a glass to the rim then gulped it back, almost emptying it straight off.

She spread the toast with hummus, but her hands shook when she lifted it to her mouth and she returned it to the plate and gripped the corner of the work surface. She counted to ten before releasing her grip. But the shaking started again, a tremor that seemed to take hold of her. She felt the hot nip of tears and lifted her fingers to her cheeks. Her sobs, quiet at first, hardened with each intake of breath, until she sank to the floor and let the tears flow.

Gilchrist was first into Old Willie's flat.

He walked through to the front room, Tyke trundling around his feet, and found Old Willie seated in his favourite armchair, his mouth and eyes open as if Death had stalked into his home and caught him by surprise.

A paramedic brushed past and pressed the back of his hand against Old Willie's neck then looked up and shook his head. Gilchrist said nothing as the paramedic kneeled on the threadbare carpet and pushed the old man's trouser legs up. He squeezed the right leg first, then the left, then moved to the right arm and slid the shirt sleeve up.

Old Willie's arm looked like bone clad in skin. How anyone could find a muscle, let alone determine if it was slack or tight, defied the imagination.

'Looks like he just slipped away,' said the paramedic. He leaned forward as if to stare into Old Willie's eyes, then pressed the lids down. But Old Willie remained as stubborn in death as he had been in life. His lids refused to close settling into a heavy-lidded stare like a stunned drunk.

'Would anyone like a dog?' Gilchrist asked. 'Goes by the name of Tyke. And house-trained.'

'Sorry, mate. Four kids is enough for me.'

Gilchrist turned to the others. 'Anyone?' he asked.

No one took up the offer.

In the kitchen, the smell of faecal matter was thick enough to taste. He raised the sash window and let fresh air waft in. He found the source of the smell under the work surface in a space that had once housed a washing machine, but in which now lay a shallow-lipped plastic tray. Old Willie had been proud of having house-trained Tyke. Tyke's got mair sense o' hygiene than some o' thae mucky louts that roam the streets, he had once told Gilchrist.

Gilchrist removed a plastic bag from the cupboard under the sink and tipped Tyke's litter tray into it. He twisted the top of the bag and sat it beside the hall doorway. From there, he listened to the metallic clatter of a gurney being unfolded and wondered if Old Willie's body would oblige them by straightening out from its seated position.

No one in the front room seemed to notice Gilchrist's absence, so he closed the kitchen door. To the side of the kettle, tucked underneath the wall cabinets, sat three white ceramic pots. Embossed lettering on each cracked lid led Gilchrist to the sugar container.

He removed the lid, tipped the sugar through his fingers into the sink. A plastic bag fell into his waiting hand. He shook it, scattering trapped sugar crystals into the sink, then removed the tight roll of twenty-pound banknotes and slipped it into his pocket. Next, he turned on the tap, returned the emptied pot to its spot, and popped the lid back on.

Fifteen seconds later, he had the sink cleaned.

As he made his way along the hall, Old Willie was being

gurneyed from the front room inside a black body-bag, zipped up and strapped down. From the angular protrusions, he saw the team had been unsuccessful in unfolding him.

In the front room, Tyke sat on the window ledge, nothing more than a wooden shelf Old Willie had mounted level with the bottom of the window so that his tired old dog could look out at the activity on the street below. But now Tyke had no interest in the outside world and eyed his master's empty chair with a cataract look of uncertainty.

Gilchrist leaned down and smiled as Tyke's tail squirmed. 'There's a good boy,' he said, scratching the dog behind its ear. The fur was thick and matted and had about it a smell of old age and oily clothes. He dug his fingers deeper. Tyke twisted his head and grumbled with pleasure, and together they watched the ambulance take Old Willie's body away.

It felt odd being alone there with Tyke. This had been Old Willie's home for as long as Gilchrist had known him. As if sharing his concerns, the old building creaked. At the sound, Tyke lifted his head and peered glassy-eyed at the empty chair, then gave a whimper and returned his head to his paws.

Sadness swept through Gilchrist at the thought of having to take Tyke to the vet. But in his chirpiest voice, he said, 'Walkies?'

Tyke's head lifted and his ears tweaked up. Then he jumped from the ledge, ran across the room and sat under a leather lead on a hook behind the door.

Gilchrist kneeled and attached it to Tyke's collar. 'We could both do with a bit of fresh air, Tyke. What do you say?'

Tyke trundled along the hallway, Gilchrist behind him, the old dog coming alive with the promise of a walk into a world of different smells. And Gilchrist wondered when his own life had last been as unencumbered. He called the vet to confirm the surgery was open, and to explain about Tyke. The receptionist told him to come whenever he was ready. An idea struck Gilchrist then, and he decided to take Tyke for a long walk first, before darkness fell.

On the grassy slopes by the West Sands, Tyke scratched the

ground with grumpy growls as if he knew his time to kick up clawfuls of sand was coming to an end. On the return journey, Gilchrist visited each of the spots where the Stabber's seven victims had been found. Not that he expected to uncover anything new by doing so, but the Stabber's case had become such a force in his life that it seemed he might suffer withdrawal symptoms if he did not think about it. He puzzled that Tyke livened at each infamous location, as if his canine senses picked up the scent of their brutal history.

By the time they reached the vet's, Tyke's fur smelled like damp wool. Gilchrist handed him over, and his parting image of Old Willie's dog was of sad eyes looking up at him, fearful of what was about to happen.

CHAPTER 29

SOMETHING IN HIS walk with Tyke fired Gilchrist's mind, and being the stubborn fool Gail had always taken him for, he determined to give Maggie one more go.

Back at her cottage, he tried the doorbell, once, twice, then wondered if she had decided to work her last two nights at Lafferty's after all. He was about to turn away when a movement on the high stone wall that bordered the cottage caught his eye.

A black and white cat, more white than black, eyed him from the top of the wall, its coat glistening in the light from a coach lamp on the gable end. Gilchrist held out his hand, intrigued that the cat's markings seemed oddly familiar.

'Here, puss, puss,' he whispered. 'Here, puss.'

The cat arched its white back in a slow stretch and let him chuck it under its chin. Gilchrist smiled as it purred. 'There's a good puss,' he said, and felt his fingers catch on the cat's collar. He tugged at the name tag and in the light from the coach lamp read the name etched into the disc.

Patter.

Gilchrist pulled the tag closer, felt the cat resist, but held on and read the tag again. He was not mistaken. Patter. Pitter patter, he heard Garvie's voice whisper in his mind.

Patter. Pitter's twin. If cats had twins, that is.

'I know your sister Pitter, Patter,' he said, and smiled at the formation of his words. 'I know where she lives.' He chucked Patter under the chin some more, then stopped, his mind all of a sudden firing with something improbable.

I know where she lives.

Pitter? Patter? Two cats in two homes?

Connected by a common thread?

I know where she lives, his mind echoed.

Wild thoughts flashed through his mind, the logic trying to spin away from him. He pulled out his mobile phone and called Terry Leighton.

Four rings, and he was through.

'It's Andy Gilchrist here. I left a message.'

'Oh yes yes. Sorry I never got back to you.'

Gilchrist ignored Leighton's apology. 'Beth gave you a photograph. Were you able to determine what was wrong with the cat's face?'

'Oh yes yes. It's a scar from a cut. Quite a horrific cut. You can see it quite clearly using a magnifying glass.'

'Were you able to digitally enhance the image?'

'Oh yes,' said Leighton. 'The poor creature appears to have suffered a severe injury. It has a scar running from above its left eye, down through the eyeball. It must have been completely blind in that eye. The scar misses the nose and splits the lip. Judging from the shape of the cat's face, it must have been quite deep. Particularly around the nose. I suspect, with such a deep cut, considerable force was used.'

'So, it's not an accidental wound?'

'Impossible to say with certainty, of course. At first, I thought the scar wasn't straight enough to be done by an axe, for example, but the cat's face was turned slightly to the side, which exaggerated the scar's crookedness and when I digitally adjusted the face, the scar looked much straighter. Also, it's possible that the wound healed in a quite irregular manner.'

'How would that happen?'

'It's only my opinion, but it could have been caused during the healing process itself. The wound could have become infected and reopened, in which case parts of it might have taken longer to heal, causing disfigurement.'

'You seem to have more than a passing knowledge of the medical side of things.'

'My father was a surgeon, Mr Gilchrist. As a boy, I always thought I would follow in his footsteps. Then along came computers.'

'Would you put the cat's wound down to an accident? Or not?'

'Not,' said Leighton.

'And you think it could have been hit with an axe?'

'Impossible to say.'

'Best guess.'

'An axe, maybe. Or a heavy knife. Someone else might see it differently. Although I fail to see quite how.'

'Could I have a copy of the enhanced photo?'

'I've already returned it,' Leighton said. 'I had it couriered to Beth, along with my handwritten observations.'

Gilchrist thanked Leighton and immediately called Beth, but her answering machine cut in. Next, he called Lafferty's, but Maggie had not made an appearance and was not expected to return. On a long shot, he tried the Dunvegan, but Maggie was not there either.

He walked up North Street towards the Cathedral and could tell from a glance at Garvie's house that she was out, and Maggie was not there either. He checked his watch, surprised to find an hour had passed since he dropped Tyke off. He tried Beth's number again and felt a flush of concern at the sound of her answering machine. He left no message, and decided to pay her a visit.

But first, he had to return to the vet's and settle up.

The smell of dried food in the reception area somehow reminded him of a plant shop. From the back of the building he heard the whine of a dog, the rattle of a cage. He paid using Old Willie's money, and could not hold back a chuckle when Tyke was brought from the back, fur trimmed and groomed and carbolic fresh. When Gilchrist put on his lead, Tyke gave a gruffy growl and tugged towards the door, his short tail upright and lively as a fresh dock.

Gilchrist walked him to Inverlea Cottage, where Tyke sat on his haunches as if waiting to be escorted inside. He tried the door and, just as she had said, it was unlocked. He pressed the doorbell and stepped into a tiny vestibule with an inner door of smoked glass, and locked, which pleased him. He rapped his knuckles on the glass panel.

'Mrs Granton?'

Moments later, he was pleased to see her frail shadow manifest beyond the smoked glass panel. She fumbled with the key, and when she pulled the door open, her gaze settled on the side of his head.

'Whatever happened?'

He fingered his left ear. 'Bumped into a cupboard.'

'Goodness gracious. You must be more careful. Well, in you come, dear. I've got some shortbread cooling.'

Gilchrist held up his hand. 'I can't stay.' He looked down at his feet. 'You said you liked dogs.' He held out the lead. 'His name's Tyke. And he needs a good home. I can't think of anywhere better than with you.'

The sight of Tyke's scruffy face raised a smile that took years off her. She looked back up at Gilchrist. 'For me?'

'If you want him.'

'Tyke,' she said to the old dog. 'And are you? Are you just a cheeky little tyke?'

Tyke wagged his tail.

'He's had a good walk,' said Gilchrist. 'It's time for his nap,' and handed over the lead. As Mrs Granton took it, he pulled out the wad of notes from Old Willie's flat, pushed them into her hand and folded her fingers over the money.

'That's to take care of him.'

Before she could object, he added, 'From Tyke's previous master. It's what he wanted,' then bent down and scratched Tyke behind the ears. 'You behave yourself now. Do you hear?' And with that, Gilchrist stepped back and closed the door behind him.

A sliver of light seeped from the edge of the velvet curtains in the front bedroom window. Gilchrist glanced at his watch and rang the doorbell. It was too early for Beth to retire, but sometimes she would stretch out and read. Light spilled into the hallway as an inner door was opened and the main door unlocked.

The rings under Beth's eyes looked as dark as bruises. Her hair had an unkempt style he could not remember seeing before.

'Did I waken you?' he asked.

She shook her head. 'I wasn't expecting you.'

From the heaviness in her words, Gilchrist realised she had been dozing. He was about to ask for Leighton's digital photograph when she blinked, heavy and slow, turned her head and stared back along the hallway. For one disconcerting moment, he wondered if he was interrupting her evening with Armstrong, then she swayed, and he realised she had been drinking.

'I spoke with Leighton,' he said.

'Sorry..?'

The word had been spoken with effort, but left no taint of alcohol in the narrow space between them. He hated having to ask, but said, 'Are you alone?'

She nodded, as if speech was beyond her. Then she frowned, as if remembering something from a long time ago, and pushed the door towards him, the move so unexpected that he almost had no time to shove his foot in the way.

The door bounced back.

Beth looked at the tiled floor in dazed surprise. She pushed again, but the door hit Gilchrist's foot and she stumbled against the doorframe.

Gilchrist leaned forward, pushed an arm behind her knees, and lifted her. By the time he placed her on her bed he knew what had happened.

He called an ambulance.

'Can you identify the problem?'

Gilchrist picked up the plastic-backed foil from the floor by the bedside table. 'Cuprofen,' he said. 'Ibuprofen tablets. Maximum strength. Both packs. That's twenty-four in total. She's conscious. But only just. Get someone here as fast as you can.'

'Mr Gilchrist?'

Gilchrist opened his eyes. The doctor's hair was snowy white, as if to match his gown. A navy-blue waistcoat and starched shirt with tightly knotted tie made Gilchrist run his tongue over his teeth. He pushed himself up out of the chair.

'There's no need to get up.'

'It's better if I stand.' His spine seemed to have locked, and the fire in his side refused to let him flex. 'How is she, Doctor...' He eyed the name tag. 'Ferguson?'

'Resting. We've pumped her stomach and given her a sedative. She's sound asleep.' The corners of Ferguson's eyes creased. 'Your fast action went a considerable way to saving her life.'

Gilchrist nodded. After calling for an ambulance, he had managed to make Beth swallow a large glass of warm salted water, then held her head over a plastic basin and pushed his fingers to the back of her throat. By the time she made it to Accident and Emergency, she was unconscious with skin the waxy pallor of the terminally ill.

'Can I see her?' he asked.

'I think we can arrange that,' Ferguson said. 'But it's important she rests.'

Gilchrist followed Ferguson as he strutted along the corridor, his firm steps as tight and precise as his shirt collar. They passed a row of curtained consulting rooms and entered a ward that rang with the clatter of cutlery and the rattle of trolleys. The smell of vegetables and cooked meat did nothing for him, and he knew he would have to force himself to eat later.

Ferguson led him to a small anteroom. 'Five minutes,' he said. 'That's all.'

Beth's eyes were closed. A clear drip was connected to her left arm. A monitor stood at the opposite end of the bed, with a wire that led to one of her fingers. He took her other hand and pressed it to his lips. Her skin smelled fresh, felt oily smooth, and he felt deeply troubled that she would step to the edge of her psychological precipice and take a leap that would end her life. He saw, too, how close he had come to doing that with his own life after Gail left him.

What he did know for sure was, that when Beth had needed him, he had not been there for her.

'I'm sorry,' he whispered.

Her dark lashes fluttered, as if her subconscious had heard his voice and was signalling her awake. But after several seconds she settled, and he laid her arm by her side and left the ward.

CHAPTER 30

CRICKET BAT.

It seemed such an odd weapon, but in the hands of someone wild enough, a cricket bat packed a punch and a half and took a lot of stopping.

Gilchrist touched his wounds, felt the evidence of his recent beating at the hands of a crazed batsman. Except that the man who had assaulted Beth, then Gilchrist, was no English gentleman, but a scruffy lout with nae sense o' hygiene.

Gilchrist pushed his sodden hair off his forehead, and shivered. The wet weather seemed to trigger his thoughts. Or perhaps his sixth sense was working at some subconscious level in his brain. His ribs hurt, his head hurt, and he was not sure if the dampness that seeped down his neck was blood, or rain.

How could he have been so blind? Not blind, but stupid. He had never given it a thought. It was the damned cricket bat that had got him going, the one that had beaten him half to death and which used to hang from hooks on the wall in Beth's bedroom.

He reached Garvie's ten minutes or so after seven. The curtains were now drawn, so she was at home.

The drizzle had turned to a steady downpour, the sky as dark as a prison blanket.

He stopped at the first gate in Gregory Lane. The paint looked new, but the wood rotted near the ground. He gripped the metal handle. How much noise would it make if he burst it open? The wall was too high to climb over with damaged ribs, and a quick look along the lane made him reach his decision.

He put his shoulder to the gate and gave it a hard thump.

The lock popped, tearing the screws from the weakened wood. He stepped from the lane, pulled the gate behind him, pressed the screws back into the frame. They held. Far from perfect. But anyone passing in the lane would not notice.

He wasted no time in pushing through the sodden shrubbery until he found himself crouching behind Garvie's perimeter wall.

No choice this time but to climb over.

Around him, rain pattered gardens that lay mid-winter black. Despite the gloom, crossing Garvie's garden to the ventilation grille without being seen would be almost impossible.

Over the wall, he saw Garvie in the kitchen, the motion of her hands suggesting she was chopping vegetables. He pulled out his mobile, called Directory Enquiries, and asked for her number. If she had a phone in the kitchen, he was snookered.

As the connection was made, Garvie turned, grabbed a hand towel, and left the kitchen. Through the living room window, he saw her reach for her phone.

Now.

He gripped the top of the wall and pulled himself up, almost screamed, then fell back. He heard Garvie say Hello as he slumped onto the wet grass. His breath burst from his mouth in short bursts that burned his ribs. He disconnected and fumbled in his pockets, found the painkillers and poked one out of its foil packaging. And another. From the fire in his ribcage he knew he had damaged his fractured ribs. The pills had been taken too late to prevent the pain from what he was about to do. But they would help later.

He willed himself back to his feet and peered over the wall.

Garvie was back in the kitchen. He caught a glimpse of something orange, and guessed she was making a fruit salad. Once again, he placed his hands on the wall, let his arms take the strain, then pulled. He felt the pain increase until it reached some kind of limit. With his hands free and his weight on his elbows, he pressed Redial.

Same scenario.

This time, as soon as Garvie was out of the kitchen, he slid his legs over the wall and stifled a grunt as he fell onto the grass.

He got onto his knees, disconnected, and stumbled towards the door. If Garvie reached the kitchen too soon, she would see him.

His mind screamed, *Now*.

He rolled to the right, away from the kitchen window, towards the ventilation grille. The thick grass softened his landing, but did nothing to cut back the pain that stabbed his side, forcing him to stifle another grunt. He rolled onto his back, pressed hard against the wall, his face only inches from the wire mesh that covered the grille.

The first thing he noticed was the mesh had been moved. Someone had tampered with it. Was his hunch correct? He gripped the edge of the chicken wire and pulled—

The back door opened.

Light flooded the grass and slabs by Gilchrist's feet.

He froze.

Garvie bent down to place something on the back step. From where she stood it seemed impossible for her not to notice his shoes. He fought off the urge to pull in his legs, knowing that the slightest movement would register on Garvie's peripheral vision. Pain forced tears to his eyes, but he dared not move.

Garvie straightened up, her sharp profile dark against the backlight from the kitchen. 'Here, Pitter, Pitter.'

Something landed with a quiet thud behind him and he knew without looking that Pitter had leapt from the wall and was loping through the tall grass towards her keeper.

He held his breath.

If Pitter stopped...

If Garvie turned her head...

'There you are, Pitter. Who's a clever puss?'

Gilchrist watched Garvie lift Pitter to her face. 'Who's a clever Pitter?' she said, casting a look towards the boundary wall, before closing the door.

The garden settled into darkness once more.

Gilchrist felt his breath leave his lungs in a long sigh. He shifted his position, trying to find some way to ease the pain. But it was no use.

He gritted his teeth and tugged the ventilation grille free from the wall. He had to roll onto his side to place the concrete block behind him and gasped as the pain hit. The block slipped from his grip and dropped onto the grass.

When the fire faded, he pushed his arm back through the hole in the wall. The still air under the flooring felt warm and he wondered why, during his earlier search, he had thought of only down, and not up. Was he slipping? Would Stan or Sa have been more thorough? And was it not strange how it had taken being hit with an old cricket bat and remembering how the bat hung on hooks on Beth's bedroom wall.

Hooks. Or nails hammered in and bent up like hooks.

Like the nail he had found the day before. Not an old nail, but a nail tarnished by rust light enough to brush off and expose metal as fresh as new.

Gilchrist's fingertips searched the side of the wooden beam, its surface as dry and bristled as a pig's hackles. He patted the beam, stretched as far as he could manage.

Nothing.

He tried the other side, felt a flush of disappointment.

Was he wrong?

He shone his torch through the hole, and peered in. But the opening was too small, the angle too tight. He shifted his body, pushed his arm back through and reached for the beam on the left. The surface bristled with splinters of wood—

He touched something.

Something cold and slippery, something that shifted in his prying fingers. Plastic. A sheet of plastic. A sealed package.

Hanging on nails for hooks.

He lifted the bundle up and off its hooks and out through the opening. He felt the cold shiver of horripilation as he clicked on his pencil-torch.

Wooden staves glistened beneath the plastic sheath like rods of gold with unmistakable ridges. Bamboo. Thirteen in total.

Gilchrist fingered the ends.

Blunt. All of them.

None sharpened to a point. Not yet.

His investigation teams held differing views on why the Stabber used shaved bamboo staves. The general consensus was that natural ridges of bamboo provided an excellent handgrip.

But why were they shaved?

Gilchrist had seen each of the staves after they had been removed from the eye socket of the victims. Now he could see they came from a piece of bamboo furniture. But he saw, too, why they had been shaved.

The ends of several were discoloured where they had been bound together, probably as the corner of a coffee table, perhaps. Or a bookcase. Shaving the varnished surfaces, at the same time as whittling one end to a point, obliterated all trace of the bindings.

All of a sudden, Gilchrist was aware of the seriousness of his predicament. If he took the lot to the Office, in all likelihood the staves would not be permissible as evidence. He had no search warrant, no right to be on Garvie's property, not to mention being suspended. Patterson would have a field day. And so would any defence lawyer.

Alternatively, he could make an anonymous call. But doing so, would not serve his own needs. He would still be viewed by Patterson as persona non grata, his reputation vilified. The prospect of Patterson's own career being exalted at Gilchrist's expense sealed it for him. He would not, could not, go that route. Two days on the case and the Scottish Crime Squad exposes the identity of the Stabber. How right Patterson had been to bring in DeFiore. And how wrong Gilchrist's supporters had been to believe he was the right man for the job.

The more Gilchrist thought about it, the more he saw he had no choice but to keep his find to himself and continue with his investigation alone. And God help him if victim number eight turned up before he caught the Stabber.

Gilchrist decided he would wait. And watch.

Sebbie finished the last of the six-pack. He glanced at the digital clock on the microwave.

8:11. What had happened? Margo said she would be round at eight. Had she—

The doorbell rang.

Then again. Longer this time.

He slunk into the kitchen doorway in case someone looked through the letterbox.

The telephone rang, then the answering machine cut in.

He listened to Alice's voice end her recorded message with her stupid Have a great day, then Margo's voice say, 'Alice? Dieter? Me and Jim are outside. If you're there, can you pick up?' A pause for several seconds, then, 'Did you get my message?' Something thudded against the door.

Sebbie tightened his grip on the knife, held it up before his eyes. In the moonlight, the serrated blade glinted like burnished steel.

A man's voice joined the woman's, their words indecipherable. Then, 'I'll call later, Alice. Okay?' Another pause, as if the woman was still hopeful of an answer, then a click as they disconnected.

Sebbie lowered the knife. He was about to return to the hallway when he heard a metallic rattle, a light tinny sound like a lid closing. From the front door.

He heard it again.

A key being slotted into a lock?

Did Alice's friends have a key?

How stupid he had been not to jam the lock. He should have stuck a hairpin in it, a bit of plastic, something, anything he could have snapped or torn off to block the mechanism.

A heavy sound reverberated along the hallway. Sebbie half-expected the door to burst open. He drew back, knife raised, ready to strike. But when the digital display read 8:20, and the door had not exploded open, and the telephone had not rung again, and the whispers and rattles and thuds had vanished, he lowered his weapon.

He was safe.

In the darkness, he listened to the sounds of the house, felt the hair on the back of his neck rise as he heard something, a low moaning sound as if...

Knife in hand, he crept from the kitchen, across the hallway and into the back bedroom. The room felt cold, and his nostrils filled with the stench of decaying meat.

Alice and Dieter lay on the floor, their wax-like bodies twisted into two hapless heaps. The wind moaned past the open window. Sebbie pushed the sash up until the moaning stopped. Then he heard a laugh escape his lips as he looked down at Alice's bloated face.

'Cat caught your tongue,' he cackled.

Gilchrist stood on the cliff path, his back to the metal railing, the sea wind brushing his neck with fingers of ice. Garvie's upper curtains were open, those on the lower level were drawn. The house looked dark, save for a faint glow from the door by the landing. Garvie said she worked at night on her computer in her study off her bedroom, but as the upstairs rooms lay in darkness, he guessed she had finished for the day. Was she in bed? Or downstairs?

Was she alone?

He remembered the shadow he thought he had seen flit past her bedroom window. If she had company he needed to know, and who. But after fifteen shivering minutes, with the house showing no signs of life, he decided to pay Garvie a visit.

What could Patterson do? Fire him twice?

The doorbell chimes echoed back at him. He gave another press then waited until the chimes faded to silence.

No response.

He waited thirty seconds then stepped to the lounge window.

A glimmer of light slipped through the tiniest of gaps between the curtains.

He pressed his face against the cold glass.

In the thread of light he could make out only the wall opposite the sofa, but enough to confirm the fire was out and the fireguard was in place. Snow was forecast. If Garvie was in, would she not have the fire on?

He tried the doorbell again, ringing once, twice, then realised Garvie must have slipped out. He was about to turn, when he heard the tinkle of a tiny bell. He searched the shadows but saw no twin moons shining back at him. The thought of the cats' names brought a smile to his lips. Pitter, Patter. Two cats, two owners—

He stiffened. Why had he not thought of it before?

Pitter, Patter. Two cats. Two owners.

Or a third person common to both?

His mind powered through the labyrinth of what-ifs and maybes, the fogs of detection giving glimmers of probables, possibles, maybe nots, until they thinned to leave the visual remnant of a cat with a disfigured face, and Fats Granton standing beside a young Maggie Hendren. He listened to Fats curse him in the front room of his mansion, heard the whisper of voices replay the words, Whose cat's she holding?

Not mine. Hate the fuckers.

And at that moment, Gilchrist saw his error.

He remembered puzzling over why the top of the photograph had been cut, and saw now that its edge had not been trimmed to fit the frame, but to centre the images of a snapshot taken by someone unfamiliar with photography.

All of a sudden the fog lifted.

CHAPTER 31

Wind whips icy blasts across open fields.

I pull my anorak tight and turn to face the cottage. Through the kitchen window I watch Patterson's wife move into the dining room. I can tell from her vacant look that her expectations of life have passed her by. She is a beaten woman. In body, as well as in mind.

I see in her actions the same lifeless movements of my mother, her body and hands going through the motions of day-to-day existence. Another dead soul. It is disgusting how her husband has treated her. On the surface, he is someone regarded in high esteem, a man who holds one of the highest offices of public trust. But he is a hypocrite, a betrayer of his profession and of those who placed their trust in him.

He is the worst kind of misogynist.

Soon he will suffer the consequences of his hypocrisy.

'This is Detective Inspector Gilchrist. Put me through to Stan, please.'

'He's not here, sir. Have you tried his mobile?'

'Of course I've tried his mobile. It's switched off.'

'Well, all I can do is—'

'Who's he with?'

'DC Wilson.'

'Could you give me her mobile number?'

'I'm not allowed to give that out, sir.'

'Who am I speaking to?'

A pause, then, 'Constable Greg James. Sir. I can get DC Davidson on the radio and have him give you a—'

'Forget it,' snapped Gilchrist.

Why had he not asked for Norris, or any other of a number of detectives and officers for that matter? But he trusted Stan. Simple as that. Over the years, his level of trust in others had deteriorated. Then a thought struck him.

He trusted Alyson Baird, too. She worked as a secretary in the upper office, providing support for Patterson and others.

But at that time of night, was she still there?

Gilchrist pressed Redial. He had often puzzled over his affair with Alyson. Gail had left six months earlier and drink had played its usual will-weakening part. The affair had been short-lived but its sexual passion had been the much needed lift for Gilchrist's emotional nadir. More importantly, its secret survived Patterson's interrogation. Alyson had denied it all with a barefaced ease that had astonished Gilchrist at the time.

His call was answered once more by Constable James.

'Alyson Baird,' he said.

It took four rings before Alyson's curt voice clipped, 'Crime Division.'

'Alyson?'

'Yes?'

'It's Andy.' A pause, then, 'Andy Gilchrist.'

She gave a salacious chuckle and he fought off an image of her slipping off her stockings.

'How many Randy Andys do you think I know, then?'

Gilchrist tried to steer the conversation away from her favourite subject. 'Listen, Alyson. I need a favour.'

'Let me wish. A blow-job?'

'Mobile telephone number.'

'Any bitch I know?'

'I'm trying to contact DS Nancy Wilson.'

'That slut?'

'Please, Alyson. I'm trying to get hold of Stan. His mobile's off. Nancy's with him.'

'Well, seeing as how you're so friendly,' she said, 'I've got it right here.' She recited the number.

Gilchrist assigned it to memory. 'One other thing.'

'I'm all ears.'

He could not mistake the huffiness in her voice, but he had already tired of her banal innuendoes. 'Would you happen to know where Sa is?' he asked.

'Meeting with Patterson.'

Sa meeting with Patterson? 'Just the two of them?'

'I believe so.'

'When?'

'8:30.'

'Where?'

'Doesn't matter. Sa's just called to ask where he is.'

'Patterson didn't turn up?'

'According to Sa.'

'Do you know what the meeting was about?'

'Something to do with the Stabber case. Other than that, I haven't a clue, big boy.'

Gilchrist's mind crackled. Was Patterson simply running late? Or had something more sinister happened?

'Alyson,' he said, 'can you reach Patterson right away? Make sure he's okay.'

'Don't need to.'

'What d'you mean?'

'He's just called, too. He says Sa never turned up.'

What the hell was going on? 'Is Patterson on his way back to the Office?'

'Afraid not. He's done for the day. He's going home.'

'Home?'

'Yes, Andy. Home. You know? Where he lives. With his wife.

She called. He's to be back for nine.'

'Thanks, Alyson. You're a darling.'

'Yeah, I love you, too, Andy.'

Did he have it all wrong? Had Patterson and Sa simply confused the place they were meant to meet? Then he saw it with a clarity that stunned him. He glanced at his watch. Just after 8:45.

Less than fifteen minutes.

Could he make it in time?

The clouds are shifting, giving a glimpse of a wan moon and a frosted sky. Again I am reminded of Timmy. Of my mother. Of the three of us staring out through a frosted bedroom window. And of snow falling. I watch Timmy's face break into a smile. My mother's, too. And I realise we were a close family once.

I feel the weight of sadness overwhelm me as I imagine how it might have been to have led a normal life, a life with Timmy in it, an older brother to talk to when our mother died. I imagine visiting Timmy's home, sitting his children on my knees, hearing their voices whisper words of love.

An icy breeze covers the moon with tattered strips of clouds. I can almost hear Timmy's children call out to me.

And I wonder why the raindrops no longer feel cold.

Maybe it was driving at speed that honed his mind razor sharp to make sense of the most tenuous of connections. In all his years as a detective, he had never been able to put a finger on it and say, Yes, now I understand how the mind rationalises the irrational. Perhaps that was how a sixth sense worked, brain cells sorting through nonsensical jumble, calculating improbables at a subconscious level while five other senses were tuned in to the real world. But no matter how that tenuous connection was made, Gilchrist knew he had made another.

Beth's attacker. And trainers. That's what he had seen from Stan's car on the way to the hospital. Someone walking past wearing trainers.

White. Clean.

He tucked his mobile under his chin and powered his Merc through a tight bend. 'Nance,' he growled, 'Put Stan on.'

Nance obliged.

'Yes, boss?'

'Where are you?'

'Just pulling into the Office now, boss. DeFiore's called for a debriefing.'

Damn. Even if Stan could get out of the debriefing, it would take him ten minutes to catch up. Gilchrist would have to go it alone. But Stan could help in other ways.

'It's come to me, Stan. He was wearing trainers.'

'I don't follow.'

Gilchrist was not sure he followed the rationale himself, but said, 'When you drove me to the hospital, I remembered seeing something odd. I couldn't place it. Not until a moment ago. A pair of trainers, Stan. They were new. Not old. They didn't fit.'

'You all right, boss?'

'Not the size. The profile.'

'Profile?'

'Of the person. They didn't fit the profile. An old man wearing new trainers. It looked all wrong.' He twisted the wheel, accelerated up the hill, felt his back press into the seat. 'That's when it clicked. Like the scruffy guy I saw from the Victoria Café. He was wearing trainers. And they were clean.'

'Would you like me to make you another appointment?'

Gilchrist almost laughed. He floored the pedal. He whipped past two cars and a van and hammered through a wide corner. 'I didn't recognise him at the time. But I do now. Sebastian Hamilton. The man who attacked Beth. And me.'

'You sure?'

Yes, Gilchrist wanted to say. I'm dead sure. But he wasn't. He was nowhere near sure. 'Sure I'm sure,' he lied, and heard only silence come back at him. Not quite the reception he expected. 'Norris did speak to you, Stan. Right?'

'He did.'

'And told you to bring in Hamilton for indecent exposure?'

'He did.'

'And?'

'He's been evicted.'

'What are you telling me, Stan?'

'He wasn't home, boss.'

'So where is he?'

'No one knows.'

'Hang on.' Gilchrist braked for a tight bend then accelerated out of it. Ahead, the road rushed at him from tunnelled darkness, its wet surface glistening under the glare of his headlights. A glance at the speedo, almost eighty, had him easing back a touch. He would be no use to anyone wrapped around a tree. But the thought that he was already too late made him press his foot back to the floor.

'Eh, boss?'

'Still here.'

'Has anyone told you what they found at Hamilton's?'

The unusual softness in Stan's voice made Gilchrist lift his foot from the pedal again. 'Go on,' he said.

'I've only just heard about it myself, boss.'

'I'm listening.'

'In his bedroom. A right mess it was. Paper clippings. Reports about the murder. The body on the beach. All in an album. And of the investigation, boss.' A pause, then, 'And photographs of you, boss. Old ones. New ones. You name it, you're in it.'

Gilchrist dipped his lights for an oncoming car. He could sense Stan was holding something back. 'And?' he tried.

A cough, then, 'There's also several of you and Beth.'

Gilchrist frowned. He and Beth had started dating about three months after the body was found on the beach. But he could not remember the pair of them ever being photographed by the press. 'Paper clippings, you say? Of me and Beth?'

'That's just the problem, boss. The ones of you and Beth are originals. And there's some of Beth by herself. We think Hamilton shot them.'

Now it made sense. Now he knew why Beth had been attacked. To get at him. For failing in a murder investigation. 'Didn't Hamilton have a girlfriend?' he snapped. 'When his father was found? Remember? On the beach? Wasn't she with him that morning?'

'Yes, boss. But don't ask me her name. It's been a while.'

Having spoken to Alyson reminded Gilchrist. Not Alyson... 'Alice,' he hissed. 'That's it. Alice. Alice somebody or other.'

'McLay, McKay, McKee...'

'Check it out, Stan. Find out where she lives.'

'McGhee,' shouted Stan. 'Alice McGhee.'

'That's her. Track her down. Maybe she'll know something. Maybe Hamilton's still going out with her.'

'You're forgetting DeFiore, boss.'

Gilchrist felt a flush of anger heat his face. Not that it was Stan's fault. He was only doing as instructed. 'Stan, listen, I know you're working all hours, but I need someone to run with this for me. For Beth, too.'

'I could have Alasdair Burns take it on, boss. He gets right up DeFiore's nose.'

Gilchrist grinned. Alasdair had been on the verge of retiring every year for the last five years and had little interest in pursuing a case with the ardour of old. Which was probably why DeFiore was pissed off with him. But he was an experienced detective and could handle himself well.

'Get him on it right away, Stan.'

'Will do, boss.'

Gilchrist tried to convince himself there was nothing he could do about Hamilton, that he had to focus on the problem at hand. But something in Stan's tone reconfirmed the danger he was about to face, and made him wish Stan was with him.

For if his suspicions were correct, he was going to need all the help he could get.

CHAPTER 32

I hear a car and know it is time.

I slide my hand under my anorak. My fingers wrap around the bamboo stave. It feels comfortable, like a part of me, as if it is an extension of my being. I glance at the sky, but the stars and moon are hidden by cloud.

Rain drums around me.

I step from the hedgerow and move towards the gate. It always surprises me how calm I feel before a killing, as if the need to take someone's life is as basic to my existence as breathing and eating.

Headlights sweep the hedge by my head, twin beams that pierce the wet darkness, startling me with their brightness. Then they spin away, and the hedge returns to shadow.

I approach the gate, my gaze grazing over the side of the bungalow, searching for movement. I am aware that Patterson's wife might hear the car and peer through the curtains. I lie low and watch the car emerge from the forest road and enter the clearing in front of the house. The engine sounds as if it is idling, the driver in no hurry. Another flash of light as the car pulls in to face the house, then darkness again, like a stage curtain being lowered.

The car door slams. Footsteps crunch the gravel. A cough, a wet spit of phlegm. Even from that most basic of functions I recognise Patterson.

I steal forward, hidden from view by the hedgerow. I am less than three steps from the gate when I hear another car, the high whine of its engine above the rustling of the rain. Someone in a hurry. But Patterson seems not to have heard. He grasps the gate and pushes it open.

A horn blares, long and drawn out.

Patterson frowns and looks towards the forest. But the car has not crowned the hillside yet. Then he closes the gate and fiddles with the latch. I hear the car clearly now, much closer. Its engine revs and whines as the driver fights his way over the rutted road.

Patterson hears it and faces the darkness.

I can just make out his profile.

My fingers tighten around the stave.

I shift forward into his line of sight.

He steps back.

In the rain, his eyes sparkle. But I know the look of fear.

'For God's sake,' he hisses. Then he recovers. 'Who the hell are you?'

I lower my anorak, let him see my face.

'You?' he says.

The car crowns the ridge. Headlights flicker between the trees by the forestry fence, twin beams that jump through the rain like jiggling flashlights. Then they steady and pierce the sodden darkness and sweep the driveway.

For one confusing moment the lights blind me. I blink, decide to strike.

The car horn blares again, this time a rat-a-tat-tat.

'What the?' Patterson stares off towards the forest.

Too late.

I lower the stave, slip it from view.

The horn rat-a-tat-tats, closer now. Headlights dance behind *the trees.*

Patterson glances at me and steps back, as if aware all of a sudden of how close I am to him. He brushes a hand over his balding pate and growls, 'What are you doing here?'

I smile at him. I want to whip the stave out from under my anorak and drive it deep into the socket of his left eye. But the car is so close I can hear the metallic rattle of its suspension, the splash of puddles at its wheels.

My mind is in turmoil. Should I strike? Or wait?

But I feel such a burning need, that I know I have to do it. I decide to do it. And to do it...

Now—

The night explodes with light.

The car swings our way.

Patterson looks to his side.

I freeze. The stave is out, and I wonder for one crazed moment if I should plunge it into his ear, kill him that way.

'Who the hell is this?' he growls, and moves to the gate.

I return the stave to its hidden pocket, and pull up my hood as twin beams bounce towards us. Now I know I will have to kill to survive.

Gilchrist drew the Merc to a sharp halt that had his tyres scattering gravel. He did not switch off the engine and kept the lights on at full beam and the wipers running.

He opened the door and stepped out.

From where he stood, he could make out the stocky figure of Patterson and next to him, in shadow, someone smaller. He was unable to see the face, but he knew who she was. She wore an anorak with the hood up. Just as MacMillan had described.

Something fluttered in his chest.

He had the Stabber.

He stood with his hands at his side, not wanting to move for fear of breaking the moment and letting loose a disaster. Drops of rain ran down his collar like beads of ice. No one seemed willing to speak, until Patterson snarled, 'Gilchrist?'

'That's me.'

'What in God's name are you doing here, man?'

'I need to speak to you. Right now.'

'Now? On a night like this?'

'Especially on a night like this.'

'What about? Dammit.'

Patterson's failure to decipher the meaning of his words, or detect any danger, annoyed Gilchrist. He struggled to keep his tone level. 'Could I ask you to come over to my car?'

'No. Dammit. Say what you have to say, Gilchrist, then get the hell out of it before we all catch our death.'

The Stabber shifted her stance. Doubts flashed into Gilchrist's mind. Surely she was not going to carry out her grisly act in front of him. Or was she? Surely she did not know he had figured it out. Or did she? But the longer he talked to Patterson, the sooner she would realise it was over for her. Of that he was certain.

God only knew what she would do then.

Gilchrist pulled the gate open, but did not enter the garden area. Nothing stood between the three of them.

'Well?' said Patterson. 'I'm waiting.'

From behind him, Gilchrist heard the angry hiss of water on the exhaust pipe, the sleepy beat of the windscreen wipers. His own faint shadow lay over the ground before him, falling between Patterson and the Stabber like some physical divide between life and death. He turned to the Stabber and smiled at the irony of it all.

'It's raining,' he said.

'Lord above us,' muttered Patterson.

As if to confirm the accuracy of Gilchrist's statement, the Stabber held out both her hands, palm up. But Gilchrist knew she was trying to lull him into thinking she was unarmed.

He focused on her eyes. 'Like you,' he said, 'I love the rain.'

'What the hell are you talking about, man? Dammit.'

Gilchrist ignored Patterson. 'When I was a little boy,' he said to the Stabber, 'whenever it rained, my mother would recite a rhyme to me. She would almost sing it to me. Rain, rain, go away, come back here another day. Then she would run her fingers up and down my body to imitate the rain falling. And do you know what she would say as she did that?'

'What?'

'Pitter patter, pitter patter.'

The Stabber stared at him.

'It got me thinking,' he said, 'about a little group.'

The Stabber frowned.

'Pitter. Patter. The connection,' he said. 'Now. And way back then.' He almost smiled. 'It kept me thinking about cats. Or one in particular.'

Gilchrist could see the meaning of his words shift across her features. She slipped one hand inside her anorak and he realised how foolish he had been to confront her unarmed.

With calculated finality, she said, 'The photograph.'

Gilchrist nodded. 'You held the camera. You took the photograph. I had it digitally enhanced to find out what caused the scar.' He stepped through the gateway. He was closer, but not close enough.

'What scar?' roared Patterson. 'Would someone tell me what in the name of God is going on?'

Gilchrist kept his eyes on the Stabber. 'We're talking about cats.'

'Cats?'

'Cats.'

'Have you been drinking again?'

'One's called Pitter. The other, Patter.'

'Lord above us. Now I've heard it all.'

The Stabber pushed her hand deeper inside her anorak.

Ice tickled Gilchrist's neck. He stood still.

'You're wasted as a detective,' she said to him.

'I take that as a compliment.'

'You're far too clever.'

'Which is why you fabricated the complaint against me,' he said. 'To get me out of circulation.'

'Among other things.'

'But you made a mistake choosing Maggie.'

'Maggie wouldn't have said a word,' she snapped. 'I won't believe you if you say that.'

'She did better than that. She left Lafferty's.'

The Stabber shook her head. 'Not for another month.'

'She's gone.'

'I don't believe you.'

'She couldn't wait to leave for the south of England with all that money you gave her to keep her quiet.' He saw from her eyes that his words were hurting. 'How much?' he asked.

'Too much, it seems.' Her hand pulled out.

'I wouldn't do that,' said Gilchrist.

The Stabber froze.

'I found the plastic wrapping under the floorboards.'

'Good Lord. How many different ways do I have to say it, Gilchrist? You are suspended. Do you hear?'

Gilchrist was so focused on the Stabber's eyes that it seemed as if Patterson was no longer there in physical form, but in voice only, like the verbal remnants of a fading dream.

The Stabber narrowed her eyes. 'I knew when you started snooping around it would only be a matter of time. What gave it away?'

'A cricket bat.'

'Now you've lost me.'

'It's a long story.'

'I'm not going anywhere.'

'Don't bank on it.' Gilchrist thought if the Stabber was going to make a move, she would do so at that moment. But she stood still.

'That's it,' shouted Patterson. 'Cats. Cricket bats. I've heard enough. I'm ordering you off my property, right now, Gilchrist.'

'Ask her why she shortened her name.'

'Her name?' spluttered Patterson. 'I know her name.'

'Humour me.'

As if to pre-empt Patterson's question, the Stabber said, 'Timmy had a stutter—'

'Timmy? Who in Heaven's name is Timmy?'

'My older brother,' said the Stabber, keeping her eyes on Gilchrist. 'Timmy witnessed our father beat our mother. The attacks shocked him so severely that he developed a stutter.' Then her eyes flickered at Gilchrist. 'How did you find that out?'

'I didn't,' said Gilchrist. 'But when I accessed your file and saw your full name, it got me thinking.'

Silent, the Stabber stared at him.

'And with his stutter, Timmy couldn't say your name, could he? So he shortened it.'

The Stabber narrowed her eyes.

'Sandra became Sa.'

Sa gave a distant smile, as if thinking back to the days before Timmy's affliction. Then she looked at Gilchrist. 'How did you know to come here?'

'Your missed meeting. Your call to the Office. That was to be your alibi. No one would place you within twenty miles of here. That's when I knew.' Gilchrist felt his muscles tighten. They had come down to it. And Sa had nowhere to run. He eased closer. No more than a few feet separated them. He wondered if he was close enough to make a move, but Sa's hand remained inside her anorak. He raised his arm chest high in front of Patterson. 'Could I ask you to step back?'

Patterson glared at him.

'Back. Please. She's armed.'

But Patterson's mind had locked. He stood silent, his mouth opening and closing with piscine absurdity. From the corner of his eye, Gilchrist caught a movement and turned in time to see Sa pull her arm from her anorak.

And at that instant, he knew she had him beaten.

CHAPTER 33

'DON'T.'

But he was too late.

Sa had the bamboo stave out, shoulder high, arm pulled back.

Her face glowed with hate.

Gilchrist stiff-armed Patterson to the ground and dived at Sa as she struck. His right shoulder thudded into her stomach in a heavy-hitting rugby tackle that would have made his gym teacher proud.

They hit the damp lawn with a force that brought back the pain in his ribs with a hard grunt. He rolled to the side, searching for the hand with the stave, found it, and held on.

But Sa was strong. Fast. And smart.

Instead of resisting, she pulled Gilchrist towards her, causing him to roll over. Then with a rush of strength and a move as acrobatic as a gymnast's, twisted her body, so that in the time it took Gilchrist to realise she had thrown him, he found himself beneath her.

Instinct told him to pull to the side.

With a wet thud, the stave drove into the grass next to his ear.

Sa pulled it out and up, and he managed to catch her arm as the stave powered down at him again, the dirt-smeared point only inches from his eyes.

Her agility stunned him. He gritted his teeth and gasped at her strength, too.

She raised her buttocks, pressed down with all her body weight. Gilchrist turned his head, felt the tip of the stave dig into his cheek, fought to pull his head away. His breath exploded from his mouth. 'Christ.'

Sa's face twisted with hatred.

'It's over,' gasped Gilchrist.

'Bastards,' she hissed. 'Bastards.'

Gilchrist's chest burned. Without the prescription painkillers the pain from his ribs would have been too much for him. But even doped up, he knew he could not hold Sa off for long. He pushed to the side and almost cried with relief as the stave thudded into the lawn again.

Sa freed the stave, rolled away from him, readied to pull herself to her feet.

Gilchrist could not allow her to stand. She was too fast, too strong.

He scrambled forward, stumbled as he dived at her, and with a frightening flash of fear realised his fatal misjudgement as he saw her body twist, her hand juggle with the stave and turn it towards him.

He could do nothing to stop himself.

He slammed into her.

Together they hit the ground.

They landed hard, Gilchrist on top. He felt the stab of the bamboo stave as it punched into his chest with the force of a steel rod, and he waited for the explosion of pain as its whittled point pierced his heart. He took two gasping breaths before he became aware of the limp stillness of Sa's body beneath him.

He pushed himself to his knees.

Sa lay still, save for the puzzled blinking of her eyes and the silent movement of her mouth. Gilchrist felt his hand on the stave and saw it protruded from a point high in Sa's chest, near the base of her throat.

'No, Sa,' he gasped.

He wrapped his fingers around the bamboo ridges, felt her body's reluctance to release the stave from its fleshy grip, and tightened his hold. The stave pulled free with a damp sucking sound and he threw it into the darkness.

Blood bubbled and foamed from the hole in Sa's chest.

Gilchrist tore off his jacket and ripped out the lining, pressed it to her throat. 'Don't talk,' he said, and dabbed at her wound, trying to staunch the flow of blood that pulsed through his fingers like a living thing. He pressed harder and realised he had never felt such helplessness. He glanced over his shoulder.

Patterson was pulling himself to his feet.

'Call for an ambulance,' Gilchrist shouted. 'Now.'

Without answering, Patterson stumbled along the path to the house.

Gilchrist heard the sound of a door cracking open, then the unmistakable barking of orders. He turned his attention back to Sa, tore off another strip of lining and pressed it against her wound. The stave must have sliced an artery. His fingers felt warm and wet. He looked into Sa's eyes, thought he caught a glimmer of a smile, then noticed tiny flakes falling around them and melting in the damp grass. He stared up into a swirling darkness that fell towards them in thickening flurries.

Sa's throat gurgled. Her lips parted, and he thought he heard her whisper, 'Timmy.'

He pressed his ear to her lips. 'What about Timmy?'

'It's... snowing.' Her voice was as hushed as the wind.

'Yes,' he whispered. 'It's snowing.'

'Snowing...' She coughed, choked, then tried to smile. 'Snowing... for Timmy.'

'For Timmy,' he said, and watched the light die behind her eyes. He turned away then, felt the burn of tears and thought back to the times they had argued, to the bitterness in her voice, the feistiness in her spirit, and wished she had told him of her pain, her troubles, her loneliness. He could have helped her. If she had only told him.

When he opened his eyes, the snow flurries had thickened. Flakes were landing on Sa's face, the tiniest of white feathers that settled on the cornea of her eyes and melted into tears. He lifted his hand to her eyelids and closed them.

He stumbled to his feet and staggered onto the path that ran along the side of the house, feet crunching and slipping on the tiny pebbles. He reached the back door and stepped inside.

Patterson's wife let out a short scream.

'For God's sake, woman. Shut up.' Patterson turned his glare to Gilchrist. 'Where is she?' he asked.

Gilchrist shook his head, too exhausted to be troubled talking.

'Good God, man. Did you let her get away?' Patterson opened a kitchen drawer and pulled out a long-bladed knife.

'She's dead,' said Gilchrist.

'Dead?' Patterson's chest seemed to inflate, and his back straightened. 'Did you kill her?'

'She killed herself.'

'Well, then,' said Patterson, and laid the knife on the work surface.

It was then that Gilchrist noticed a tear in Patterson's uniform. 'You're bleeding,' he said.

'It's just a scratch. Lucky for you.' Patterson turned to face his wife. 'Why don't you make yourself useful for a change? Get me a whisky.'

She turned to obey.

'Mrs Patterson?'

She stopped in the doorway, her face tense with uncertainty.

'I'm sorry to have given you a fright,' he said, 'when I barged in like that. I must look a mess.'

She shook her head, then returned to the sink, ignoring her husband. She grabbed a cloth and wet it under the tap. 'Here you go,' she said, and dabbed the side of his face, close to the ear with the stitches. 'You've got yourself in a right old mess. And you've cut yourself. Oh, dear. Quite badly.'

'Do you mind if I use your phone?' he asked her.

'For God's sake, Gilchrist. I've already called for an

ambulance.'

Gilchrist ignored the outburst. 'May I?'

'What in Heaven's name for, man?'

'Oh, for goodness sake. Can't you see he's bleeding?' And with that, she removed a cordless phone from a cradle on the wall.

It felt so heavy that for one dizzying moment Gilchrist thought he was going to have to lay it down. He felt a surge of relief when he heard a booming voice say, 'McVicar.'

'Sir,' he whispered. 'It's Andrew Gilchrist.'

'Andy? You sound...' A pause, then, 'Is it..?'

'No, sir. It's the Stabber.' The words seemed to come at him from a distance, as if they had been spoken by someone else. His peripheral vision was darkening and he knew he was running out of time. 'You need to get over here,' he said.

'Where are you?'

But McVicar's voice had already faded from Gilchrist's senses and he had time only to pass the phone to Patterson's wife before his legs gave out and he sank to the floor.

CHAPTER 34

VOICES CAME AT him, faint and indiscernible, then faded from his hearing, like birdsong carried off by the wind. He tried to open his eyes, but the effort seemed too great, as if his eyelids had clotted. Then he felt a sickening sensation of spinning, falling, floating down into some deep, dark place.

He returned to the same dream.

She stood before him, her arms outstretched, beckoning him to her. He held her gaze, uncertain of her intentions, his heart swallowed up by her beauty. Wisps of blonde hair framed her face like threads of gold. She smiled, and in her smile he saw she wanted their lives to be the way they had been before their marriage broke up. He walked up to her, and she lifted her arm and struck at him with a bamboo stave. He saw it coming down at him, down at his eyes, hard and fast, its point bloodied and bright. But he could do nothing to stop it. He tried to scream.

The voices returned.

'Easy. Easy. Keep it level.'

He was lying on his back, his head lolling, body rolling as if from the motion of some small boat negotiating choppy seas. He opened his eyes, blinked against fluttering snow, and said, 'What time is it?'

'Hey, big guy.'

He tried to pull himself up.

'Take it easy, take it easy.'

'What time is it?' he asked again.

'Not a rat's tail short of ten.'

Something clattered hard and loud, metal against metal, like the sound of an extension ladder collapsing. Then the movement steadied, and he felt himself sliding forward into some capsule, like being closed in a mortuary drawer.

He swung his feet to the floor, held steady while it tilted off to the side, then righted. It took several seconds for him to realise he was in an ambulance. He stood, shot out an arm for support, felt someone clutch it. 'I need to go,' he said.

'Hey, steady. Steady.'

'I'm all right. I need to go.'

'You're going nowhere.'

He patted his hand against his chest. No leather jacket. He remembered the lining, ripping it out. He glanced at his wrist, wondered what had happened to his watch. It must have broken off during the fight. He stared at the paramedic. Then he remembered white flakes falling into Sa's eyes.

'I need a phone,' he said.

The paramedic put pressure on his arm, as if to lead him back to the stretcher. 'You need a hospital.'

'You're hindering a murder investigation. I can have you charged.'

'Charge me all you like, but I don't have a bleeding phone. Okay? Now, sit down.'

'Sorry,' said Gilchrist, and shuffled to the back of the ambulance.

Dragonlights stood in the garden like a makeshift studio. The SOCOs were already on the scene. Four of them, clad in white coveralls, combed the grass like dogs. A camera flashed in the hedgerow, causing Gilchrist to divert his gaze. Over by the back porch, he recognised the military-like figure of McVicar talking to Patterson. Off to the right, the suited silhouette of DeFiore, mobile phone pressed to his ear.

Gilchrist jumped to the ground. Pain shot across his chest. His legs gave out. He collapsed against the rear of the ambulance, and shouted, 'Sir?'

Patterson scowled.

McVicar turned to the sound of Gilchrist's voice then marched towards him. 'What the hell do you think you're playing at, Andy?'

'I need to—'

'You look like hell.' McVicar beckoned the paramedics. 'What's going on here? Why isn't this man being taken to hospital?'

'We can't force him into—'

'Sir? I need to talk to you.'

'Andy, you need to—'

'Now, sir.' Gilchrist struggled to stand erect. 'Before we're too late.'

'Too late?'

'You drive,' said Gilchrist, and stumbled over the gravel driveway to McVicar's BMW. He grabbed the door handle, gave a tug, but it was locked. He glanced back at McVicar who now stood with Patterson by his shoulder. McVicar's head twitched as Patterson whispered to him.

Then McVicar frowned and walked alone to his car.

'We've no time, sir. We need to get going.'

'Where to, Andy? Mark tells me if he hadn't stepped in when he did, you might have been killed.'

Gilchrist had no time to waste trying to reason with McVicar. He could do that later. Right at that moment, he had other matters to resolve.

'Mark said he was about to arrest the Stabber when you turned up. Despite being suspended.'

Gilchrist shook his head. 'Can we go, sir?'

'Gilchrist.' It was Patterson. He stepped closer, took a deep breath, then said, 'For your gallant effort in helping me put an end to the Stabber's reign of terror, I've decided not to ask for your resignation.'

'And the trumped-up charges for my arrest?'

Patterson's eyes narrowed. 'I'm pleased to say you can have your position back.' His lips pressed into a tight line.

Gilchrist heard a click and pulled at the door handle. He was about to sit inside, when McVicar said, 'What's this all about, Andy? Where are we going?'

Gilchrist nodded to Patterson. 'Why don't you ask him?' he said. 'He says he's solved it.'

McVicar gave a half-smile. 'Well, Mark? What's next?'

Patterson frowned. 'I, eh...' He blinked at Gilchrist, then McVicar. 'I, eh...'

'I see,' said McVicar. He opened the door and slipped behind the steering wheel. 'We'll talk later, Mark. And this time you'd better come out with the truth.' He let his words sink in, then added with a growl, 'Or so help me God, I'll have your job and your pension.'

Gilchrist clutched McVicar's mobile. 'Eddy, it's Andy.'

'How's it going, mate?

'Did Maggie turn up?'

'Demanded her wages like she owned the place. Gave them to her and told her to piss off and never come back.'

'When?'

'About an hour ago.'

'Walking? Or driving?'

'Driving. Why? What's the problem?'

'What car's she drive?'

'Used to have a Volkswagen, but got rid of that for a Land Rover. One of those new ones. Discovery. Second-hand, though. Don't know where she got the money. Not from doing overtime here. That's for sure.'

'Blue?'

'Blew what?'

'The colour of the Land Rover. Was it dark blue?'

Fast Eddy gave a fast chuckle, and said, 'Think so. But don't quote me.'

'One last question.'

'Shoot, mate.'

'Was she with anyone?'

'Can't say that I noticed.'

Gilchrist bit his lip. 'Thanks, Eddy.'

'Gotcha.'

Gilchrist laid the mobile on the central console. 'We may already be too late, sir.'

'Let's give it a try,' said McVicar, 'shall we?'

They pulled into Market Street after quarter past eleven. Gilchrist thought he had missed her, then saw a Discovery parked near the Whyte-Melville Memorial Fountain. He could not be sure if it was Maggie's. He walked towards it, brushed his hand over the driver's door, and felt the dent.

McVicar stood beside him. 'Care to share your thoughts, Andy?'

Gilchrist shrugged. 'Another one of my hunches, sir. I could be wrong.'

'I see. Do I need to call for reinforcements?'

'Not yet,' said Gilchrist, and crossed the street.

The painkillers were wearing off and the fire had returned to his side. He tried to hide his discomfort from McVicar, but once, when he almost tripped and grunted in pain, McVicar said, 'Is this a good idea, Andy?'

'Probably not.'

They reached Maggie's cottage, and Gilchrist was pleased to see a light in the dormer window and Patter sitting on the boundary wall. Once again, he worried that he had it wrong. He chucked Patter under the chin, felt the throat vibrate and his own lips tug into a smile. 'Do you like cats, sir?'

McVicar gave a wry grin. 'Prefer to have a dog if it came down to it.'

'Ever had a cat solve a murder case?'

'Can't say that I have.'

'Say hello to Patter.'

McVicar looked at Gilchrist as if he had lost his mind. But Gilchrist ignored him, pressed the doorbell, and kept his finger on it.

From within, a voice complained, 'All right, all right, hold your bloody horses.'

The door opened with a jerk, and Maggie Hendren stepped onto the threshold.

'What the bloody hell's the... oh, it's you.' Her anger softened into bewilderment as she took in his condition. 'What do you want?' she asked.

Gilchrist knew he looked dreadful. The paramedics had covered his stitched wounds with a bandage, which he had not even noticed until McVicar commented on it in the car. He caught Maggie's shock of recognition as she noted McVicar's uniform.

'May we come in?'

'What for?'

Gilchrist ignored her defiant tone. 'It's to do with Sa.'

'What about her?'

'She's dead.'

Maggie's lips threatened to purse, then broke into a forced smile that showed large teeth. 'This is a joke. Right? A sick joke.'

'I'm sorry,' said Gilchrist, and watched tears well in her eyes. 'We'd better come in.'

Maggie gave the slightest of nods.

Gilchrist ushered McVicar ahead, then followed him into a small lounge with a low ceiling. The room lay dark, despite the woodchip wallpaper. A table and chairs sat at one end, a sofa and single seat at the other. Three suitcases lined the back wall. Near the corner by the front window, a faded rectangle of wallpaper, as tall and narrow as a bamboo bookshelf, overlooked a strip of clean carpet like a spectral shadow of what used to stand there.

Gilchrist waited for Maggie to wipe the tears from her eyes, before asking, 'When were you intending to leave?'

'In the morning.'

'Early?'

She sniffed. 'About six.'

Gilchrist noted an airline ticket on the table. 'Not the south of England.'

'Majorca.'

'Flying out of Glasgow?'

'Edinburgh.'

'You never told Sa?'

'No,' she whispered.

Gilchrist glanced at the suitcases. 'Plan on staying long?'

'You could say.'

'One-way ticket?'

'You've got one guess.' Maggie sniffed. 'How did she..?'

'She didn't suffer,' said Gilchrist. 'Her last words were for Timmy.'

Maggie squeezed her eyes shut then, and shook her head. 'She loved him,' she whispered. 'She missed him more than anything else in the world. He came between us, you know.' Her voice trembled. 'I think it was that more than anything that hurt.'

Gilchrist watched tears spill from her eyes. 'What were you going to do with Patter?' he asked.

Maggie frowned, as if confused. 'Patter?'

'Were you going to leave him?'

'He's an outside cat. He doesn't need us.'

'Us?'

'Humans.'

'Would Lex not take him?'

She tutted. 'One's enough for that bitch.'

'You don't like Lex, then?'

'She tried to steal Sa from me. Before Patsy.'

Now Gilchrist understood. Hell hath no fury like a woman scorned. 'So,' he said, 'when Sa fabricated the charge against me for harassing Garvie, you jumped at the chance to get even with her, and lied about being a witness.'

Maggie's nostrils flared.

'Were you not concerned you'd be found out?' he asked.

'Who cared? I was leaving anyway.'

He glanced at McVicar to make sure he had caught it all, then said, 'Lex didn't know you were going to Majorca?'

'No one knew.'

'Not even Patsy?'

Maggie lowered her gaze.

'Was Patsy going to travel with you?'

'She's meeting me out there.'

'Were you going to tell Sa?'

'Eventually.' She sniffed. 'When things settled down.'

'What sort of things?'

Maggie's gaze flickered to the grate.

Gilchrist glanced at McVicar. 'I want you to be careful how you answer this, Maggie.'

Maggie stared at him, as if not understanding. 'Do I need a lawyer?'

'That's your prerogative.'

'But I didn't do anything.'

Therein lies the problem, Gilchrist wanted to say. 'Who stashed the bamboo staves under Garvie's floor?' he asked.

'Sa did. She thought no one would find them there. And she had a house key. From when she and Lex were close.'

'And Lex never knew?'

'No.'

'How long had you known about Sa?' he asked.

Maggie's gaze darted to the grate once more, and Gilchrist made a mental note to have the ashes tested for traces of bamboo shavings. 'We met after she came up from England. We were no more than ten or eleven at the time. But it seems as if I've known her forever,' she whispered.

'You should have come forward,' he said.

Maggie seemed to stare through him, as if his eyes were portals through which she could read the memories of her past. 'Sa had no one to talk to. She was lonely. She used to tell me things she told nobody else.' She giggled then, and the pitch of her voice rose. 'Just the two of us, you know. Me and Sa. It's always been me and Sa. We were close. Really close. We used to keep pets. When we were little girls. Rabbits and guinea pigs and mice. White mice. Lots of mice. I liked the mice. And cats. We used to feed the mice to the cats.' She giggled again, a high-pitched sound, like a little girl, then sadness glazed her eyes. 'They never lived long, the cats. Or the rabbits. They always ended up dead. I used to blame Alex.

Or the other boys. But it wasn't them. Sa told me. That was our secret,' she whispered. 'Me and Sa. It was our secret.'

CHAPTER 35

'CAN I DRIVE you home, Andy?'

'No thanks, sir. I'll walk.'

'To Crail?'

Gilchrist shook his head. 'To see a friend.'

'Local?'

'Fairly close.'

'Well, in that case, if you don't mind, I'd like to walk with you.'

For some meteorological reason, the snow had failed to reach the town. The streets glittered with frost as if the cobblestones were riddled with gems. McVicar insisted on covering Gilchrist's shoulders with a tartan woollen blanket he kept folded in the boot. When Gilchrist pulled it around him, he caught the faintest smell of perfume.

'Never know when you're going to need it.'

'Thank you, sir.'

Normally, McVicar strode with military-like authority, but he paid deference to Gilchrist's wounds and eased along beside him.

'This friend of yours, Andy. Anyone I know?'

'Beth Anderson.'

McVicar seemed to lose his stride for a brief second, then said, 'Wasn't she the lady who was—'

'Afraid so.'

'Of course, Andy. Of course. Now I understand.' He paused. 'Don't know if anyone told you, but they arrested a young man earlier this evening. Turns out he was the son of that couple, the man found murdered on the West Sands and the woman who disappeared. You remember them?'

'I do indeed, sir.'

'He's to be arraigned tomorrow morning for murder.'

Gilchrist almost stumbled. 'Murder, sir?'

'His ex-girlfriend. Alice McGhee. And her boyfriend. German-sounding name.'

Hearing how close Beth had come to being murdered sent a shiver the length of Gilchrist's spine.

'Expect his lawyers will plead not guilty by reason of insanity. Apparently the man's a wreck.' McVicar shook his head. 'Sometimes I wonder what the world's coming to, Andy. I despair. I really do.'

'Mind if I ask a question, sir?'

'Not at all, Andy.'

'You don't believe Patterson's version, do you?'

'Not one bit. The man's proven he's a damned fool. I had the opportunity of speaking briefly to his wife. Becky witnessed the whole incident from the bedroom window.'

Gilchrist almost smiled. It had troubled him that in the absence of a witness, Patterson might have convinced those who mattered. 'Will she be expected to say what happened in front of her husband?' he asked.

'I wouldn't put her through that.'

'What'll become of him, sir? Patterson.'

McVicar sighed. 'Not quite sure yet. Need to listen to what he's got to say for himself, of course. Always try to be fair about that sort of thing. But he made a serious misjudgement in pulling you from the case. That'll weigh heavily against him. Probably pull him under in the end.'

They walked on in silence and reached the hospital ten cold minutes later. Gilchrist slipped the blanket from his shoulders and handed it back to McVicar.

'Keep it, Andy.' McVicar gave Gilchrist's shoulders a tight squeeze then turned and strode into the night.

As Gilchrist pushed through the hospital entrance, tiredness swept over him in a wave and he fought off the ridiculous urge to lie down on the cold tarmac and let sleep take him.

Dawn broke to a grey-tinged sky and white-edged roads.

Gilchrist opened his eyes. The waiting room had filled, but space either side of him lay clear.

Doctor Ferguson stood before him.

Gilchrist pulled himself to his feet. 'I know, I know,' he said, and took hold of Ferguson's outstretched hand. 'No need to stand.'

'But you feel better upright.'

'I do,' he lied. 'How is she?'

'Better than you, by the looks of it.'

'Put it down to old age and the rigours of a job meant for the young. Can I see her?'

Ferguson shook his head. 'She'll be out of it for the best part of the morning.' He frowned at Gilchrist's head, and said, 'Follow me.'

They reached a row of rooms lined with curtains on rails, and Ferguson pulled the first one open to reveal a young woman in hospital scrubs writing on a medical chart.

'Nurse Simmons will attend to your head wound,' he said, then closed the curtain before Gilchrist could respond.

He sat, eyes half-shut, and let the nurse unwind his bandage. As she eased it from his crusted wound, she said, 'Now, how did you manage to do this to yourself?'

'Got into a fight.'

'At your age?'

'Didn't know I looked that old.'

Nurse Simmons let out a staccato chuckle that he found

refreshing, and began to work around his head like a hairdresser. She clipped off more of his hair and gave him an injection above the ear before cleaning the wound and sewing in an additional ten stitches, telling him the others looked like they'd been ripped out by the roots. When she finished, she gave him a couple of pills for his headache.

'There you go,' she said. 'Good as new.'

Gilchrist fingered his ear. He had no feeling on most of the left side of his face, all the way to his lower jaw.

'You can go home,' she added.

Why? thought Gilchrist. And it struck him then how empty his life had become, how he missed his family, how he longed to hear their voices and be surrounded by the careless clatter and rattle of everyday life. How nice it would be to have a pint with Jack, or a meal with Maureen, or just phone them up and say, How about I pop round and take you out? My treat. And he saw that with Gail's impending death, a huge part of what had been his family, his life, and what was to become his future, would simply vanish.

'Do you have a car?' Nurse Simmons asked.

Gilchrist frowned, then remembered he had left his Merc in Patterson's drive. 'No,' he said.

'Just as well. I wouldn't want you to be driving in your condition. I can call a taxi, if you'd like?'

Gilchrist shook his head. 'I have someone I'd like to check up on.'

'I'll be here for the rest of the morning,' she said, 'if you need anything else.'

She smiled, and Gilchrist wondered if she would still manage a smile after thirty years of attending to the walking wounded. Perhaps she would become inured to the endless barrage of needless brutality and treat life with the cynicism it seemed to deserve.

Outside, the morning air lay still and crisp as an Arctic frost. Gilchrist's breath clouded before him in short puffs, visible signs of how cold he felt. He pulled McVicar's blanket around his neck and decided to take a taxi.

MacMillan answered the door in a creased plaid shirt that hung over brown corduroy trousers with knees worn as smooth as flannel. White stubble dotted craggy cheeks and wattled neck, the growth at least several days old.

'Thought you were going to call, Sam,' Gilchrist said. 'Or were you hoping I'd forget?'

'You're a right pushy wee bugger getting.'

'Seems to be the only way around here.'

MacMillan contemplated the bandage around Gilchrist's head. 'So what's the other guy like?'

'Worse.'

MacMillan frowned. 'Can I finish my breakfast? Or are you going to arrest me on my threshold?'

'Finish your breakfast, Sam.'

MacMillan grunted then shuffled along the hall.

The kitchen was bright and open, which somehow surprised Gilchrist. Glossy posters and framed photographs of an avian repertoire filled the walls. Two pairs of binoculars sat on an open shelf by the refrigerator. One pair Gilchrist recognised. Beyond the kitchen window, three bird feeders flapped with feathered life in a small walled garden.

MacMillan screeched a chair up to a light oak table that seemed more suited to a modern house than one centuries-old. He faced the patio window and followed the line of Gilchrist's gaze. 'Once they know where to find food,' he said, 'they keep coming back.'

'Almost like keeping pets,' said Gilchrist.

'But without the buggeration factor.' MacMillan kept his gaze on the activity outside. 'See that one there? That's a wren. See it? You don't find too many of them in town. Had a nest of them a few years back, in that wee bittie privet hedge in the corner. Cats chased them away. Should have shot the buggers.'

All of a sudden, MacMillan tapped the window so hard that Gilchrist thought the glass would break. The feeders exploded in a wild flutter, three clouds of feathers that burst into the air like smoke. 'Go on,' he growled. 'Get out of it.' Then he sat back, a scowl bending his lips. 'Starlings. Bloody pests. You'd think they own the place.'

One by one the birds returned, the starlings leading, oblivious to the hatred levelled their way.

Without being invited, Gilchrist pulled a chair opposite and sat. He said nothing as MacMillan bit into a hardened crust of toast as if it were the skull of a starling. Crumbs crackled onto his plate. MacMillan glanced up. 'You look like you've been hit by a bus,' he growled. 'And what's with the blanket?'

'Lost my jacket.'

'It's chilly to be out without a jacket.'

'Hence the blanket.'

As if taking sympathy on Gilchrist's condition, MacMillan said, 'Help yourself to some tea. There's another slice of toast in the toaster. If you don't want it, it'll no go to waste.' He thumbed to the window. 'They'd eat you out of house and home, so they would.'

The birds had recovered from their temporary scare and were pecking at the feeders with renewed vigour, it seemed. Gilchrist tugged the blanket over his shoulders and rested his elbows on the table. 'Tell me about Louise, Sam.'

'What's there to tell? She's my daughter. Mentally retarded. Lives in a home in the outskirts of Dundee with specialist care that costs too bloody much. Scandalous, so it is.'

'Do you visit?'

MacMillan looked up at him, then eyed the toast again. 'Not as often as I should,' he confessed. 'But it's not the kind of place you'd queue up to see.'

'When were you last there?'

'A month ago. Maybe two. You lose track of time at my age.' He bit into the toast.

'You said your wife left you.'

'She couldnae cope.'

'With Louise?'

'And me.'

'What happened, Sam?'

'When the wheels start falling off in life, it's often difficult to keep pedalling.' MacMillan crunched the last bit of toast with a determination that spoke of bitter memories. Maybe the pedals had fallen off, too, Gilchrist thought. Silent, he watched the old man take a mouthful of tea that emptied his mug.

'You've got two kids, son.' A statement, not a question.

'Jack and Maureen.'

'I know. I seen you over the years.' MacMillan's eyes narrowed, and gave Gilchrist the impression he was trying to recall the last time he had seen Gail and him walk the streets with their children. It seemed so long ago to Gilchrist that he imagined buckets and spades and sand-covered feet.

'She left you,' MacMillan said.

'She did, Sam. Yes.'

'Why?'

Things never seemed to go the way he intended with Sam, but Gilchrist decided that a bit of give and take was as good a policy as any, so he said, 'For someone else.'

'You miss the kids?'

Gilchrist felt his lips tighten. More than anything, he wanted to say. But all he dared allow himself was, 'Yes.'

'How would you feel if something happened to them?'

'I wouldn't want anything to happen to them.'

'That's not what I asked.'

'What's your point?'

'How would you feel if one of the kids was in an accident and left brain damaged?'

'It doesn't bear thinking about.'

MacMillan grunted and turned once more to his feeders, glaring at them as if he no longer found pleasure in watching birds. 'It's the worst thing that can happen to a parent.'

Silent, Gilchrist watched the old man's lips tighten, as if he was torturing himself with the memory of something he could perhaps have prevented.

Still facing the feeders, MacMillan's voice lowered to a grumble. 'How would you feel if the accident turned out to be no accident at all, and that the brain damage had been caused by someone you thought you loved? Someone who then buggered off and left you holding the baby, so to speak.'

A frisson ran the length of Gilchrist's spine. 'Is that what happened, Sam?'

MacMillan took a deep breath, and sadness spilled from his face in shuddering waves. 'Aye, son,' he said. 'That's what happened.'

'Louise was no accident?'

MacMillan raised a thick-fingered hand to his eyes and dug in his thumb and forefinger. Then he lifted his chin and whispered to his birds, 'She tried to hide it from me. But I could tell something was wrong the moment I set foot over the threshold. Louise was asleep. But she never woke up when I kissed her. I loved to do that. Waken her up, like, and play with her. I seen something was wrong from the look on Margaret's face.'

'Your wife?'

'Not any more.'

'Go on, Sam.'

'Louise fell in the bath. She hit her head against the side. That's what Margaret told me. Except I didnae believe her. I seen the way she treated her. She'd a right temper on her, so she had. When she lost it she would shake Louise till you'd think her head was gonnae come off at the shoulders. I done nothing about it and regretted it ever since. Should've clouted her into the middle of next week.'

MacMillan's hands had curled into white fists that he used to dab spittle from the corners of his mouth. Then he looked down at them, as if surprised, opened them and placed them on the table, palms flat. He stared at his fingers for several seconds, then said, 'But I couldnae hit a woman.'

'Would it have made any difference?'

'She would have thought twice about doing what she done.'

'Did you not try to talk to her?'

'Talk? I shouted myself hoarse.'

'Did you not report her?'

'What good would reporting anything have done back then?' He shook his head. 'We took Louise to the hospital, Margaret and me. Told the doctors she'd cracked her head on the side of the bath.'

'And they believed you?'

'Aye, son. They did.' MacMillan stared dead-eyed at his birds. 'Louise widnae waken up. The doctors said she was in a coma. For three whole days I prayed to God. I never missed a minute, not one minute. But when she woke up, her eyes were glassy like. God was nae bloody use to me then and he's been nae bloody use to me since.'

Gilchrist waited several seconds before saying, 'And what did your wife say?'

'Say?' MacMillan shook his head. 'She said bugger all. I told her to bugger off out of it.'

'And you told no one?'

'Not a soul.'

'Where did your wife go?'

'Last I heard she was in London.' Thick fingers dabbed at his eyes again. 'But by then the damage was done.' He faced Gilchrist then. 'I'm not a wealthy man, son. Taking care of Louise drained me of every penny I earned. I worked weekends, nights, every hour that bugger of a God gave me.' He looked at the table, fingered the crumbs, and whispered, 'So, when the chance came up to make a wee bittie money on the side...' He hung his head. 'I took it.'

'From Granton?'

'Aye.'

'And your midnight forays to the pier was Granton's way of getting something in return.'

'You could say.'

Gilchrist found his gaze eyeing the bird feeders. A starling fluttered onto one of the trays, its opened beak chasing smaller birds away.

'Which brings us to why you're here.' MacMillan's eyes glistened. 'They say this'll be her last Christmas. She'll no see another one. I've done my bit. I cannae do anything more for her.'

Her last Christmas. Hearing these words struck a chord with Gilchrist, as if the old man's troubles paralleled his own. Gail would not see another Christmas either. How many others would suffer the same? He understood MacMillan's need to pay for his daughter's care and could understand his helplessness over the imminent loss.

But the twisted irony of it all did not go unnoticed.

Bill Granton, a bank manager whose life was lost because he was an abuser of women. Sam MacMillan, a painter and decorator who thought his life was lost because he was not an abuser of woman. If Sam had clouted his wife, would she not have harmed their daughter? Could that be argued in any rational sense of the word? And if Louise had not suffered brain damage, would Sam have been involved in embezzlement? Gilchrist did not believe so.

MacMillan stood, the move so sudden that Gilchrist started. 'Let's get it over with, son.'

Gilchrist frowned.

'I'll no be defending the charge. I took the money. So I'm guilty. I've been found out.'

'Sit down, Sam.'

MacMillan stiffened, as if in defiance, and Gilchrist could almost read his mental turmoil. MacMillan had committed a crime. An accomplice in embezzling funds. He had known the money was stolen from a bank. And he took it. It did not matter that the money was used to care for his daughter. It mattered only that he had broken the law. And now he had been found out, he was going to pay the price. It was his way of making amends, making peace with his conscience, perhaps. Then MacMillan blinked, and his face softened, as the meaning of Gilchrist's words sunk in.

'Louise needs you, Sam.' Gilchrist eyed the bird feeders, and smiled. 'And they need you, too.'

'Why, son?'

The question seemed simple enough. The answer proved otherwise. Gilchrist felt as if his life was a collection of failures. He had failed Gail, failed Jack and Maureen, failed Beth, too. But MacMillan had not failed. He had been dealt a cruel hand, but succeeded in looking after his daughter despite everything life set against him. How could Gilchrist in all conscience arrest the man? MacMillan was no crook. Putting him on trial towards the end of his life would not serve the law. It might even be argued an injustice.

Gilchrist shrugged. 'What do I know, Sam?' He pushed his chair back and stood, its legs making a screech that sent a signal to the birds. 'You should visit your daughter,' he added. 'Enjoy what time you have left with her.'

MacMillan's lips tightened, and his nostrils flared. A tremor seemed to play with his chin. 'Aye, son, I will. I'll do that,' he managed.

'You asked me to call, sir.'

'Yes, Andy. Thank you.' McVicar paused, then said, 'Could you face a press conference?'

'Would you like the truth, sir?'

'No.'

'Well, in that case, I'm ready and willing.'

McVicar chuckled, a deep rumble like the lazy growl of a large cat. 'It comes with the new territory, Andy.'

Gilchrist gripped the phone. 'Define new, sir.'

'Promotion. I'm putting your name forward for Detective Chief Inspector. Congratulations.'

'Thank you, sir. I'm... I'm—'

'Pleased your efforts are being recognised at long last?'

'Surprised, actually.'

'Well, don't be.'

'What about Patterson?'

'He's moving on.'

Gilchrist fiddled with the bandage where it had slackened by his ear. He could feel his hair short and stiff, close to the stitches. McVicar, true to his word, had wasted no time in finding out the truth. Last night, Patterson had lied. Now he was being given a choice. Take a sideways step, or get out.

'I need you here at 11:30 for a debriefing, Andy. I'd like to hear your side of it all before we face the press. We're in for a rough time, let me tell you. But all things being equal, we can announce your promotion then.'

'Very good, sir. But there is one other thing.'

'What's that?'

'I had been planning to take some leave. A couple of weeks.

To spend some time with Jack and Maureen. And a long lost friend.'

'I think we could live with that. But I need you to complete all reports before you go.'

'Not a problem, sir.'

And with that, McVicar disconnected.

Gilchrist glanced at his wrist then remembered he had lost his watch at Patterson's. He was less than a mile from the hospital and estimated the time to be about ten o'clock. Doctor Ferguson had told him Beth would be out of it for the best part of the morning.

When she wakened, would she remember what she had done? Would she feel regret at her past? Or fear for her future? Would her memory reveal itself with all its hidden horrors? However she felt, Gilchrist knew she would need someone to be with her, someone to tell her it's all right to make a mistake, all right to fail from time to time. Failing is part of life. It's what makes us human. And sometimes we have to learn how to fail before we learn how to succeed. He would tell her that. He would not fail her this time.

He leaned into the wind and started walking.

The Glasgow Dragon

Des Dillon

ISBN 1 84282 056 7 PBK £9.99

What do I want? Let me see now. I want to destroy you spiritually, emotionally and mentally before I destroy you physically.

When Christie Devlin goes into business with a triad to take control of the Glasgow drug market little does he know that his downfall and the destruction of his family is being plotted. As Devlin struggles with his own demons the real fight is just beginning.

There are some things you should never forgive yourself for.

Will he unlock the memories of the past in time to understand what is happening?
Will he be able to save his daughter from the danger he has put her in?

Nothing is as simple as good and evil. Des Dillon is a master storyteller and this is a world he knows well.

The authenticity, brutality, humour and most of all the humanity of the characters and the reality of the world they inhabit in Des Dillon's stories are never in question.
LESLEY BENZIE

Des Dillon's turn at gangland thriller is an intelligent, brutal and very Scottish examination of the drug trade.
THE LIST

Undead on Arrival

Nick Smith

ISBN 1 905222 51 3 PBK £9.99

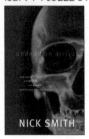

In an egotistical world of violence and deceit even the dead can't rest in peace.

Glen Glass is living a tedious existence; bickering with his wife and resentful of his kids, until death hands him the opportunity to become the hero he never was.

Whilst re-evaluating his new-found freedom, Glen inadvertently becomes involved in a plot worthy of one of his beloved spy movies. Battling his inherent idleness and the drawbacks of his new condition, he determines on finding the cause of his death, winning over the woman he loves and fighting against the forces which are increasingly endeavouring to restrict him and his kind.

As compelling as it is original, *Undead on Arrival* challenges our attitudes towards life, death and everything in between.

Writing in the Sand

Angus Dunn

ISBN 1 905222 47 5 PBK £12.99

At the farthest end of the Dark Isle lies the village of Cromness, where the normal round of domino matches, meetings of the Ladies' Guild and twice-daily netting of salmon continues as it always has done.

Down on the beach, an old man rakes the sand, looking for clues to the future. The patterns show him the harmony of the universe, but they also show that there is something wrong in Cromness. Strange things are beginning to happen.

Because this is no ordinary island. Centuries ago, so it is said, the Celtic gods and godesses took refuge here. Now, behind the walls of the world, there are restless stirring sounds. Soon everyone is drawn into the struggle against the shadows that threaten the Dark Isle. But is anyone truly aware of the scale of events? And who will prevail?

...a hallucinogenic soap... the humour at first has shades of Last of the Summer Wine, *alternating with the Goons before going all out for the Monty Python meets James Bond... a grand read. It's an entertainment. It alternates between compassionate and skilful observations, elegantly expressed and rollercoaster abandonment to a mad narrative.*
NORTHWORDS NOW

Pilgrims in the Rough: St Andrews beyond the 19th Hole

Michael Tobert

ISBN 0 946487 74 X PBK £7.99

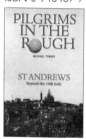

With ghosts, witches and squabbling clerics, *Pilgrims in the Rough* is a funny and affectionate portrayal of Michael Tobert's hometown. The author has always wanted to write a travel book – but he has done more than that. Combining tourist information with history, humour and anecdote, he has written a book that will appeal to golfer and non-golfer, local and visitor, alike.

While *Pilgrims in the Rough* is more than just a guide to clubs and caddies, it is packed with information for the golf enthusiast, with a detailed map of the course and the low-down on booking times, the clubs and each of the holes on the notorious Old Course. The book also contains an informative guide to the attractions of the town and the best places to stay and to eat out. Michael Tobert's infectious enthusiasm will persuade even the most jaded gc widow or widower that St Andrew' worth a visit!

An extraordinary book.
THE OBSERVER

Ideal reading.
ST ANDREWS CITIZEN

Luath Press Limited
committed to publishing well written books worth reading

LUATH PRESS takes its name from Robert Burns, whose little collie Luath (*Gael.*, swift or nimble) tripped up Jean Armour at a wedding and gave him the chance to speak to the woman who was to be his wife and the abiding love of his life. Burns called one of the 'Twa Dogs' Luath after Cuchullin's hunting dog in Ossian's *Fingal*.
Luath Press was established in 1981 in the heart of Burns country, and is now based a few steps up the road from Burns' first lodgings on Edinburgh's Royal Mile. Luath offers you distinctive writing with a hint of unexpected pleasures.
Most bookshops in the UK, the US, Canada, Australia, New Zealand and parts of Europe, either carry our books in stock or can order them for you. To order direct from us, please send a £sterling cheque, postal order, international money order or your credit card details (number, address of cardholder and expiry date) to us at the address below. Please add post and packing as follows: UK – £1.00 per delivery address; overseas surface mail – £2.50 per delivery address; overseas airmail – £3.50 for the first book to each delivery address, plus £1.00 for each additional book by airmail to the same address. If your order is a gift, we will happily enclose your card or message at no extra charge.

Luath Press Limited
543/2 Castlehill
The Royal Mile
Edinburgh EH1 2ND
Scotland
Telephone: 0131 225 4326 (24 hours)
Fax: 0131 225 4324
email: sales@luath. co.uk
Website: www. luath.co.uk